GAIA

A TELLURIA NOVEL

JODI TRASK

THE ESSENCE FUELLED engines hummed towards a place I once called home.

"Are you sure about this?" Merlin asked me for what must have been the hundredth time since we left the base.

I looked out the window and down at the shimmering blue-black of Lake Ontario. "I have to," I whispered. "Mrs. McNair was-" I paused and shook my head just as Merlin gave my hand a reassuring squeeze, "She's family. If there's even a chance she's still alive, I owe it to her to help."

Mrs. McNair was my neighbour my whole life. She was family, an aunt not by blood but in heart. It was partially my fault that her son, Grey, was no longer with her. New Atlantis killed him for helping me escape on the night I discovered I had Telluria.

Not that it would matter now. Grey was cured of Telluria. If he hadn't been killed, he would be one of *them*.

"I know, I know," Merlin sighed heavily just as the plane made the gut-lurching descent for a stretch of road near my old house. "It's just...you're only just starting to heal, Terra. Don't think I don't notice you still flinch every time you hear anything akin to a gunshot."

I looked out the window once again, "Not every time," I whispered.

"Near enough." Merlin cupped the side of my face, gently urging me to look him in the eye. "I'm just saying, Terra, it doesn't need to be you who gets her. You know you could have asked anyone on the recruitment team and they would have gone for you. That's what we do, Terra, we look out for each other."

I knew this, of course. After the cured started to act like soulless zombies, there were several missions to get other family and loved ones. Kalle and Arthur only just got back from getting Elleen's little sister when I asked to get Mrs. McNair.

I looked up into Merlin's eyes. They were lighter today, a turbulent blue-grey of the sea after a storm. "This is just something I have to do, Merlin. If you had anyone, you know I would go with you in a heartbeat."

A shadow passed over Merlin's face. He grew up with only his mother and little sister. Both died of Telluria before the cure was developed.

Before I could apologize for saying something so heartless, the cockpit door slid open and Kalle poked his head out, "Hey, get ready. I'll hold off the crazies as long as I can, but I would really appreciate you not taking too long. Remember, you can always say sorry later." At that, Kalle winked and shut the cockpit door to help the pilot, Arthur, with the landing. It always helped to have an earth elementalist to smooth the road into a perfect runway.

Merlin held my hand as we broke through the clouds. I could hear the rumble of Kalle fixing the road just before touching down on the sleepy suburban street.

"Ready?" he asked and I could only nod in reply. My mouth was dry, there was no turning back now.

"Streets are clear for now. Hurry guys!" Kalle called from the cockpit.

Merlin gave my hand one last squeeze before leading the way off the plane. We stepped out into the autumn sunshine of my childhood neighbourhood. Side by side, the houses that lined the street were identical, save for the colour of the faded peeling paint. I turned towards two houses that were the same as all the others, and yet looked as unique as snowflakes from the rest to me.

In front of these two houses were flower gardens that were once so carefully tended. It looked as though my father hadn't touched them in some time. Weeds were already strangling the valuable edible flowers and useful herbs. Would it be the same in the backyard? The food garden was in the back, protected by a fence. I wondered if they tried to grow pumpkins again this year. They would almost be ready for harvest by now.

Looking out at the houses, I found myself praying to whatever divine force that might be listening that my parents weren't home. They were the cured and I didn't want to see what they had become. If it came to it, could I really bring myself to hurt them?

"Terra? Ready?" Merlin gave me that look again, giving me one last chance to turn back. Instead, I squeezed his hand and began walking forwards.

The moment we stepped away from the plane, the ground rumbled. Looking back, I saw Kalle making a cage of raw granite, iron, and chunks of brown crystals around the plane. Arthur gave a little wave from the cockpit window and an encouraging thumbs-up.

Of the two houses, the one on the right was my childhood home. I yearned to go inside, but I knew there was no point. I wouldn't see my mother making a batch of winter apple sauce in the kitchen , and I wouldn't see my father in the backyard weeding or working in his little greenhouse. They wouldn't be there, just the shells of what they once were.

Instead, we approached the McNair house on the left. Mrs. McNair was the mother of my childhood friend, Grey. He was healed of Telluria shortly before I fell sick with it, a disease that dissolves you into one of the four elements of nature; earth, air, fire, or water.

Grey was Type E, earth, like me. Even after the cure, he was left with the thin lines of quartz on his shoulder. It was the remainder of his mark, the scar of Telluria.

On the night I contracted Telluria, Grey spotted the symptoms first. But instead of sending me to the clinic, he begged me to run. His last words to me were a warning, 'The cure changes you' he said, 'Run.'

The cure did more than just change him, it created a compulsion. Even as he was pushing me out the door, he confessed that he had already contacted New Atlantis—the corporation who created the cure—and that they were on their way. He was still begging me not to get cured when they arrived. He was screaming at me to run, and New Atlantis muzzled him with a bullet.

Grey was the only reason I escaped the cure. Without him, I would have been like the rest of the cured now; bloodthirsty and savage. Some people back at the base would joke that it was a zombie apocalypse, if all zombies were made from serial killers. For letting me avoid the same fate, I felt as though I owed it to Grey's memory to help his mother. She was the only person I knew who was never cured. I just hoped that status hadn't changed while I was away.

"Let's get this over with," I whispered to Merlin, leading the way up the cracked and neglected driveway. Weeds and grass were growing up through the pavement. Not that it mattered. The McNair's sold their car for scrap when the oil prices first began to skyrocket before the Telluria outbreak. We walked up the front steps and I reached for the door, half expecting it to be unlocked. But when I tried to turn the knob, it didn't budge.

I took a small step back and glanced up and down the street. I guessed that nothing I did now would attract as much attention as an airplane landing in the middle of the road. I turned back towards the door and slammed my fist against the unyielding surface, "Mrs. McNair! It's Terra!"

We waited in the still silence of the suburban street for a long moment. By long, I mean we waited roughly the time span of two heartbeats. *Please, just let her be here.*

I knocked harder the second time, pounding my fist against the wood door so hard that my hand ached when I pulled away, "Mrs. McNair! We're here to take you someplace safe! Please! Grey would kill me if I left you alone. Open the door!"

In the buzzing silence, we waited for the length of two more heartbeats. In the corner of my eye, I thought I saw the living room curtain move. By the time I stepped over to the window, the curtains were still again. Even so, I pressed my hands against the glass and leaned in to try and see inside. Through a crack in the curtains, I was able to see Mrs. McNair's familiar living room with all it's crystal figurines and lace doilies. I didn't see her, or anyone else for that matter.

With a deep sigh, I went back to the door and pressed my hand against it, "I really didn't want to do this..."

"No extra keys lying under a rock or something like that?" Merlin ventured. He reached up and ran his hand over the top of the door frame as if expecting a key to magically appear there.

I shook my head, "No. There used to be a trick to opening the cellar door, but Grey fixed that years ago. Even this far from the city centre, raiders would come by all the time."

Merlin gave something of a grim nod, "Might as well get it over with then. The faster we can do this, the better."

I couldn't argue there, we were too exposed. Even if the street was empty, the monsters could be lurking in any of the houses.

With a resigned sigh, I waved a hand towards the greenery just beyond the patio. Creeper vines grew towards me, crawling so fast across the wooden boards that it looked like something out of an old documentary time-lapse. The vines crammed into the lock, not so much picking it but, rather, shattering the internal mechanisms with a sharp crisp clank. The lock fell open and Merlin reached past me to give the door a nudge, letting it swing open with a soft creek.

There were no lights on inside or any sign that anyone was home. We stepped inside the silent house. "Mrs. McNair?" I called out, my uncertain voice just barely above a whisper.

At first, there was nothing. Just as I was starting to wonder if I imagined the curtain moving, I heard a soft thud from upstairs. I motioned to Merlin to follow me towards the sound.

There were four doors at the top of the landing. Grey's

bedroom, the bathroom, and the guest room all stood with open doors. Only Mrs. McNair's was closed.

"Wait here." I whispered to Merlin, gesturing to the staircase, "In case she thinks we're one of them and tries to bolt."

I knocked on Mrs. McNair's bedroom door, hoping she might just answer it, "Mrs. McNair? Are you in there? It's me, Terra."

"Go away!"

Ice shot through my veins. It was Mrs. McNair alright, her voice high and squeaky with pure terror. I hadn't heard her sounds like that since Grey got sick.

I pressed my hand against the door, "Mrs. McNair! Thank God. Are you okay? I'm coming in—" I turned the handle and the door opened almost two inches before it brought up on something solid. As I peered through the crack in the door, it looked like her dresser was barricading the door.

"Please, just go away!" Mrs. McNair sobbed from inside the room, "I was always kind to you, Terra! Why would you —I treated you like a daughter!"

A heavy weight dropped into my gut. I knew where this was going. "Mrs. McNair, I'm just here to help you. It isn't safe here—"

"After what you did to my baby, did you really think I would go anywhere with you?!" Her voice was so brittle, so full of malice, it wasn't the gentle Mrs. McNair I had grown up with. She was someone else, poised on a precipice, ready to snap.

"Mrs. McNair I—"

"You killed my son! You put a bullet in his head! He was only trying to help you! You're sick, Terra! You're sick and you—"

Every word was a knife directly to my heart. While she was still yelling, I motioned for Merlin to come help me. She was freaked out enough. No need to traumatize her with vines and waves of water appearing from seemingly nowhere.

"Mrs. McNair, I didn't—" My voice broke. I looked to Merlin and he came up to the door beside me. "Mrs. McNair, we're coming in. It's just the two of us. We don't have any weapons or anything."

Merlin tapped on my shoulder and put up three fingers. He mouthed to the count of three and we both shoved against the door. With the screech of the dresser sliding across the hardwood floor, the door jittered open.

Mrs. McNair started screaming as we forced our way in the room and something heavy and glass shattered against the doorframe. Shards rained against Merlin and I, scraping against any exposed skin.

Hoping that she didn't have anything else glass within reach, I put my hands through the small opening in the door, holding them up so she would see they were empty. When nothing else was thrown at me, I made my way inside.

Mrs. McNair was huddled against the far wall. She was clutching an ancient wooden baseball bat that had Grey's name carved along the length of it in large pointed letters. I guessed it was a small blessing that a bat was easier to deal with than a knife or a gun.

"Mrs. McNair, please, it's not safe here." I pleaded, keeping my hands open and raised for her to see.

"St-stay away!" Her eyes were wide and glassy as if she were staring at a ghost, not the girl she had practically raised. Tears streamed down her face as she swung the bat at me in a wild arc.

Merlin touched my shoulder, "Terra, we need to go. Can you grab her?" I could hear the strain in his voice. I knew he was trying to give me as much time as he could, but every second was a bigger chance of someone else coming.

I looked back at Merlin and just gave him a silent nod before turning back to Mrs. McNair, "I'm really sorry about this Mrs. McNair. I pro—"

Downstairs the front door crashed open. The three of us all looked in the direction of the sound as a clear strong voice rang out, "Terra, sweetie! Come give your mother a hug!"

"WHAT DO WE DO?" My whisper was a small squeak as panicked tears stung my eyes. I was usually so calm and collected during normal missions, but this was different. This was my parents.

"Is there any way to sneak out without them seeing?" Merlin asked, looking from me to Mrs. McNair in case she felt the need to chime in. She was still watching the door in mute horror.

"I don't know. They would know any way I could think of."

"Ter...we might have to—" Merlin started but I put my hand up to stop him.

"We are not hurting my parents, Merlin. I don't care if they aren't...themselves."

Merlin pulled his hand over his face, fighting a look of exasperation. "Terra...they won't care that you're their daughter. They will tear us apart if they get up here," he whispered, in a tone like he was trying to explain why the sun rose.

I bit my lip. I knew this, of course. It'd been like this for weeks. The husks would treat us the same if we were mortal enemies or the closest of family.

"Oh, Terrrrrraaaaaaaa sweetie. We know you're up there. Come now, we need to have a little chat." My mother's voice sounded closer now, maybe at the bottom of the stairs.

I thought I was going to be sick, this was the last thing I wanted. I couldn't face my parents, not now. I didn't want to see the monsters they had become.

"W-we can go out the window," Mrs. McNair stammered from the corner. "I don't know what happened. They were so sweet before, everyone was. And then a few weeks ago everyone...changed."

I blinked, a little taken aback that she said anything. She still looked scared, but at some point in the last thirty seconds there was a silent agreement that Merlin and I were not the real problem right now.

"Excuse me, Mrs. McNair?" Merlin approached her slowly, "My name is Merlin, and I'm a friend of Terra's here. We know about the change...it's why we're here. It's happened all over the world, to everyone who was cured. As soon as Terra realized what was going on, she wanted to come get you," he explained in a tone like talking down a frightened bunny. It was the same voice he used with people rescued from the clinics. "We have a plane outside, I'm sure you saw it. We just want to take you somewhere safe, then we can talk. Okay?"

Her grip tightened on the bat, "And what if I don't want to stay after we've talked?"

Merlin smirked, "Terra asked the same thing when she first came to us. And I'll give you the same answer. You are free to stay in the base as long as you wish, just as you are free to leave. You can pick anywhere in the world and we'll do everything in our power to help you start a new life." He gave an easy shrug as if it wasn't a big deal at all, "It is completely your choice."

"Fine then," Mrs. McNair watched me wearily as she got up from the corner and pulled a bulky package out from under the bed. An emergency ladder. "Grey found this for me in one of the abandoned houses when your mother fell sick. We heard Type F was starting fires, and sometimes homes would burn down. We wanted to be prepared..." She nodded to Merlin as she approached the window, "Young man, block the door while I set this up."

"Right away, Ma'am!" Merlin went back to the door and started replacing the barricade.

While Mrs. McNair had her back turned, Merlin mimed to me to use my powers to help him. With the faint sound of creaking and groaning, the wood of the door came to life. Branches grew out of the frame, crossing over each other in a tangled mess that my parents would need patience and an axe to get through.

Mrs. McNair opened the window and hooked the ladder on the frame. She let it unravel and fall to the ground, "Hurry now. Before they realize."

"Terra, you first. I'll take the rear," Merlin said, turning full-business. He brought us back to our comfort zone. This was just another mission. We knew how to handle this.

"Okay." I nodded and went for the open window. I swung my leg over the ledge and caught the first rung of the ladder with my foot. I eased my weight onto it, making sure it would hold.

"Terrrrrraaaaaaaaa. Are you in here?" My mother was at

the bedroom door now. I could feel through my branches that she or Dad was hitting the tangled entrance with something hard and blunt. "Terra, honey this is your mother! Let me in this instant!" A shiver cascaded down my spine at the voice. It wasn't her. It was cold and careless, like an animal enjoying the chase.

There was a loud thud on the wall next to the door. Were they trying to break through the wall?! "Terra!" my father shouted, crisp and furious. "There is nowhere for you to go. Just come out."

I bit my lip, hesitating on the window ledge. Merlin waved for me to go. We didn't have time to waste like this. Tears stung my eyes and I pulled the rest of my body through the window. I tried to block out their continued screaming as I scurried down the ladder and landed in the overgrown grass below. I motioned for Mrs. McNair to come next. She seemed much less sure about her footing but scrambled down to the best of her ability.

Upstairs the sound of my parents crashing against the wall was getting louder. They were relentless. I could hear the drywall splintering just as Merlin started to make his way down. He dropped the last few feet, landing in a soft crouch before motioning for us to start moving again.

I couldn't hear my parents anymore as we made our way out onto the street, but I did realize we had another problem. The stone cage was still around the plane. There would be no avoiding that Mrs. McNair was about to see true Telluria in action. "Mrs. McNair, what you're about to see might be a bit of a shock but—"

Before I could finish, she noticed the plane and her eyes went wide, "What happened to it? How do we get out?!" The earlier hysteria was returning to her voice.

I put my hands out, trying to calm her. Or in the very least, trying to keep her from getting any louder. Mom and Dad already knew we were here, we didn't need any more husks coming out to play. "Mrs. McNair it's okay. We'll explain it once we take off. Please just-"

Kalle picked the worst time to drop the cage. The ground rumbled beneath us and I looked over to see Kalle waving from the open door of the plane just at the cage was slinking back into the ground.

"Wh-what...what..." Mrs. McNair was backing away slowly, "Magic..."

I reached out to grab her hand, but she wrenched it away from me. She looked at me as if I were a stranger, "What are you?" she whispered, turned, then ran.

"Mrs. McNair, no!" I broke into a run after her, swiping at the air to catch her hand. "Please, we don't have time for this! We have to go!"

"Let go of me!" she screamed, struggling in my grip and trying to get away from me. "I am going nowhere with you! I'll be safer here than with...with..." She looked back at the plane as if it were some kind of metal demon.

Kalle was still waiting in the open plane door when he shouted, "Terra just drag her in if you have to! You can apologize later!"

Merlin caught up with us as well then, "He's right. We need to go. Your parents will realize we're gone soon."

Soon being...now.

The front door of the McNair house burst open and out came both of my parents. They looked worse for wear. Both were covered in drywall dust and blood, though whose I couldn't say. My father's left arm was hanging limp at his side as if it were dislocated. Did he just do that? My mother was carrying a knife from the kitchen, her lips curling into a razor smile as they got closer. Despite her expression, there was nothing in her eyes. "Terra sweetie! Oh, and you brought friends! How lovely. Come give your mother a hug."

"M-mom." My mouth went dry seeing that dead look in their eyes. I took a shaky step back. Rationally, I knew that they were husks now, but why did they have to wear my parents' faces? "Dad..."

A few months ago I would have loved to see them. I would have been able to run to them and hold them. My eyes drifted to the bloody knife in my mother's hand. How many people had she already killed with it? Did she wear that soulless smile when she did it? Would she wear that same smile when she killed me? My chest felt like it was going to crack open, spilling out my insides to be trampled.

My hand dropped from Mrs. McNair as they came closer. I watched them, locked in those dead eyes.

"Terra, no!" Merlin grabbed my arm and pulled me against his chest. "Terra, it's not them. Look at me."

I couldn't tear my eyes away from them. They were coming towards us leisurely, their faces starting to gain an amused hunger. Merlin cupped my chin and forced me to look at him.

"We don't need to hurt them if we hurry. Do you trust me?"

I knew I was shaking. I couldn't feel it but I knew I was. I nodded only once.

"On the count of three," there was a promise in his voice that everything would be okay. My parents seemed to sense that something was happening and they picked up their pace. Merlin held me so that I couldn't turn to them, "One...

two..." He kissed me hard then pushed me towards Mrs. McNair. My parents were running towards us, the bloody knife raised high as water gushed out from beneath the pavement. Merlin held out his hand and the water washed across the road, swirling around my parents. The knife was knocked out of my mother's hand as they were pulled by a terrestrial whirlpool away from us.

I ran for Mrs. McNair and grabbed her hand. The action broke her out of a kind of trance as I pulled her towards the plane. She wasn't fighting me now at least. "What is this? I can't...I..." Her words came out in small gasps and she put her hand to her chest.

"It's okay. Just come with me." I tried to sound soothing, but my throat felt tight and everything I said sounded small and far away in my own ears. "Please...I'm still Terra. Don't make me lose you too. Please..."

Her eyes were wide and glassy when I glanced back at her, "Terra—"

"Terra! Merlin! Behind you!" Kalle shouted from the plane.

I looked over my shoulder to see other cured were arriving on the street, attracted by all the noise and chaos. Most of them held makeshift weapons and had the same dead eyes as my parents. One had a gun...

I started pulling Mrs. McNair towards the plane as fast as she would let me. Merlin came up behind us, using the swirling waters to keep a wall between us and them. The voices of the cured rose up as they fought against the water to get to us.

We reached the steps of the plane and Kalle stepped aside, "About time!"

I pulled Mrs. McNair up the stairs and all but pushed her towards the seats. Merlin was in a second after us, darting for a window so he could continue to control the water while Kalle closed the door.

"Arthur, we're ready!" Kalle said, locking the door.

"On it!" Arthur called from the cockpit and the engines roared to life.

WATER SWIRLED around the plane as I moved to a window to get a glimpse of my parents. They were fighting against the wall of water. They and the other husks were hell-bent on getting to the plane. Merlin kept pushing them back, a thin layer of sweat forming on his face.

"Kalle! Merlin! Clear the runway!" Arthur called from the cockpit.

Merlin merely nodded, keeping his gaze locked outside. He moved his hands and the water pushed the husks off the road, parting them like the red sea. I kept looking for my parents in the pandemonium as we started moving. In the shifting waves, I lost sight of them. We were pulling further and further away. By the time the plane left the ground, I knew I wasn't going to see them again.

I bit my lip, tearing my eyes from the window. What would happen once we were gone? Husks had the tendency to turn on each other. What would happen to my parents?

"Ter, careful. You're putting nail marks in the armrest." Merlin said gently, sitting next to me.

He was still catching his breath and there was a thin

sheen of sweat on his forehead from the exertion of moving all that water. He didn't show it, but I knew that place over his heart where his mark was must be hurting.

I looked at him but didn't say anything. I tried, but the words got stuck in my throat. My eyes stung and despite the success of the mission, I regretted coming. Merlin was right. Anyone else could have, should have, done this.

"It's okay," Merlin whispered, reading the expression I must have held in my eyes as he reached up to touch my face. "It's okay, Terra. Just breathe, okay? You did awesome! You are the strongest woman I know for what you just did. I don't think anyone else would have had the strength to face that."

In spite of myself, the smallest of smiles twitched in the corner of my lips, "You did all the hard work."

"I did all the heavy lifting. You did the big stuff though." He poked me lightly over where my heart was. "Your parents are feisty like you. They'll manage until we can turn them back."

I couldn't help but give a hollow laugh, "Yeah...feisty. That's what we'll call it." My voice was as dry as week-old toast. "Did you see them...when we were taking off. I couldn't—"

At that Merlin grinned a little brighter.

"What...?"

"Well, you wouldn't have seen them, would you? I pushed them into their house."

At first, I blinked. After the day we had, it took a minute for my brain to register what he had just said. And then I suddenly threw myself at him, kissing those smirking lips with tears in my eyes. Happy tears. "Thank you!"

Merlin chuckled lightly and wrapped his arms around me, "Of course. They're going to be my in-laws someday after all. I kinda was obligated to do what I could to help them out, yeah?" He asked, making light of the situation.

Wordlessly, I nodded. I was so thankful for him thinking of that, for putting in that extra effort for me.

"You know...they were really working as a team out there. Did you see them? From everything we've learned about the husks, that's really uncommon." Merlin mused aloud as if he was just mentioning a trivial fact.

"...Your point?" I asked.

A small grin pulled at his lips, "My point, dear Terra, is that they are stronger together. So long as that fact remains, they'll survive.

"But my Dad—"

"He dislocated his arm trying to get in the door, yes. As you know, normally the weaker husks are picked off. But I could hear your mom saying she would set it for him." There was a faraway look in his eyes, as if he were just realizing something, "They didn't seem completely inhumane. I wonder if—"

I lurched forward, not sure if I wanted to hear what Merlin was going to say, "What?"

His eyes focused on my face again, "Nikolai said that the cured always had some residual essence left. Something like 1% of Tellurian remaining. Enough to leave that scar, but not enough to maintain any kind of link to the earth. Maybe...maybe for people like Grey, and your parents, maybe that residual amount is enough for them to hold onto some part of themselves. Like their relationship. Plus you said Grey was able to fight the compulsion."

It felt too good to be true. I wanted it to be true so badly. "Maybe..." I said, and turned back to the window, "Have you told Nikolai this theory?"

"No. It only just came to me. But I'll ask him when we

get home." Merlin said, though there was a slight bitter edge to his tone at the mention of talking to Nikolai. "Speaking of in-laws..." Merlin pulled back a little and we both looked over to Mrs. McNair. She was as far away from us as she could possibly be in the small plane cabin. She was sitting huddled on her seat.

"Mrs. McNair..." I began but stopped when she flinched at the sound of my voice.

"Just because I came with you dear, doesn't mean that I will forget what you did." She said in a shrill voice, ready to break.

"But I didn't—"

"They showed me the video feeds. There were cameras on their uniforms, did you know that?" Her voice was so full of malice. How long had she been holding onto her anger and grief all on her own? "They showed me how you shot my baby in a crazed state. How you ran away after you... I can't forgive that, Terra. You...my sweet baby boy...he only tried to help."

I couldn't believe this, and yet I could. Surely a corporation that had once mind-controlled nearly all the world either directly or indirectly, would have no problem doctoring a little footage to fit their narrative. "But I didn't! They altered the footage." While I wasn't surprised at this news, heat still ran through my veins. She flinched as my voice rose, as if she was afraid I would snap at any moment. "I didn't shoot him! I would never—"

"Terra..." Merlin put his hand on my shoulder, "Maybe give her a little time, hm? She's scared. Let's wait until we can get her settled at the base and then we can talk about this."

Mrs. McNair eyed us both and fidgeted in her seat as if trying to get further away, "There is nothing to talk about, young man. I know what I saw." She said simply and looked out the window.

I stood up, "But—"

"Terra..." Merlin nudged his head down towards my seat. I bit my lip, knowing there was nothing I could do right now. Not while her whole world was flipped so upside down.

Reluctantly, I sat back down. Merlin scooted closer and pressed his forehead against mine in gentle reassurance, "Just wait until we get back, okay?"

"What if she never wants to listen?" I whispered, barely able to get the words past my lips, "What if she never looks at me the same again?"

"Well," a tiny smile pulled at his lips, "I would hope she doesn't look at you the same way. You've come a long way from the scared little girl we picked up in Niagara. But, as for trusting you again, give it time okay?" He sat back and looked almost sheepish, "Maybe Nik can convince her the footage could have been altered."

"Oh, I'm sure he could do that if he deigned to grace us with his help," I muttered under my breath and sat back against the seat. My hand went to the jade stone I wore around my neck as I looked out the window at the patch-work green landscape far below the plane.

"Yeah I know...I don't like it either." Merlin murmured. Nik was polite enough, even while prone to spells of mania, but I knew that wasn't what Merlin was talking about. Over the past few weeks, Cyrus has been giving the former head of New Atlantis more and more freedoms. While he wasn't truly free, Nikolai had been given unlimited access to the library and was permitted to walk the base so long as a guard remained with him. Cyrus had promised me that it was only while Nikolai was being well-behaved. Yeah... didn't make seeing his flame-lit face any easier.

It was around then that Kalle called back from the cockpit, "Hey guys, you can move around now if you want."

Merlin immediately stood up and looked down at me, "Want to have a game of chess?"

A small tired smile pulled at my lips, but I shook my head, "Ask Mrs. McNair. She used to compete as a teenager. Maybe she could teach you a thing or two."

He chuckled and winked. I knew he was trying to cheer me up, but I wasn't feeling it just yet. "Great idea. Only if you promise you'll watch."

MERLIN, as always, had a gift with people. Mrs. McNair didn't agree to a game at first so Merlin played a couple of rounds by himself, turning the board around to be both black and white.

After a couple of games, Mrs. McNair would start to pipe up with better moves or mistakes. "Don't move your queen there, boy," and, "You could use that white knight to take the black bishop."

He played a couple more rounds of chess like this before resetting the board and asking her to play with him. I watched silently from the distance of my seat. That seemed to suit Mrs. McNair just fine. She completely slaughtered Merlin every game they played together, but after five rounds it was clear he was starting to get better. By then we were almost back at the base.

"You learn quickly, young man. Do they have a chess-board at this place you keep talking about?"

"A really nice one, actually," Merlin agreed as he moved his castle. "The base is built under an old mansion. The owner had a chess table in one of the sitting rooms. Me and

Terra have a game sometimes. Arthur, he's the pilot, is usually good for a game too."

"Terra and I, dear," Mrs. McNair corrected gently, and moved to take his queen, "Check."

"If you decide to stay for a little while, perhaps we could play more? I think I'm getting better," Merlin offered. "Terra said that you used to play the piano as well. There is a grand piano in the music room."

"My, my, it really must be a mansion." She moved her knight again, "Checkmate, dear. Another game?"

"Hey, guys! Sorry to break up the party but we're going to start landing soon," Kalle called from the cockpit. He had left the door open during the flight just in case he needed to help with Mrs. McNair.

"Looks like we'll need to raincheck until later," Merlin said with a note of regret in his voice.

"I haven't asked, where is this mansion of yours?" Mrs. McNair said, looking at me for the first time in ages.

"We can't actually tell you that. For security reasons," Merlin answered. "We've only been flying for a couple of hours and we've been going south-ish. I like to think we're in Maine."

Mrs. McNair tilted her head, "You don't know? Who does?"

"The exact location?" Merlin lifted his hand, "Oh, Arthur of course, and his copilot Kalle. And then there is Cyrus and Ember."

Merlin put the chessboard away and returned to his seat next to me. Mrs. McNair buckled herself into her own seat, "More friends of yours?"

"Cyrus is the current leader of the resistance. He took over after his father passed away. Ember is his sister."

The plane began to make the gut-lurching descent

towards the base. I watched the sweep of red and orange trees below us. It was certainly far enough north that it reminded me of my home in Toronto. Perhaps Merlin was right, we were probably somewhere in Maine. I remember I asked Cyrus once, but even though we were friends, he wouldn't tell me. Markus always wanted to let as few people as possible know to reduce the chance of the leak.

Mrs. McNair had a curious yet dubious expression on her face, "So how do people find you then, if you won't tell them where to go?"

"Well, typically we find them. There's a small team of us who go out and find other people with Telluria before they get the cure. Terra's on the recruitment team as well. Or at least, that used to be our job."

There was a strained silence that followed Merlin's answer. It lasted until we descended through the clouds and touched down at the base. Arthur drove the plane up to the hangar doors before coming to a stop.

"Alright, we're home," Arthur called from the cockpit, "Go on inside, I need to refuel Bessie here."

I gave a little nod and stood up. As I did, Mrs. McNair flinched. I never thought I would see so much fear and hate in her eyes directed at me. In an attempt to make it easier for her, I kept my head down and stepped off the plane. The moment I did, I was tackled by a petite flaming redhead.

"Terra! Oh, we were so worried! Did you get her?"

A small tired laugh escaped me and I wrapped my arms around Ember, "Hi, Em. And yeah, we did."

She pulled back and looked at me in the face, "Oh, what's the matter? Did someone get hurt?" Not waiting for my response, she looked over my shoulder at the others coming off the plane. I could see her making a mental tally of Merlin, Arthur, Kalle and Mrs. McNair before the worry in her eyes disappeared.

"It's complicated. I'll explain later, okay?" I promised. She seemed to accept that for now and took a step back.

Ember was not the only member of our welcome party, Cyrus was there as well. He approached Mrs. McNair and put out his hand to shake hers, "Welcome, Mrs. McNair. I hope you had a pleasant flight. I am Cyrus Chiaro, the current head of this facility." Cyrus greeted her with a charming smile. It was weird seeing Cyrus act this way. So diplomatic. Markus could have taken a pointer or two. " Terra told us all about you and we have a room prepared. I hope it'll be to your liking."

Mrs. McNair looked a little surprised to see Cyrus. No doubt she was expecting someone older to be the leader, rather than a child little older than me. "Thank you, Mr. Chiaro. Though I didn't have much choice in coming here."

"Oh, please, just call me Cyrus," he offered gently, ignoring part of her statement.

"Well, Cyrus then. That is most generous of you, but I'm not sure..." she clutched her hands together and I could see her fiddling with her wedding ring. "Well, it is only that I may not be staying for very long. I would hate to be a bother."

At that, Cyrus smiled warmly and shook his head, "It's no bother at all. We always have extra rooms ready for those who need them. This facility's main objective has always been to help people get back on their feet. You are welcome to stay as long or as short as you like."

Mrs. McNair let out a little huff, "Very well, young man. Just know that if you or yours try any funny business, I am quite able to put up a fight."

Cyrus' lips quirked like he was holding back a laugh,

"From everything that Terra has told us about you, I have no doubt." He then gestured towards the building, "Shall we?"

I stood with Ember and Merlin as Cyrus and Mrs. McNair turned to leave. I had to admit that it was good to see a little of her old spark come back.

"Terra, what on earth did you do to that woman?" Ember asked, tilting her head as she watched her brother and Mrs. McNair disappear into the base. "She looked petrified to be here, and she wouldn't even look at you."

"Ember..." Merlin cautioned, but I shook my head as if to say it was okay.

"That's sort of part of the long story." I began, and nibbled my lip, "She thinks I killed Grey, and she was pretty spooked by the whole...magic...thing." I waved my hand in the air to gesture using the elements. "We met some company on the way out. We had to use some of our power to get away."

Ember's amber eyes widened and she looked between us quickly, "Company? The husks? Are you okay?" She then gasped sharply, "Oh burning skies, was it anyone you know?"

I looked away, not really wanting to have this conversation right now, "Just my parents." I whispered and quickly began to walk away.

"Wait! Terra, wait! Merlin!" Ember was jogging to keep up with me, "Terra, are you okay?"

"Fine," I said in a tone that suggested I was anything but. "I'm just...going to go to the solarium for a little while."

"But-"

"Alone," I added and hurried inside before Ember could protest some more. I could hear Merlin saying something softly to her. No doubt he was keeping her from following me. I felt bad for leaving but I just needed a moment to decompress. Just to think. I felt jittery and agitated. I wanted to scream but I felt like I had caged myself in for the whole duration of the flight. I felt trapped and hadn't yet clawed my way out.

The moment I was inside, I broke into a run and bolted up the stairs.

The solarium was on the second floor of the mansion and was easily one of my favourite rooms. It was one of the only places I could feel truly at peace. There was floor to ceiling windows that arched up overhead. It was decorated simply with white wicker furniture, like something out of a garden. Merlin brought me here when I first started staying at the base. When Merlin first started bringing me here, there were rows of flowers and herbs against the windows that gave the room the air of an English garden.

It wasn't quite like that anymore. After my change in power from earth to nature, I no longer had a proper isolated space to train. There were the gardens, sure, but I didn't want to risk messing up the food garden. Instead, the solarium became my refuge. In my attempts to gain control over my new powers, the small English style garden was converted into something more akin to a jungle. Vines and flowers grew across every surface. The plants covered every inch of window, dimming the light in the room. The other plants didn't seem to mind, they made due.

When I walked in, I could feel them. It was like a thousand faces all turning towards their own personal sun. I remembered when I first got these powers the feeling was unnerving and downright overwhelming at times. Going outside was nearly impossible, at first, without feeling over-the-top paranoia. But it got better and I got stronger.

I reached a hand out towards the hanging vines, letting them wrap around my hand like an embrace. I reached out another arm letting more vines wrap around me. Soon, they lifted me into the air twisting around my body until I wasn't hanging by just my arms. The plants made a seat for me among them, almost like a swing. I could have even rocked back and forth if I wanted to.

"You're getting overgrown again. I can't have you getting out of the room." I murmured, looking up at the branches. "I certainly can't have you breaking the glass..." I tried to focus on just one plant, one small lemon tree. I motioned with my hand, moving and shaping this one tree to shrink down a little. As I did, lemons dropped to the floor with a dull thud. I would bring them to the kitchens later. Normally lemons wouldn't be able to grow this far north, so they were nice to have.

I managed to get the lemon tree under control, but as I did the other plants were shifting and groaning around me. That was part of the reason everything was so overgrown. If I used my powers, or even just stood in the room, they were growing at an impossible pace.

I continued to try to get some semblance of control over the room for the next hour. By that time, I was drenched in sweat and aching. The several Telluria scars I had, two for each element, were sending shooting pains through my flesh. The one on my neck was particularly troublesome. I didn't want to stop, but I knew I would have to. There were risks with pushing yourself too far. Cyrus, who had his mark on the small of his back, would occasionally go paralyzed from the waist down when he pushed himself too far. Ember would get horrible migraines with her mark in her eyes. And Merlin...his mark was over his heart.

Gently, I allowed the vines and branches to lower me back to the ground. They lingered on my arms, my hands, as if they didn't want me to leave their embrace. A small creeper vine was trying to entangle itself in my hair but I gently persuaded it to return to the others. I looked up at my work. In the hour or so of training, it didn't look like I did much. The solarium still looked like an overgrown jungle, but those who visited often enough would be able to see the difference. The lemon tree was small and tamed in its pot. The roses in turn, which had been under control, were wild and filled every spare inch of space. It was hard to tell if it was getting better or not. I liked to think it was.

"Nice work on the roses."

I jumped, looking towards the doorway before immediately breaking into a tired smile. "How long were you watching?" I asked Merlin as he came further into the room.

"Not long, just enough to see you come down from the ceiling," he answered with a small half-smile. "Why do you always train up there anyway?"

I gave a little shrug, "That's where they want me to be. They cooperate more." It was hard to explain, really. This wasn't the first time we had this conversation.

His lips quirked and he reached out to touch a vine that was brushing against his shoulder, "Strange to think that they have opinions. But...I get that." He walked closer to me and lifted a rose off the top of my head. "I feel that way with the water sometimes. Maybe not in the same way, but like it's calling. I can't go near an ocean without feeling like a thousand voices are yelling on the inside of my head."

With a tiny movement of my hand, the rose he was touching fell from the plant and into his hand. A new one quickly grew in its place on the bush. "You never told me that before. Is that why you always get anxious on the longer flights?"

He chuckled and tucked the rose into my hair, "Noticed that, did you?"

"Kinda hard not to, to be perfectly honest," I pointed out with a small smile of my own. "You get all agitated unless you're distracted by something, chess, puzzles, anything. Except for reading, that doesn't seem to work for you." They were just general observations I made from the two overseas flights we had made. Well, mostly just the one. The time we went to London, England. I didn't remember much of the flight back.

"Yeah well...I didn't want to worry you." He mumbled and rubbed the back of his neck before taking a seat on one of the wicker couches. Well...the only wicker couch that hadn't yet been taken over by plants. Half of this couch still had some plants on it, leaving just one solitary seat left. "Come sit with me."

I crossed the room and curled up on his lap. I could have perhaps moved the vines and branches that were taking up the rest of the couch, but I liked this better. An excuse to be close, not that we ever needed one before.

"How's Mrs. McNair doing?" I asked, pressing my forehead against his. I had put off the question long enough.

Merlin reached up and laced his fingers through my curls, gently brushing them back from my face. "She's okay," he assured me. "She calmed down once she made it to her room. She said she was going to lie down for a while."

I hesitated again, though I was happy she was doing better. She must have been exhausted from the constant fear of living in that house with the husks all around for months. With the escape on top of that, it was a sign of her good health that she hadn't needed to rest sooner. "Has she been given the talk yet?"

Merlin looked up into my eyes and shook his head, "No. Not yet. She was exhausted, all the fight just drained out of her the moment we got her to her room. Cyrus was going to wait until she had some time to rest and get used to her new surroundings." He sighed softly and kissed my forehead, "One of the doctors, you know Abi? She said that it'll take a little while for Mrs. McNair's fight or flight instincts to calm down. After living out there, surrounded by those things all the time, she is constantly on high alert. It'll take a little time."

I nodded, knowing the feeling. I remembered when I first came to the base, it took a long time to get used to being free, to not being hunted. It took me a while to realize that I was safe here. "When do you think you'll do it?" I whispered.

"When she's ready. Long answer short, soon. Within a day or two seeing as she can't join the general population until she knows." Merlin put a finger under my chin and looked me in the eyes, "Did you want to be there when it happens?"

I shook my head at first, but then stopped and bit my lip, "She won't want me there. She's terrified of me."

"Not you..." Merlin sat back a little in thought, "She's not scared of you. She's scared of what she thinks you are. But you're not that, you aren't the person who killed her son. You know that I know that, and soon she'll know that. Maybe if we can get Nik on board, he could probably tell her how the video was doctored and verify what we say about the compulsion. She'll come around..."

I could hear the promise in his voice, but I still wasn't sure. "It might be too soon. Even if she comes around eventually, she is terrified of me now." I took a breath, "Do you think it would be okay if I just stayed outside of the room? I want to be there...I just think it might be better if she didn't know I was there."

After a moment of thought, Merlin gave a little nod, "Sure, why not. And if she shows any sign that she's starting to come around, maybe I can mention you're there?"

"I don't know..."

He smiled gently and tucked his arms around me, "Okay, okay. I'll play it by ear. Do you trust me?"

I buried my face into the crook of his neck and wrapped my arms around him, "Always."

WE SAT like that for a while, me curled up in his arms while all the plants inched closer. We didn't say anything, we didn't need to. It was starting to get late and the sun was blazing red over the trees. "We should go for supper," I said eventually, "And I need a shower..."

"Thank God!" Merlin chuckled and helped me to my feet, "I'm starving."

I couldn't help but grin and punched him lightly in the arm, "Why didn't you say anything?"

Merlin laughed, "You were having a moment! And I was being a good boyfriend or whatever."

"Pfft," I rolled my eyes but felt touched by the sentiment. "Well come on then. Help me with these lemons first though."

We dropped off the lemons at the kitchen before going back to my room so I could have a quick shower. He waited on my bed, flipping through an old atlas that I had borrowed from the upstairs library. My roommate, Ember, was sitting on her bed and chatting with animation about all the travelling she did before Telluria happened. She had lived a life of privilege before the pandemic had set in, and her mother had loved to travel.

Once I was ready, the three of us left to go to supper. Ember explained that Cyrus was already there saving our seat. I was glad, that even though he had taken over running the resistance, that he didn't take his father's spot at the centre table. Cyrus used that table from time to time for announcements, but usually, he sat with us. In his words, just because some things changed, didn't mean all things needed to change.

The scent of shepherds pie wafted down the halls before we even made it to the cafeteria. It was made with potatoes from the garden and game meat hunted from the nearby woods. When the husks first appeared, we thought it would be harder to get food. We raided the nearest New Atlantis warehouses for anything we could get, but they were barely touched. The husks didn't care about the systems New Atlantis had put in place. They didn't care about the stores of food just ripe for the taking. They scavenged and ate as they went like animals. They had no desire to horde, to prepare, to plan. They just didn't care anymore. No one cared.

We, meanwhile, built up a stockpile that could last for months, on top of what we grew and hunted ourselves. So far, the husks had been leaving us alone, but if that changed, we would be prepared.

Ember, Merlin, and I got in line for food and went back to our table. Cyrus was already there, some papers spread out in front of him while he nursed a cup of tea.

Ember looked at her brother, then at the table where

there was no sign of Cyrus having supper. She put down her plate with an exasperated huff, "Do you ever stop working? You did remember to eat, right?"

Cyrus chuckled and put his cup down, "Hi, sister dearest. Nice to see you too," he remarked with only a hint of sarcasm. There were dark circles under his eyes, and despite his banter, I could see the bone-deep weariness that seemed to follow him everywhere these days.

"What are you working on?" I asked and took a bite of my shepherds pie.

"Trade agreements," Cyrus said and took another sip of his tea, "With Florida. We have some surplus at the moment, and they're struggling. They have some supplies, but they have a lot that isn't a necessity. Like they have coffee and we don't. We have more flour than we'll use in a year. Arthur is going to make a flight down tomorrow with some supplies. Kalle is going with him."

Ember's brows went up a little, "Goodness, do those two ever stop?" She asked. "Arthur and Kalle only just got back a few hours ago. Before that, they were out with Frank getting Elleen's sister."

Cyrus shook his head, "They don't seem to mind. If anything, Arthur is happiest in the air. He and Kalle are becoming very close as well."

Merlin snorted into his supper, "If Arthur could find a way to permanently stay up in the air, he would. If he ever got Telluria, I bet my socks he would be air."

Cyrus offered a tired smile, "I think so too," he agreed. "Plus, he's been teaching Kalle and Frank how to fly as well. We've been on the lookout for a new plane. If we can get a couple of pilots and a couple of working planes, we could do more." He took another sip of his tea, "Imagine being able to send out two or three groups at a time. We would need more recruitment members of course but—"

I continued to eat as Cyrus continued to talk. He did this sometimes, just letting his thoughts flow out-loud. Merlin was listening with rapt attention and Ember sat with a look of amusement. She told me once that Cyrus was always like this. If you got him started on something that he was passionate about, he would keep talking about it for ages until he was completely exhausted on the subject. Merlin joined in, asking questions and making suggestions while Ember was mostly silent. However, I thought I noticed a shine of excitement in her eyes at the idea of getting a new plane. When we weren't out on missions, she worked as a mechanic for the base, and I knew she would just love to get her hands on new toys.

I looked across the room while the others were talking. Normally I would have joined in, but my head wasn't in it today. I zoned out, watching the crowds of people come and go. Then I saw him.

He glided into the room like a man on fire. His skin was blackened and cracked, glowing just under the surface like magma. Nikolai Wolfe, the ex-leader of New Atlantis. His guard was trailing behind him, a middle-aged woman named Sara. She looked unassuming enough, but I knew she had great control over her water abilities and was once in the army. I wasn't sure which army, but one of them.

Upon seeing them, I lost my appetite. I put my fork down and looked away. I still couldn't believe he was allowed to walk free. He always had a guard with him, of course, but just seeing him made ice crawl up my spine.

Merlin noticed my agitation and stopped talking to Cyrus, "Ter, what—"

I heaved a sigh and picked up my fork again. I didn't say

anything at first, but rather pushed my food around, "I understand that you need to get on his good side or whatever, but must he be here at mealtimes?" I muttered under my breath so that only the people at our table would hear. Cyrus still had hope that something could be done about the husks. He hoped that Nikolai would be able to reverse what happened to them if we could just get him to cooperate.

Cyrus put his pen down and looked over at his uncle for a moment before turning back to me, "I thought of that, Terra, I really did. I didn't think it would be fair to the cooks. They would have to stay late to fit his schedule. This way...well...he'll be here for a while. I need people to get used to him being here."

I ground my teeth to keep myself from saying the first five things to come to mind. "Fine," I settled with.

Ember looked tense and unhappy about it too. I knew she blamed Nikolai for her father's death. I knew that Cyrus did as well, but he had a duty to the resistance. As he kept reminding us, sometimes he had to pick the resistance over what he really wanted.

"Terra, I don't like it either. Believe me. I know what he did. I was there, I remember it. But...I think this is the right thing to do. Just trust me, please?" Cyrus asked, lowering his voice so only we would hear the uncertainty in his plea.

"I trust you, Cyrus. You are not the problem." I corrected, but paused and nodded, "It's fine. I'll deal with it. It's fine." I went back to my supper, but mostly was just pushing the food around. I didn't like to waste food, so I tried to eat more. Eventually, I gave up and gave the rest of my portion to Merlin.

Noticing that we were done, Ember chirped up, "Does anyone want dessert? Tea?"

I shook my head, "Not really."

"What if we didn't eat it here?" She countered with a small grin.

I paused and looked over where Nikolai was sitting. He was talking to Sara in that dumb suave way. I hated that he practically looked like he was enjoying himself.

Merlin looked from me to Ember, "What did you have in mind, Ember?"

She flipped her crimson curls over her shoulder and flashed a dazzling smile, "What about the music room? We haven't been there in ages. I recently found out that William was a concert violinist back in the day." She pointed out an older man with a full head of pale blond hair. "He's been maintaining all those instruments. They're all tuned and cleaned now! I've been dying to play the piano again."

I tore my gaze away from Nikolai and tilted my head at Ember. I knew she loved music, but her talk of instruments had me a little surprised, "You play?"

"Mama taught me and Cyrus to play when we were kids. I can also play the violin, and Cyrus the cello. Or...used to. As I said, it's been so long."

Cyrus chuckled, "I doubt I would remember any of it now. But if there's some sheet music, we can give it a try." At that he stood up, "I'll meet you up there. I have to finish something first, okay? Save a spot on the bench for me, Em."

He ruffled his sister's hair and walked off. I nodded to Merlin and Ember, "Let's go then."

It was a lovely evening. We brought up a tray of tea and lemon cakes from the kitchens and put them on a small table in the middle of the music room. I didn't know how to play an instrument, but I was more than happy to curl up in one of the worn leather chairs and listen to Ember try to remember the violin. She told me it was something like falling off a bike. Your fingers will always remember once you pick it back up, even if you are a little rusty at first.

Merlin brought in the chessboard from the parlour, and we played a couple of games while Ember worked her way through a book of beginner songs for warm-up. By the time Cyrus arrived, she was playing the theme song of some old TV show about dragons by ear.

Cyrus sat down at the piano and picked up the song as she played, weaving an intricate melody under the violin. Both Merlin and I stopped our chess game and watched with identical looks of awe. After playing the last few notes, Cyrus met our gaze with a sheepish grin, "Okay, so I might have been practicing a little."

Ember put down the violin and swatted at her brother playfully before sitting next to him on the piano bench. "Why didn't you say anything? How long have you been coming here?"

"Oh...since William asked me if it would be alright for him to maintain the instruments. I said on one condition, do the piano first." There was a stack of sheet music on top of the piano and Cyrus opened one up in front of them.

"And you didn't tell me?!" Ember was aghast, "Why not?"

There was a smirk on Cyrus' lips, "So I wouldn't be rusty when you realized all the instruments were fixed."

"You are by far the worst brother ever." Ember flipped some of her curls over her shoulders and looked down at the keys. She started playing something, presumably whatever sheet music Cyrus had put up. Cyrus started to play as well, playing the other half of the duet.

To me, it sounded like a battle played by music. "Whatever they're playing sounds like war via piano."

"I wouldn't expect anything less." Merlin chuckled and moved his queen, "Check."

"At least the end of the world as we know it hasn't brought their mood down," I said as I looked over the chessboard. I bit my lip and moved a bishop, "Checkmate?"

Merlin looked down in surprise. After all of thirty seconds, he broke out in a grin, got up, and leaned over the board to kiss me. "You're getting better! Must be from having someone as good as Mrs. McNair around your whole life."

I felt a bit sheepish but smiled all the same, "I only ever played with her a couple of times. She's way above my level."

"You got better via osmosis then." Merlin declared, and started clearing the board, "Another game?"

The music stopped and Ember leaned back on the piano bench to look over at us, "Terra, don't you mind that stuffy old chess. Let the boys play and I'll teach you how to play the piano!"

"Wow, gee thanks, sister dearest. Nice to know you appreciate my company." Cyrus said as he got up from the bench and traded places with me at the chessboard.

"I've been playing piano with you my whole life. It'll be fun to teach Terra! Maybe Merlin can pick up an instrument too! We could form a whole orchestra."

"Four an orchestra does not make." Cyrus pointed out as he moved the pieces to reset the chessboard, "You want to play white, Merlin?"

Ember rolled her eyes and scooted over closer to me. "A

quartet then. I mean we're practically squad goals as it is. Imagine if we became the ultimate triple threat. Tellurians, musicians—"

"And master chess players?" Merlin piped in with a chuckle as he moved his first pawn. "I will get you to play with me eventually, Ember."

"I highly doubt it," Ember assured him and started showing me where to place my hands on the keys.

I DIDN'T GET much sleep that night. The little I did get was filled with dreams of my parents. I kept seeing them as they were, the bloodthirsty monsters who stood just beyond Merlin's waves. I didn't want to remember them like that, and yet I couldn't get it out of my head.

In the morning I rose, exhausted but thankful the long night was over. I went about my normal routine; shower, dress, go with Ember to breakfast. The smell of brewing tea and the rare treat of sausage was wafting down the hall. Merlin was already at our table, halfway through a plate of sausage, eggs, and toast. The chickens must have really been generous lately. Cyrus wasn't there yet, but that wasn't odd for him. He seemed to be late for meals more often than not these days.

Merlin, Ember and I chatted over our breakfast, speculating what would come next for us. There were still so many requests to get family members from all over the world. But with only one plane at the moment, Cyrus and Josh were being careful to make sure Arthur got some rest in between saving people and checking on the other bases.

As the missions of getting family members worked best with only a couple of people, the rest of the recruitment team found themselves with time on their hands. We made sure to get plenty of rest and training in between going out, but we also had to find other ways to fill the time. Ember, of course, worked in the garage. Even though the plane was the only vehicle that went anywhere lately, there was still work for her to do. Merlin and I spent most of our time in the med bay. On days when I felt like my powers were cooperating, I would also go for a walk in the gardens to help them grow.

Cyrus didn't appear until we were finished eating and nearly about to leave. He didn't have a plate in his hand as he approached our table. Ember put her hands on her hips, "Cyrus aren't you going to eat anything?"

"Can't yet, Em. I will soon, promise," Cyrus said dismissively and turned to me, "Terra, Mrs. McNair will be given the talk after breakfast."

Merlin looked up at Cyrus between sips of tea, "She's ready?" He asked, a little weary.

Cyrus nodded, "She's calmed down considerably since yesterday and she doesn't want to be cooped up in her room like some kind of prisoner. Her words, not mine."

I almost smiled at that. It sounded like her. "Okay, I'll be there. Well...I'll be in the area. I told Merlin I think it would be better if I just waited outside the door."

"That's understandable," Cyrus replied with a small nod of his head, "I didn't mention you, but I told her Merlin would be in after he finished breakfast. She's eating in her room at the moment, so feel free to take your time."

Cyrus was just about to leave when Ember grabbed his hand, "Cyrus, they have toast today. Just eat one piece.

Please? Here, take mine if you don't want to wait in line." She pushed a piece of buttered toast into his hand.

He didn't answer at first, but eventually sighed and sat down next to Ember, "Fine I'll eat this one piece of toast. But then I need to get back to work."

"Then let me help you," Ember argued. Cyrus gave her a look that suggested that this wasn't the first time she said that. Though, it was the first time I was hearing it. "You don't have to do everything on your own."

Cyrus nibbled half-heartedly on the toast, "Father managed fine on his own. There's no reason for you to help, Emmy. They need you in the shop."

"Ember is right, Cyrus," Merlin chimed in, hiding his own mask of surprise better than I was. "You haven't even taken an assistant yet. You and I both know that Markus had help. Why not let Ember help if she wants to."

"I don't need it," Cyrus argued, two spots of colour appearing on his cheeks. It wasn't like him to get so agitated so quickly, "I have this handled." He got up from the table, toast in hand, "I have to finish up something in the office. You can find me there when you're ready to speak with Mrs. McNair." Without another word, Cyrus walked away.

I bit my lip and moved closer to Ember. She was watching her brother leave with the flames in her eyes flickering with a mix of exasperation and worry. "How long has he been like this?"

She turned back to her food but didn't seem to want to eat anymore. "Long enough, ever since he took over for father. He wants to prove to everyone that he can be as good as father was, better even. He insists on doing everything himself, even when father always had help. He barely sleeps. He doesn't eat..." Ember paused to add more honey to her tea. She stirred it slowly, the soft clink, clink, clink of her spoon against the mug breaking the tense silence, "People...people are talking..."

"What are they saying?" I asked. I couldn't help but look over the crowd. The base was still running smoothly, but were people really starting to doubt Cyrus' ability? He was so young, but he also knew his father's vision better than anyone. "Ember?"

Ember didn't answer. She took a long sip of her tea, not meeting either mine or Merlin's gaze, "Mmm never mind. I'm sure he'll come around eventually. His office is a disaster. He's barely keeping up. He'll see reason eventually."

Here I was hoping that Cyrus didn't have the family trait of being more stubborn than a pile of rocks like Ember and Markus. The Cyrus I met so long ago seemed like he had more reason than this.

Ember wouldn't talk about it any further, so we finished our breakfast and went our separate ways. Ember went to the garage, and Merlin and I went to find Cyrus in his office. Merlin held my hand as we walked, gently rubbing his thumb against my index finger.

"It'll be alright, you know? The talk with Mrs. McNair I mean," he murmured just before we reached the office. "People are always the most scared of what they don't understand. She'll come around once she knows what's going on."

"The opposite also tends to be true," I reminded him. "No matter how much people are told the truth, often they won't accept something so far outside of what they already believe."

Merlin chuckled softly, "True enough. But I don't think that's the case this time," he said in a light-hearted tone.

"From what you've told me about Clara, well Mrs. McNair, and after speaking with her myself, she seems like a reasonable person who's willing to change her views if the evidence supports it." Merlin's light smile turned into a grin, "I know these things. I've been doing it longer than you after all."

That almost made me smile back, "You're horrible and you're right," I muttered.

We reached Cyrus' office and Merlin knocked once on the door before we went in. The last time I was in this office it still belonged to Markus. When he had run the resistance, the office was meticulously organized. I could still remember the day of my interview with him once I had finished my probation period. The interview was to decide if I would stay with the resistance or go my own way. At the time the faded green industrial metal desk was empty but for my file.

Cyrus was...something else. The office was chaos incarnate. He looked flustered and was working away at one of the stacks of paper on his desk. The stacks weren't so much as sorted in piles as they were strewn haphazardly across every surface in the room.

"Hey, Cy? You ready?" Merlin asked, "Don't want to leave Clara waiting."

I might have asked when Merlin got on a first name basis with Mrs. McNair, but my attention was more on Cyrus at the moment, "Is something wrong, Cyrus?" I asked as he flipped through the mountain of papers.

"I can't find the bleeding letter from London. They asked for a few things, and I can't remember..."

I glanced around but I didn't see anything that shouted London at me.

Merlin beat over and picked something up off the floor, "Do you mean this?" He asked, and glanced at it, "Something something, Kay and Charlotte have been forced to move the group into Heathrow airport after an attack by the husks." He looked up at Cyrus, "Is this true?"

"Yes, that! Thanks!" Cyrus took the paper from Merlin, "The base we established for them was working perfect but it was too open. Husks found it and it was too hard to defend. They've moved into the airport and have been living off the supplies that New Atlantis left. They know they won't be able to keep going that way forever but...well, we'll figure it out."

He got up and put the letter directly in the middle of the desk so that he would be able to find it when he came back. "Let's go talk to Mrs. McNair first. I can come back to this. Arthur isn't making another flight across the ocean for at least a week anyway."

"A week?" I asked, "What's he doing in the meantime?"

Cyrus ushered us out of the office and we started making our way down the hall, "Some of the other chapters are in worse condition. Plus, more family members need to be found and brought back."

"Why haven't we heard anything about this?" Merlin asked, "This is sort of our job."

Cyrus pushed a hand through his hair, "I've spoken to Josh." Josh was the head of the recruitment team, "We're working on a plan. I suspect you'll hear something soon."

I didn't like it. I caught Merlin's gaze and I could tell he was thinking the same thing. Where had all this secrecy come from?

I wiped the palms of my hands off on my jeans once we made it to Mrs. McNair's room. My mouth felt dry. Sure, I wanted to be here, but I was starting to doubt that it was a good idea. What if she found out I was just outside the door and threw a fit? What if she talked about me and said something horrible? I wasn't too enthusiastic about being called a murderer again. Least of all, being accused of murdering my best friend. Grey was like my brother. Sick or not, I never would have hurt him. Ever.

Mrs. McNair was being housed in one of the newer resident areas. I stopped just outside the door and waved for Merlin and Cyrus to go inside. Merlin gave me a questioning look and I merely nodded. I was sure I didn't want to go in. I would be fine out in the hall where she couldn't see me.

Cyrus knocked on her door, "Mrs. McNair? It's Cyrus and Merlin. We would like to have that chat now if you're ready."

I pressed my back against the wall as she opened the door. I didn't even dare breathe.

"Oh, hello dears. I was wondering when you might turn up. That sweet dear, Elleen, just took away my breakfast tray and said you wouldn't be long."

Cyrus smiled, though as I looked over at him it was a different smile than the one I was used to. It was cool, professional, very much like the one Markus used to use. Merlin, of course, was the same as ever, that same easy grin that always seemed to light his face.

"May we come in, Clara?" Merlin asked, hands in his pockets.

"Oh, certainly dears. I made up the other bed for you to sit on. Come in, come in."

The two moved inside and I could hear the sigh of the mattress as Merlin and Cyrus must have sat down. They didn't leave the door wide open but closed it just enough to let me still listen in while giving the guise of a private conversation. Merlin told me once that the talks tended to go better if the person didn't feel trapped. Maybe they should have thought of that when I was given the talk.

"I would offer tea if I could but...well I suppose it would really be up to you to offer tea." I could hear her laugh. It was tight and nervous, but with a hint of her usual warmth. She was starting to act herself again, busy and nurturing, the epitome of mother hen. "Alright, dearies. Now you were going to explain all this...voodoo nonsense."

I grinned to myself a little. It was so achingly familiar to hear her speak like that.

Cyrus was the first to begin speaking. "If I may, Mrs. McNair, it's not voodoo, or really even magic. It's just the transfer of energy. If you would sit down, we'll explain everything."

I could hear the faint squeak of her bed as she sat down. "Well whatever it was, it looked like magic to me. You said Telluria causes this?" She sounded dubious.

"Yes," Cyrus answered, "The way we explain it to newcomers is that it's a different kind of cure. What New Atlantis did, while effective, had some unfortunate side effects. Have you ever noticed, Mrs. McNair, that people who received the cure seemed...different? Something about their demeanour."

There was a pause. The silence went on for several long seconds, "Yes, I have. My son, he was so different when he returned. He was so affectionate before. And my friends, like Terra's parents..." She paused again, "But that's just the effect of the trauma, PTSD from being sick."

There was another long silence before Merlin began to speak, "Telluria is the manifestation of our connection to the earth. That's why the scars are the elements. The 'cure' is basically sucking out that connection and bottling it in the form of essence."

"Essence? Like the power—"

"Yes. New Atlantis has been using people more or less as batteries."

I could hear Mrs. McNair scoff at that, "Batteries. Did these scientists never watch the Matrix?"

Merlin chuckled along with her, "I've heard that one a few times. Unfortunately, as you know, essence is a very powerful fuel. It's manufactured from the sick."

"That doesn't sound so bad. They offered the cure for free, at least they are getting something out of it." Mrs. McNair was, as always, thinking of things in a practical light.

Merlin made a humming noise in the back of his throat, "If it were just that, I would understand too. Most people would. But it's not just that. You see, you never see people right after they receive the cure. There's always a recovery period. That's to mask the other side effects. A fully cured person loses their connection to the earth, and it causes them to lose all of their humanity. They are, more or less, exactly like the husks."

"Husks?"

Cyrus took over speaking again, "That's what we had been calling the cured since they stopped acting normal." He explained.

"I see..." I couldn't tell if Mrs. McNair believed them or

not with that tone. It sounded like she was thinking it over, "Why weren't they like that all along then?"

Merlin picked up the explanation again, "When New Atlantis was still administering the cure, they implanted a small device in the back of the neck. It controlled the cured to act like their normal self. As normal as the programming allowed."

"Are you suggesting my boy, my Grey, was being mind-controlled?!" The hysteria was starting to rise again in Mrs. McNair's voice. I held my hands together, squeezing so tight that my knuckles were going white. I wanted to be able to go in there, to help her through this. I felt utterly useless stuck outside the door.

Cyrus' answer was solemn, "I'm afraid so, ma'am."

I looked towards the door, waiting for her reply. There was another silence that stretched on for a millennia before I finally heard her say, "W-well if that's so, then why is it no longer working?"

I had a feeling Merlin and Cyrus were exchanging a look. They didn't answer right away, my guess was they were thinking about how best to answer that. Merlin eventually spoke up, "The main transmission was coming from the New Atlantis headquarters just off the coast of the Azores. That building...blew up."

"And that was when everyone started to act like psychopaths?" Mrs. McNair huffed with agitation, "Dears, I may look young but I wasn't born yesterday. What is this—"

"It's completely true." Cyrus continued, "I am willing to offer proof if you like. Several eyewitnesses, along with Nikolai Wolfe."

Mrs. McNair let out a barking laugh, "You have the leader of New Atlantis here? What is he? Another prisoner?"

"I will remind you that you are not a prisoner, Mrs. McNair," Cyrus stated with deadly calm, "You will be given leave to explore as you like after this chat. I only ask that if you should decide to leave the base, that you will give me some notice so that we may be able to help you prepare for your new life. But yes, Mr. Wolfe is a prisoner. He is also my Uncle, which is why I chose to keep him here."

I was starting to hate the long strings of silences. I understood that everything was a lot to take in, but I couldn't even see her face to know how she was taking all this. I was blind and I hated it.

"Fine, tell me about this magic first. Then perhaps you can show me your proof about New Atlantis."

"Very well. Merlin, care to do the honours?"

Merlin coughed under his breath, "You remember the way the water acted near your home, yes? And that stone cage that was around the plane?"

There was a small strained laugh, "How could I not?"

"As you know, Telluria has four types, well normally." Merlin amended, and I knew he was thinking of me when he said that, "Types E, A, F, and W, for earth, air, fire, and water. I was told you lost someone before the cure was made?"

"Y-yes, my husband. He was Type A. Terra's parents both got very close as well."

I jolted at hearing my name. I looked over my shoulder as if I could see through the wall I was leaning against. I couldn't tell if there was malice in her voice or not this time.

"There is another way, other than the cure. It's a type of treatment." Merlin paused, "That power you saw, it was a manifestation of Telluria. Rather than taking over the body, we can manipulate our element. It takes some practice, of course, but when we use this power, it keeps the mark from spreading. It keeps us alive. It means we don't need to get the cure. A lot of people here have had Telluria for years and it's never spread beyond the original mark."

I wish I could see her face. I knew she couldn't deny what Merlin was saying because she had seen it.

"Can you show me again?" She asked.

I heard a soft gasp and I could only assume that Merlin conjured a small ball of water in his hand. He likely turned it into a small animal, as he was so fond of doing. When he first showed me his power, he made a small bird.

"Goodness. And this...this is why Terra is still alive?"

I bit my lip, pressing harder against the wall. I didn't even want to breathe if it meant not hearing this next part of the conversation.

"Yes," Merlin answered, softer this time. "We found her in Niagara. She was running from New Atlantis and her marks were very far along. We brought her here and taught her how to harness her power. Cyrus was her tutor."

I felt tears sting my eyes, though I wasn't sure why. Dammit, I just wanted to go in that room.

"She had a difficult start, but she quickly became one of our strongest elementalists. She's been vital to the team."

"But why would she run?" Mrs. McNair sounded perplexed, "She trusted the cure. It saved her parents and Grey..."

"If I may," Merlin began again, "Perhaps Terra would like to answer that?"

"If she were here certainly but—"

"Clara," Merlin cut her off, "She's been sitting outside. She wanted to be here while we explained everything, but she didn't want to upset you. Just say the word and she can come in and explain what happened."

I waited, and finally, "T-Terra dear?"

I pushed against the wall and went to the door. I pressed a shaking hand against it and slowly pushed it open. Tears were starting to slip down my cheeks as I stood in the doorway looking at the three of them.

"Terra...tell me what happened. Please..."

I CLASPED my hands together to hide how much they were shaking. Mrs. McNair looked at my face, my marks, and her eyes widened in shock, "Terra what—"

"I didn't want the cure because Grey...because Grey told me not to. That night Grey found out I was sick. He woke me up and told me New Atlantis was already on the way. He begged me to run." The words spilled from my mouth. I couldn't seem to say them fast enough. I was worried if I stopped, I might not have the nerve to say it at all. "He said the cure changes you. He kept begging me to run. He was pushing me out the door when New Atlantis came. They...he..." I stopped, trying to catch my breath around lungs that were suddenly too tight. "What they showed you was all wrong. He pushed me out the door and they... they couldn't stand that he was helping me. Th-they shot him. Before I even made it over the fence. They—" I shut my eyes, hearing that gunshot ringing through my head again. "I'm sorry. I'm so sorry. It's all my fault. I as good as killed him. If I... if I just..."

"Sweetie, come here." Mrs. McNair opened her arms to me.

I couldn't stop myself. I went to her and let her envelop me in her embrace. A tiny sob shook through my throat, "Y-you believe me?" I whispered.

She smoothed a hand through my curls, "All I know for sure is you would have never hurt Grey. They told me that the sickness gave you a kind of mania."

"B-but it didn't—"

"Shhh... I don't know what to think, sweetie. But at the moment all I can think of is you were all alone. You are just a child and you had to go through all that alone. I'm so sorry, Terra. Your parents would be so proud."

"I thought you would be safe with them. I'm so sorry that I didn't come sooner," I sobbed into her shoulder. I couldn't seem to hold it back anymore. Hours, days, weeks of worrying if she was alright. I was still worrying if my parents would ever be the same. It was all crashing down at once.

"It's okay, sweetie. I'm here..." Mrs. McNair shushed softly in the same way she did when I was five and I had broken my arm falling out of a tree behind the house.

After a moment Cyrus cleared his throat from where he was now standing by the door. Merlin stood with him, "I see that you two have some catching up to do. Mrs. McNair, you now have free roam of the base. If you get lost, feel free to ask anyone. Terra, perhaps you could give her a tour later? When you're ready."

I sniffled and wiped my eyes, "Th-thanks Cy."

"See you supper time, okay?" Cyrus said, and slipped out into the hallway. Merlin gave a little wave and followed him.

We waited until the door was closed to speak again.

Mrs. McNair brushed a hand through my hair, "You'll tell me, won't you? Have they been treating you well? Was everything they said true?"

I sat down next to her on the bed and wiped at my tears, "It is. I didn't believe it at first either, the 'magic' and everything. But I've seen it and I've used it myself. It really works, and it kept me alive." I pulled up my sleeve so she could see my original mark, the faint quartz lines that were so similar to Grey's. "My whole arm turned to stone at one point," I explained, remembering that night when I spent hours in the training room with Cyrus, Merlin, and Ember until it was under control.

"And that part about Grey? The mind control?" Mrs. McNair pressed.

I nodded, "I'm afraid so. You saw him, he wasn't himself. Even when he was pushing me out the door, it was as if it physically hurt him to help me. We call it the compulsion."

"I see..." Mrs. McNair went very still as the information was slowly sinking in. After a moment, she brushed back the hair from my neck, "And what about this? I saw another on you as well. Is it normal to get separate strains like this?"

A lump built in my throat. I didn't want to tell her about that, I didn't even like talking about it with Merlin. What Nikolai did to me was common knowledge in the base. Cyrus made an announcement after people started to notice my marks and the change in my power. "No...I'm the only one."

"How..."

I looked away, "I was tortured by Nikolai Wolfe. He wanted the location of this base. Plus he needed a human test subject for some research. Two birds with one stone I guess..."

"T-tortured?!" Mrs. McNair shot to her feet, "Where is

this Mr. Wolfe? I'll wring his neck." She looked to the door in horrified exasperation, "You said he's a prisoner here?"

"In a manner of speaking." I resisted the urge to roll my eyes, "He spends most of his time locked in his room, but he is allowed out sometimes, so long as he has a guard with him. Usually, he just leaves for meals and to go to the library."

Mrs. McNair jumped to her feet as if she was going to go hunt him down and punch him out. I took her hand and pulled lightly until she sat back down, "I don't like it either. But Cyrus needs his help, we all do. His knowledge of Telluria is unprecedented. He may be able to find a way to fix the husks. This..." I gestured to my other marks that were visible, "Was for research towards a true cure."

"What research? Terra, tell me what that man did to you." Mrs. McNair had that half-crazed look in her eye like a mama bear on the prowl.

"Please don't go confront him about it," I begged, though I secretly hoped someone would punch Nikolai in his smug face. "He injected me with the other strains of Telluria. I have two of each now. It made my powers change a little. I can't control earth anymore like I used to."

I reached into my pocket and drew out a small seed. Like everyone else, the power had to draw from somewhere, and it seemed like a bad idea to have plants come down through the ceiling. The seed instantly began to grow into a small oak sapling with the roots twisting around my hand for support. "Nikolai calls it Vita, the element of life. He thinks it's the secret to ending Telluria, fixing the husks, everything."

Mrs. McNair was looking at me with wide eyes torn between horror and worry. I stood up, and offered my spare hand to her, "Come on, let's find this little guy a home out in the gardens. I can give you a tour then."

Things weren't exactly fixed between Mrs. McNair and I, but it was an improvement. She told me everything that happened after I left. New Atlantis officials came and showed her the footage of me killing Grey. She was told the footage came from the cameras the officers wore on their uniforms. Apparently they never even told my parents that I was picked up in Niagara. Instead, I was declared dead after a month.

"I always thought it was odd." Mrs. McNair said as we walked outside, "Your parents were sad, yes, but their grief didn't seem real somehow. It was like watching someone who was told to look sad."

I nibbled my lip, walking towards the small graveyard out in the gardens. I thought it would be a nice place for the oak sapling. "It's what the compulsion told them to do. I guess the average person wouldn't have noticed the difference." Not for the first time I wondered if they would ever be themselves again. Nikolai thought it was possible, but I took anything he said with a mountain of salt.

"I was so devastated after Grey, I just assumed they were taking your death in their own way. It was so quiet without you kids around..."

"Sorry I left you alone. I think you understand why I couldn't come to get you sooner." I said and stopped by a spot not far from Markus' grave to plant the sapling.

There wasn't any need to dig, I just coaxed the roots to burrow into the ground. As I worked, I told Mrs. McNair everything that had happened over the last year; Quebec,

London, the Azores, everything. I was in the middle of telling her about when Merlin was shot in Quebec when I heard a soft sigh.

"You really care about that boy, don't you?" She asked, "I saw the way you were on the plane. He's absolutely besotted with you. He looks at you the same way Grey used to."

There was a sharp pain in my chest and a note of regret in her voice. I knew she always hoped that me and Grey would become a couple. She had been planning our wedding since we were kids, but I just never felt that way about Grey. I didn't have the heart to tell her that Grey kissed me the night he died. "I think I love him..." I admitted in barely a whisper while I felt the heat rise into my cheeks. "He's always been there for me, ever since the beginning. He's so sweet and smart and kind and lets me move things at my own pace. Even when I was still mourning Grey, he was always there for me."

"You told him about Grey?" Mrs. McNair asked. She was trying to sound casual but this was her son we were talking about, it was impossible for her to act completely disinterested.

I nodded, "Yes. When I first came here, I was very weak. I spent a few days in the med bay recovering. Merlin visited every day and I told him about Grey. Actually..." I brushed the dirt off my hands and looked over to Markus' grave, "It was Merlin who encouraged me to tell Markus what happened to Grey. Normally, it's impossible to fight the compulsion, but Grey did somehow. Markus didn't under-stand it, and he helped create the cure in the first place—"

"Wait. Markus? That Cyrus boy said his name was Chiaro. You don't mean he was the son of Markus Chiaro?"

At that, I walked over to Markus' headstone and

gestured to it, "I told you how he died in the Azores. Cyrus has been running the base since."

"But he's so young..."

I shrugged, "Cyrus is a couple of years old than me. He's young, yes, but he worked with his father since the beginning of the resistance. He knew his father's vision better than anyone."

We left the graveyard and I showed her the rest of the base. I made sure she knew where the cafeteria was and the med bay first. After that, we went up into the mansion. She was fascinated by the gorgeous old building that was mostly left unused. When New Atlantis was still in power, the mansion was used sparingly so that we wouldn't draw attention with the lights. We kept the same philosophy once the husks appeared, though no husks had found us yet. We were comfortable in the base below the mansion anyway.

We ended our tour at the solarium. The moment we walked in, there was a subtle shift in all the plants towards me. Mrs. McNair noticed it too, as she let out a small gasp. "So this is where you practice your powers?"

"I...try." Several vines were reaching down as I walked further in. I could feel them wanting to pick me up and lift me into the embrace of the greenery above. "With my old powers, once I accepted them it was only easy to control my element. But it's different with plants. They have a mind of their own."

Mrs. McNair stopped to smell the roses. "Your father would say that nature was never meant to be controlled." She looked up at the plants arching over the ceiling, "He would love this room."

I turned towards the overgrown herbs to try and tame them down a little, "Do you think we'll get them back?" I didn't look up at her, unsure if I wanted to see her face when she answered.

"Before yesterday I didn't think any of this was possible. But we live in a world with magic now, perhaps other things are possible as well." Mrs. McNair spoke softly. She was still facing the roses but there was a look in her eyes that suggested she was somewhere else. "If the plants react this way to you, the base must have no problem growing food."

I shook my head, "I can't go into the gardens. My powers are still too unpredictable."

"You make it sound like you're a walking bomb." Mrs. McNair said with a laugh. Her laugh was cut short when she saw whatever look I must have had on my face, "Terra what's wrong?"

"What if I am?" I felt a knot in my stomach the moment she said it. I always worried that something was wrong with my powers, that something would go wrong. It was just a matter of time, wasn't it? "All the other abilities have had years to test their limits. But this? Not even Nikolai knows how it will manifest. Everyone keeps trying to assure me it will be fine but—I don't know. I have this feeling every time I go outside. It's like hearing a million voices and—" I fiddled with the jade necklace that Merlin gave me, "I'm scared."

"Oh Terra..." Mrs. McNair put an arm around my shoulders, "You've come this far, and I'm here now. I won't let anything happen to you."

I let out a small laugh, "Didn't you throw a vase at me yesterday?" I asked, "And swing a bat at me."

"A lamp, actually." Mrs. McNair corrected then gave my arm a little squeeze, "I was scared too. I still am. You'll forgive me, won't you?"

I was silent for a moment. I pulled away from her embrace, "Will you?"

She didn't need to ask what. It was there, Grey was there, a ghost standing between us. "I suspect I will..."

I nodded and turned towards the door. "But not yet..." Even if I hadn't killed him, I had contributed to his death.

"Terra—"

I cut her off before she could say anything else. I didn't want to face Grey's ghost right now, "That's the whole tour. Do you know how to find your way back?"

"I suspect I'll be able to find my way," She answered, "But T-"

"I just remembered I was supposed to write a report of what happened yesterday. I'll see you around." And before she could stop me, I all but ran from that room.

DAYS TURNED to weeks and the base returned to its natural rhythm. Cyrus was still overworked and led on with all the chaos of a hurricane. Ember was making sure he remembered to eat and after days of nagging him, he let me help with filing. At first, I used the same filing system Markus used, thinking that would be the easiest for Cyrus. I was mostly right. Cyrus liked to keep active things in front of him, such as letters from other bases. Those stayed either firmly under paperweights on his desk or pinned to the wall to keep his air powers from blowing everything away when he got flustered.

Mrs. McNair got settled in and started working between the kitchens and the med bay. We were still working things out, but we had time.

Arthur, Kalle, and Frank were almost always gone with other members of the recruitment team to either visit other bases or get family. As time went on, rescue missions got further apart.

My solarium was still a mess, though I liked to think it

was getting slightly better. At the very least, nothing had broken through a window yet.

Nikolai had taken Markus' old notes on Telluria and spent nearly all of his time researching. This kept him in his room which was perfectly fine with me. As of yet, there was no progress on Vita, Telluria, or the husks. Although according to Cyrus, Nikolai did complain about not having any of his own research or human trials to work with. As much as everyone wanted the situation with the husks to be over, Cyrus drew the line at letting Nikolai experiment on humans again.

It was a cold and rainy day in late fall and Merlin was helping me harvest some things from my solarium. With the winter fast approaching, I started moving more food crops into the solarium. There were still lemons and herbs, but now we also had nuts, berries, and a few vegetables. If it worked, we could add more plants to other rooms in the mansion. If it worked, we wouldn't need to worry about how we were going to get through the winter.

"I can't remember the last time I had peanut butter," Merlin chirped as he loaded vegetables into a basket.

"We won't be making very much with what we have," I said, coaxing blueberries to fall into a bucket. "Not enough for everyone."

"Yet." Merlin corrected, "You're doing great, Ter. I know you're still worried about how stable your abilities are, but look at this." Merlin gestured around us, "You did all this. I don't think you realize how amazing this is."

I shrugged a little, "I'm just worried it'll stop working. I don't want the base to rely on my powers for survival. If anything changes..."

Merlin put another filled basket outside the solarium

door and came over to me. He offered his hand to help me up. "We know. Cyrus knows. The base has enough stored up to last us until the spring. What you can do will just make it easier. If anything happens to our supplies, you're our safety net."

I stood up and wrapped my arms around him, "What if—"

Merlin touched the side of my face. "We're fine, Terra. You could stop your garden today and we would still be fine. Besides, nothing is going to happen to you. I promise."

I wished I could believe him. I just couldn't shake this restless feeling, like I needed to do something. Still, I nodded and rested my head against his chest. At least if something did happen, he was right, the base would be fine.

We finished packing up the rest of the food. There were five large baskets in all and we likely could have filled more if I stayed in that room for longer. Even as we were heading for the door I could see the tiny green bulbs of new bell peppers growing where ripe ones had been removed. We took a basket each and would come back for the rest. With any luck, we would find someone on the way to help us.

Luck seemed to be on our side. We hadn't even made it down the stairs when Elleen came running up to us, "Hey, Elleen, could you—what's wrong?" Her normally calm face was red and flustered.

"You need to come quickly. Both of you. The recruitment office." Elleen explained between breaths. "I looked. Everywhere. For you."

Merlin put down his basket at the top of the grand staircase. "What happened Elleen? Is it the husks?"

Elleen shook her head, "No, someone is here. He just walked in from outside, that's all I know. Cyrus and Josh are with him right now. They said to get everyone." Everyone being the rest of the recruitment team.

I put down my basket next to Merlin's and followed him down the stairs. Elleen turned on her heel and went on in front of us. "Is there anyone else you need to find?" I asked Elleen.

"No. You two were the last ones."

Merlin and I shared a look and hurried behind her. It only took a couple of minutes to get from the solarium, down into the base to the recruitment office. The recruitment office was a large room with a table and some chairs. The walls were plastered with notes about upcoming missions or intel on other bases. The three of us rushed into the room to find the rest of the team already there. Cyrus was standing next to an exhausted-looking man with deep hollows under his eyes. He was slumped in a chair with a blanket around his shoulders and a cup of something hot in his hands.

"Terra, Merlin, good, everyone is here. Thank you Elleen." Cyrus offered a tight smile and I moved to take a seat while Merlin leaned against the wall behind me.

"Okay Cy, what's up?" Merlin asked once everyone was settled. He eyed the stranger.

"Everyone, this is Carter." Cyrus gestured to the man sitting in the chair, "He arrived an hour ago from New York to deliver this." Cyrus pulled a crumpled looking letter out of his pocket.

"I didn't hear a plane come in," Ember was the first to say with a slight crease to her brow. Considering Ember worked in the base's garage, she would have known if something new came in. There was a smear of grease on her cheek and her hair was still wrapped up in a scarf to suggest she had just come from there.

"That's because I didn't take no plane. I ran here." Carter spoke for himself between sips of what I guessed was tea.

"Wait, what? You ran? From—" A look of surprise and sheer disbelief washed over Ember's face, making the fire in her eyes flicker with interest.

"I left a month ago. I could have got here sooner but I was avoiding the husks while going through some of the most populated areas in all of the former U.S. of A."

A stunned silence ran over the group, all except for Cyrus who used the opportunity to clear his throat and give the letter in his hand a little wave. "Yes, Carter ran here, on his own, at great personal risk." Cyrus looked down at the letter, "From Moxxi, the current acting leader of the New York Alliance."

But before Cyrus could read the letter, Merlin asked, "Moxxi? What happened to Julia?"

Carter gave a shrug, "Missing, probably dead by our best guess. Let the man read the letter won't ya?"

I looked back and saw a twitch of emotion on Merlin's face. Was Julia a friend? He was barely betraying any emotion despite just finding out that someone he knew was likely dead. I could see something in his eyes that spoke of his true feelings. I reached back and took his hand in mine. He gave it a little squeeze but didn't let go as we both turned our attention back to Cyrus

"Dear Markus, or whoever is running things now. We need your help. Something has gone wrong with the cured. The compulsion isn't working anymore and they are acting like they are fresh out of the pods. New York is mayhem on an apocalyptic scale. The uncured that were in the city are now either dead or hiding. I can only hope for the latter, but I fear the former.

"Despite our resources and power, we are not doing so good. If we attempt to leave our base, they swarm like locusts. We are the few, and they are the many. We have lost so many members in attempts to leave the base. Unfortunately, our group is also divided.

"As you know, we made our home within the Museum of Natural History. In recent months our group got so big that we started a second base in Grand Central Station. We lost contact with the other group, and all attempts to get to them so far have ended in tragedy.

"I am writing this letter to plead for reinforcements. We need supplies. We need help. If you do this, I have something that might interest you. We know you have a pilot but only one plane. We have the means to access a former New Atlantis stronghold, the JFK Airport. There are supplies, data, and aircraft. Come help us and you will have first choice of whatever we find there.

Again I beg you, please send help.

Moxxi of the New York Alliance

SOS"

Cyrus folded the letter slowly and looked up at us with his burnished hazel eyes. "Well...?"

"We have to go, obviously," Merlin said at once. This was met with murmurs of agreement throughout the room.

"I thought you might say that, Merlin," Cyrus agreed with a curt nod. "Anyone else?"

"What about the base?" It was Tasha. She was one of the members of the recruitment team who didn't have Telluria. She and some of the others were trained to use more traditional weapons and were a massive help when we had to sneak under New Atlantis' radar on missions.

Carter grumbled in the corner, still holding the empty cup of tea in his hand, "What about your base? The last few hours through your woods was the most peace I've had in a month." He glowered over at Tasha, "If you're suggesting that you need to stay here to protect the place, let me tell you that you are safe for miles."

Braxton who, like Tasha, didn't have Telluria, spoke up, "Our most recent scouting missions suggest the nearest husks are a day's walk at least. I don't think everyone should go. If the husks realize we're here, the base could be swarmed within 24 hours. We need to leave some defences behind."

Cyrus nodded, then looked to the head of recruitment, "Braxton and Tasha have a point. I think a pure Tellurian team will be better suited for this. But it's your call, Josh."

Josh made a noise of assent in the back of his throat, "Tasha, Braxton, Simon, and Edgar. You will stay here and protect the base. Keep scouting to make sure they're not getting any closer. Braxton, I'll leave you in charge, okay?"

"No problem, Josh," Braxton agreed with a nod. The other three made murmurs of agreement as well.

Josh turned to Kalle who was sitting towards the back of the room with Frank, "Arthur has been teaching you to fly, right? If we get a second plane, we'll need someone to fly it back. Will you be able to do this?"

"Sure can do, Boss Man!" Kalle smacked his fists together with enthusiasm.

"Good. That just leaves the rest of us." Josh nodded at the aforementioned 'rest of us' before looking to Carter, "How long do you need to rest before you can go back? And what strain of Telluria do you have?"

"A decent night's sleep and a couple of good meals and I'll be good to go." Carter raised one hand to reveal semi-transparent skin that wrapped around his hand and rippled like water.

Josh grinned, "Oh good, a water type. You should bounce right back on your feet then."

Cyrus put his hand on Josh's shoulder, "I think I should stay here." He said with a note of regret, "I have the rest of the base to think about as well..."

Josh patted Cyrus' hand "Don't worry, we got this."

"Maybe Ember should stay too," Cyrus added.

Ember burst to her feet, the fire in her eyes sparking dangerously, "Like hell I am. You may be the leader now, but I am still a member of this team."

"Emmy..."

"Don't think for a second that I don't know what you're trying to do. No Cy. You can't put me in a box for my own protection. My place is with them. I'm going." The temperature in the room was rising ever so slightly.

Cyrus looked like he was about to argue, but Merlin moved to stand between the two siblings. He faced Cyrus, "We'll keep an eye on her, yeah? It'll be fine, I promise. Just a quick trip and we'll be back."

Cyrus met Merlin's expression and there was a silent conversation between the two friends, "England was supposed to be quick." He growled under his breath.

I felt myself sinking lower in my seat. I didn't want to think about what happened in England, but Cyrus apparently never stopped thinking about it. Merlin pulled Cyrus into a tight hug, "It won't be like that again, okay?"

Cyrus' hand fisted into the shirt on Merlin's back. It was a small crack in Cyrus' attempt to hold everything. For just a second, he held onto someone else. Too soon, Cyrus let go and marched towards the door, "Go make your preparations. I'll meet you in the hanger tomorrow morning."

Ember took a step towards her brother, "You'll still meet us for supper, right?"

Cyrus paused by the door and it seemed like he wasn't going to say anything at first. Just as he reached to open the door he said simply, "Sure Em," and left.

THE NEXT DAY I was in my room packing when Mrs. McNair came by, "Terra dear, I thought—" She stopped mid-sentence and looked down at the slim backpack that was lying open on my bed. "Where are you going?"

I usually used the duffle bag that I brought with me from my house, but Josh suggested something smaller would be better this time. With so many husks in the city, the safest way to get around was by travelling between rooftops. A small backpack would get in the way less.

"New York," I answered simply, tossing in an extra sweater. "We've been asked to help out a resistance chapter there. We're leaving tonight."

"Wh-what?!" Mrs. McNair came into the room and grabbed my hand to stop me from packing. "What do you mean New York?"

I blinked and looked from down at my wrist up to her face. She was panic-stricken as if I had just told her I was going to jump from the top of Niagara Falls. "Oh...sorry. I forgot you're new to this." I gently removed my hand from her grip and turned towards her. "Remember how I told you about the recruitment team? How we've been helping people get away from the husks? Like you?"

When I reminded her that we saved her, her face morphed into some mix between panic and conflict. "B-but Terra, it's dangerous! You're just a little girl! You could get hurt. I've seen what those things are like. You have no idea—"

I sighed and motioned for her to sit down on my bed. When she did, I sat next to her and took her hand, "Someone walked all the way from New York to get our help. They're broken up into different bases and they've lost contact with each other. They're running out of supplies. We are lucky enough to be able to grow our food, but not everyone can," I tried to explain calmly. "They need our help. Plus we might get a new plane out of it. You have no idea how much easier that will make things for us."

"No," Mrs. McNair said. "I forbid you to go. If your parents were here, they would agree with me."

I stood up again to finish packing. We would be meeting in the hanger in a couple of hours and I wanted to get a few more things done before that. "I'm sorry. It's not up for debate. I know you're worried but in the year I've been gone this has been my life. I've trained for this, I know what I'm facing out there." I zipped up the bag and tossed it over my shoulder, "Cyrus will still be here. I asked him to check in on you in case you need anything. I'll only be gone a few days at the most."

I started moving towards the door but she stopped me again by putting a hand on my shoulder. I sighed, hoping I wasn't going to have to fight her to leave. But when I looked back, her eyes were shining with tears, "You're so much like Grey. He would have wanted to help people too. Are you sure you won't reconsider it?"

I smiled and moved in for a hug, "I know there's no point in telling you not to worry but we have a good team. You know Dad would be all for it. He loved this sort of vigilante stuff. Mom would likely agree with you though."

"I hate it when you're right," Mrs. McNair mumbled and pulled back to look into my face, "Please be careful. I don't want to lose you again."

"I promise. You can come to see me off if you want?" I offered, "We'll be meeting in the hanger in about two hours."

Mrs. McNair shook her head, "No, I think it's better that I don't. I'm sure you wouldn't want me there fussing over you."

"I wouldn't mind if it was you." I gave her an extra hug, "I'll see you soon?"

"Come home safe, dear."

A few people were already in the hanger by the time I got there. Arthur and Kalle had the plane ready and were chatting with Frank by the open door. Cyrus was nearby, hands in his pockets, waiting for everyone else to arrive. Merlin, Ember, Josh, Elleen, and Carter were still missing.

"Where is everyone?" I asked as I approached the plane.

"Let me get that," Frank took my bag for me and put it inside. I gave him a murmur of thanks.

Cyrus approached me, "They're just getting the rest of the supplies from the kitchens. It'll be a bit of a haul, but you'll be bringing the New York Alliance as much food as you can comfortably carry."

I nodded, "What about Carter?" I asked, knowing he was still in the med bay that morning.

"They just wanted to give him one last look-over in the clinic. He should be here soon."

While we were still waiting, I sat down on the step of the plane and chatted with Cyrus a little more. Carter was the first to come back. He scurried towards the plane like he was in a hurry to get out of here. Not that I blamed him.

I got off the step before Carter reached me, in case he wanted to get on the plane, but he stopped and looked around at the small group. "Where are the others? Are we going yet? Weren't thinking of leaving without me were you?"

Cyrus put out a hand, "Take it easy, friend. We wouldn't have left without you. They will need your help to get around the city safely." Cyrus commented calmly, "The others will be here soon. You can find a seat on the plane if you want."

Carter looked over the plane, turning his head to take in the length of the small craft, "I can't remember the last time I was in one of these things. Before the Fall for sure, nothing like this, though. Where did you get a private jet? Stole it from the leader of New Atlantis himself or something?"

I coughed, not wanting to point out that said leader of New Atlantis was in a cell below us somewhere.

"It came with the mansion," Cyrus explained. "It and everything here belonged to the man who used to own this house. He left everything to my father when he passed. My father was still working on a cure then, he just wanted to help in any way he could."

There was a dark smirk on Carter's face, "Riiiiight. Your daddy used to work for New Atlantis, didn't he? Did he ever tell you about how they created the husks?"

Cyrus' mouth set into a hard line, "I'm well aware of the history, thank you."

"Honestly, I was never quite sure about letting a guy like that run things. No offence, of course. Just a bit too close to the enemy if you know what I mean." Carter's expression suggested that he didn't consider Cyrus to be much better.

"Cyrus is doing everything he can for this base, and yours." I bit out, "The only enemy we have now is the husks."

Carter put his hands in the air, "Easy, easy. I mean no offence."

There was a tense silence between Carter, Cyrus, and myself that was mercifully cut short when Merlin called out from the door. "We're here!" Merlin along with Ember, Elleen, and Josh were all carrying crates of food from the kitchens. It looked like a lot, but I knew it wouldn't last long in a large group like the New York Alliance.

"Are you sure we'll be able to carry all that?" I asked, eyeing the four crates of food with some doubt.

Merlin shrugged and handed his crate off to Frank. "I think so. It won't be too bad once it's all split up and it's not all heavy."

"I'm sure you'll do fine," Cyrus commented as the others got the crates loaded onto the plane. We would split it all up between our bags once we were in the air, "Well, everyone is here. Do you have everything you need?"

Several voices murmured in agreement. Ember skipped up to her brother and gave him a hug, "Don't miss us too much, big brother. And don't let the base blow up while we're gone."

"I'll leave the explosions to you, Em. Be careful, okay?"

Ember giggled and stepped back to throw her arm around me, "You won't have a chance to miss us."

Cyrus didn't look so sure about that, but he turned to

Arthur and gestured to the plane, "Start it up then, Arthur. It looks like you're good to go."

Arthur touched the tip of his baseball cap and nodded at Kalle. The two men climbed into the cockpit to get things ready and the rest of us found our seats on the plane. I watched Cyrus out the window as he walked back from the plane and stood by the door. Despite all the work he had to get back to, he still wanted to watch us go.

IT WAS GETTING dark by the time we flew over New York. After we got the food sorted into our bags, we did what we could to wait out the time. Frank sat up with Kalle and Arthur. The door to the cockpit was open so we could hear the animated conversation they were having about basketball. Frank loved old basketball stats and he dreamed of bringing back nationwide tournaments again. That is, if the world ever returned to some semblance of normal. He did organize smaller tournaments in our base from time to time. The ballroom in the mansion did make a fairly good, though small, basketball court when we couldn't play outside.

Ember and Elleen were curled up in the corner together, giggling over some book they had brought from the library. Carter was asleep. He barely had a day to rest at the base and it would be a long night yet. Josh was silently looking out the window.

Merlin and I were huddled around a puzzle. It wasn't a very long flight to New York, but it was enough for us to put the edges together. If we were careful, we could probably keep it on the table. It would only take a couple of trips to finish it.

When we were getting close to landing, Arthur turned off all lights, including the outside and the cabin. While he couldn't do much about the sound, we wanted to attract the least amount of attention as possible. "Hey, guys! I'm going to start landing now!" Arthur called from his seat, "Seatbelts and all that. You know the drill. Thanks for flying Arty Airlines."

Kalle scoffed beside him, "Arty Airlines? Is that really what you're going to call it?"

"Why not? I'm pilot numero uno after all. You, wee salad leaf, are just my protege."

Kalle laughed and swatted the landing checklist at Arthur. "Yeah because I'm the only one who can put up with you for hours at a time," he countered and buckled his seatbelt. After that bit of banter, Kalle slid right back into his role as co-pilot, helping Arthur with the landing.

I looked out the window but there was nothing to see. It was only inky blackness beneath us for as far as I could see. "My parents used to say that when you flew anywhere at night, you could look down and the city lights would shine like stars." I murmured, unable to see the ground that we were getting closer to. I couldn't see it, but I could feel it in the plants that lived there. It felt like flying into an embrace.

"I saw it once." Merlin said, leaning in close to me so he could look out the window as well, "When I was five. I remember it, just all those lights below that flew past when we were landing. I told my mom it was like being in a spaceship."

"Do you think we'll get to see it again?" I asked as I felt the lurch of the landing gear lowering.

"I don't know." Merlin reached over and took my hand.

He gave it a squeeze to help distract me from all the plant life coming so close so fast. "I'm not sure the world will ever really go back to the way it was. Too much has happened now. There will probably be lights again, maybe peace again, but those big cities that we were used to, with all the sprawling technology and stuff like that? That's the part I'm more dubious on."

We landed in what was once a small private airport near Manhattan and rolled the plane into an empty hanger. It would be safe enough until we came back for it. Normally, Arthur would stay with the plane so that he could move it if there was any trouble, but this time he needed to come with us. On the bright side, it meant another pair of hands to help carry the food.

Since I had a smaller bag, I offered to take some of the heavier stuff. I crammed a bag of flour and some vegetables into my bag. I didn't mind the weight, it reminded me of the days when I would take fruits and vegetables from my dad's garden to the market to trade for things that weren't provided by New Atlantis.

It was pitch black by the time we started our trek towards Manhattan. We guessed it would take us a few hours to get to the Museum of Natural History, so with any luck we would make it there before dawn. We walked in near silence, not wanting to wake any nearby husks if we could help it. I held Merlin's hand as we walked, enjoying just having him there next to me. Behind me, I could hear Elleen whispering to Ember the different constellations in the sky. It was a clear night with a sliver of moon, letting the stars shine in all their glory.

"You know that rhyme about star light star bright the first star you see tonight? The funny thing about that is the first stars you see at night are planets. See that one there?"

Elleen must have been pointing somewhere in the sky as Ember gasped softly.

"You mean that big orange one?" Ember asked, whispering just as softly as Elleen was.

"Yeah, that one," Elleen continued, "That orange one is Mars. It must be really close right now to be so bright. And that one there is Venus. It's usually the first one you can see at night. Um, and Jupiter is over there."

"So what's the first star then?" asked Ember, "If I'm going to be wishing on stars, I would like to be wishing on actual stars."

Elleen stifled a soft giggle, "That would be Sirius B, probably. Right....erm, there."

While Elleen continued to point out different stars to Ember, I gave Merlin's hand a soft squeeze, "Elleen has started on science. I'm surprised you haven't been telling me the history of the Statue of Liberty or something yet."

Merlin gave a little of a guilty chuckle, "Well for one, it's dark out and she would be a little hard to see. Also, I don't know a lot about this particular area. I know a little about Manhattan, though."

"Oh?" I grinned, "Like what? Give me a random fact," I dared him.

He laughed again, or rather his chest shook with silent mirth, "Not yet, patience grasshopper. I would rather you see the thing I'm talking about rather than just spitting random facts at you."

"Have it your way then." I punched him lightly in the arm, and we went back to walking in comfortable silence.

After a couple of hours we made it to the Hudson River. We were still a long way from dawn, but the moon and stars made the sky just light enough to see the faintest outline of the city in the dark.

We made it to the water's edge and Carter crossed his arms, "So what's the plan for getting across?" he asked. He missed out on a lot of the planning due to being in the med bay. "You probably don't want to swim. You're not taking the bridge, that's for sure. The husks like to sleep in the abandoned New Atlantis buses." He smirked and looked around at us, "I mean, we could take the bridge, they would love it. Not great if you want to live to see the sun again though."

Josh shook his head, "Thank you for that...assessment...Carter. But no," he stated cooly. "We're going to make a bridge."

Merlin strolled out onto the water's surface and looked down at the swirling darkness beneath his feet, "You know...I know we decided on a bridge when we were planning, but I have another idea."

"What is it Merlin?" Josh asked, totally unfazed by Merlin walking on water.

Merlin grinned and looked over at me, "What about a boat? If you can make one, I should be able to push it along."

My mouth hung open slightly, "You're kidding, right?"

"Why not? You used to be an expert at shaping stone. It's not too different," Merlin pointed out. "It doesn't need to be anything fancy. Just a raft really. You can do that."

I wanted to punch him. He smirked at me, knowing that I wanted to punch him. I hated when he was right. "I'll try...but if it doesn't work maybe me and Kalle can build a bridge or something."

"A good Plan B. How about it, Josh? Should we let Terra

build us a boat?" Merlin asked, waiting to get the okay from our leader before I went ahead and attempted this.

Josh nodded, "Why not? It'll likely be faster and more energy-efficient than a bridge. Go ahead and give it a try Terra."

"Fine..." I pulled a maple key out of my pocket and let it spiral down to the water. It floated there on the surface of the river, where I could already feel the small bundle of life starting to uncoil.

Carter walked out on the water after Merlin and looked back at me, "What the hell is she doing?" he asked Merlin, "How is she supposed to make a boat?"

"Shhh, just watch. You'll see," Merlin hushed Carter with a small chuckle. He then winked at me, "Go on, Terra."

I reached out a hand to the maple key. Slowly I coaxed from seed to seedling and encouraged it to grow wide rather than tall. Roots weaved outwards from the trunk to form a wide raft before slipping down beneath the water. The trunk itself grew sideways across the woven roots to form a seat for us. Branches arched around the trunk and upwards towards the shivering stars. My breath was starting to quicken by the time it was done and I stopped to look at my work. It didn't look much like a boat, but it floated.

"Sweet!" Merlin cheered, "All aboard, everyone. Leave the rest to me."

"The hell kind of Telluria is that?!" Carter stood back from my 'boat' like it was some kind of monstrosity. For a moment he seemed to lose concentration of his power and his foot dipped into the actual water.

Merlin laughed while Carter shook off his now wet foot, "Be careful would you. You just told us we probably wouldn't want to swim in this." He walked back to me and threw an arm around my shoulders, "This is Terra's power."

Josh looked as proud as a peacock at my creation, "It's perfect, Terra! Thank you. Come on everyone," he waved at the others to get on the 'boat.' I still wasn't sure if I wanted to call it a boat exactly. It mostly just looked like a tree that had started growing sideways in some heavy wind...that just happened to float.

"Well, it's...something," Carter said, crossing his arms.

I stood on the water's edge while everyone else climbed on the 'boat.' The wide stance of the roots was keeping it surprisingly stable with everyone shuffling aboard. "I used to be earth. This is...new," I murmured. By then everyone else had climbed on, so I got on last.

Merlin used his manipulation of water to propel the boat across the river. He and Carter walked alongside the boat, though it looked like they were using their powers to be moving faster than their leisurely pace.

Carter had his hands in his pockets and kept looking over at me, "Right, so is Telluria known for mutating like that?"

I decided to watch the city coming towards us rather than watch them. "Not exactly, no," I murmured, not wanting to get into all of the details about why my powers changed.

"Terra's been through some stuff," Merlin explained to Carter without actually saying anything. He was acting calm enough but I thought I saw something in his eyes, the ghost of the rage he showed way back then. "Don't worry, it's not catching. I doubt it will happen to anyone else."

Carter narrowed his eyes, "Then maybe you should share with the whole group huh, to make sure it doesn't happen?" Carter pressed again.

There was a spark of light and I looked over to see Ember's eyes blazing with fire, "How about no."

"Jesus, fine, calm down," Carter put his hands up defensively. "Don't burn your boat down."

I could hear Josh sigh over the sound of rippling water. "Okay, guys. We can talk about this later. We don't want to be heard, yeah? Keep it down until we make it to the museum."

"No problem, Boss," Merlin chirped, and went back to propelling the boat. All anger seemed to flow out of him with the sound of the gently lapping water of the Hudson.

We got lucky as no one was lurking on the docks when we pulled up. I had our boat anchor itself against the dock so it might still be there if we needed it again. The towering buildings of Manhattan seemed to disappear into the star-strewn sky. Carter had already warned us that we wouldn't be able to stay on the ground level for very long. If any husks were around, they would swarm us the moment they spotted us.

"Alright, Carter, you're up," Josh motioned to Carter, "You'll lead from here."

Carter started walking towards the nearest building, "Get to the top of this building, then we'll take the rooftops to the museum. It's not far now." He looked back and put a finger to his lips, "Remember to be quiet, now. You don't want to get caught." Without any warning, water erupted beneath Carter and shot him upwards to the roof.

Kalle pushed up the sleeves of his hoodie, "Let me get this one." He offered and the cracked pavement rose up from the ground to form stairs.

While the others started to climb up after Carter, I

patted Kalle on the shoulder, "Let's take every other build-ing, okay?"

"Thanks Terra, but that's fine. As Carter said, it's not far. You save your strength for the real stuff."

I bit my lip but nodded, "If you're sure." I said then started up the stairs. I knew that Kalle's powers had gotten stronger since having to go on so many flights with Arthur. Clearing runways meant big bursts of power in a controlled manner. He was likely stronger than I ever was when my powers were still earth. And, well...we both knew my endurance wasn't what it once was.

Kalle continued to make bridges between the buildings. I could hear his breathing starting to pick up but I held off on offering to help again. If he really started to get tired, then I would. The city was deadly quiet. There were times I thought I heard a scream in the distance, but when I stopped to listen it was only silence. It felt like we were being watched, maybe we were. It wasn't like we spent enough time around the husks to really understand their habits yet. If Nikolai had his way, he probably would have kept one in the base to experiment on. I wouldn't have been surprised if he had asked for that, but Cyrus likely said no.

"Being out here really gives you the chills, huh?" Elleen whispered, looking down from one of Kalle's bridges towards the distant streets. We were so high in the air there would be no way we could see anyone below.

Arthur was walking near the front of the group, just after Frank, "I get the same feeling when I fly sometimes. It's just not what it used to be."

Finally the buildings started to get lower and I could feel an expanse of greenery nearby. We must have reached Central Park, which meant we were nearly at the museum. Carter directed Kalle to make his last bridge towards what looked like a cluster of low connected roofs surrounded by a ring of trees. We went to the centre-most roof and Carter suddenly looked more chipper than he had all night. He put out his arms to gesture around him, "Welcome to the Museum of Natural History. Otherwise known as the home of the New York Alliance. Now if you'll just follow me, I'll be your tour guide this...morning?"

The edge of the sky was just starting to stain pink and the park in front of us was starting to glow with the late autumn leaves. It must have been beautiful in the day. Carter led us to the corner between two rooftops where there was a bit of exposed wall. There was a small window set into the wall that was mirrored so we couldn't see in. It was hard to tell if the window had always been there, or if an elementalist had added it later.

Carter knocked on the glass and waited. It was less than ten seconds and a section of the wall swung out like a door. A small boy who couldn't have been any older than ten barrelled into Carter. "You made it back! I knew you would make it back!"

"Hey, kiddo," Carter ruffled the boy's hair, "Told you I would be back, didn't I? Come on, let's get inside."

The boy tugged on Carter's hand and we all climbed in through the opening in the wall. Once we were all inside, the boy scurried around us to close up the wall once again.

"Do you think Mox is up yet?" Carter asked. We were in a darkened hall, only slightly lit by the coming dawn.

The boy nodded, "She'll be up for sure. I'll go get her!" He ran off, leaving us alone to follow Carter.

We moved slowly down the hallway, deeper into the museum. It was clear that the earth elementalists must have added and moved walls to suit the needs of the base, but you could still see some of the museum. As we came down a flight of steps and out into an open area, my mouth fell open as my eyes moved upwards. In the dimly lit room, the bones of a t-rex loomed over us. Glass cases were littered through the space and held artifacts from almost every era. Just from where I stood I saw jewels, wooden bowls, and scarab pins. Priceless art hung from every spare inch of space on the wall, and even more left carefully stacked against the wall.

"Jules heard what New Atlantis did to the art in Paris, so she wanted to save as much as she could," Carter explained, referencing the old leader of the New York Alliance. "Not just the art, but our history. There's another room we call the library just full of books that we managed to smuggle back here."

"What did they do?" I ventured to ask.

Carter looked back at me. At first I didn't think he was going to answer, but then he shrugged and continued forward, "Took them off the walls and carted them off somewhere. That was New Atlantis' thing. They did it to a lot of the museums. I heard the Vatican was totally emptied. They hoarded everything like dragons. Did you ever try going to a library after the fall?"

I nodded, "I only bothered to try once." After New Atlantis took over, the library was locked up. There was a computer terminal left in front of the library doors. You could use that to order books to come to your house, but the selection was limited. New Atlantis always insisted it was hard to keep a wider variety of books in stock simply because so many people wanted them. That answer never seemed quite right."

"Righty-o! Oldest trick in the book. If you want to control the world, you need to control the information." Carter tapped the side of his head and started walking again, "That's what made me join, before I even caught

Telluria. I was saying for ages that there was something sketchy about the way New Atlantis ran things. But did anyone listen to me? No sir. I was just a conspiracy theorist looking a gift horse in the face."

I laughed under my breath, but as I did Merlin squeezed my hand. "I had similar thoughts, actually," he admitted. "When New Atlantis reopened the library in my hometown, I went to find some new history books. There was...nothing. There were a few basic textbooks, the kind of things that everyone would know, but that was it. It gave me a weird feeling, so I left."

"It must have been great when you made it to the base," I murmured back. "Half the mansion library is history."

Merlin grinned and nodded. Ember was walking just behind us, "Daddy always said the library was for everyone. Though...I've been telling Cy that maybe he should look into asking someone to act as a librarian. Now that we're getting so many people it wouldn't be a bad idea to keep track of things."

"Merlin would actually have to return the stack next to his bed." I giggled.

"Arthur would actually have to return his—mmph!" Kalle's voice was cut off and I looked back to see Arthur holding Kalle in a headlock with his hand over his mouth.

I stifled a giggle and was about to say something but my attention was drawn to the sound of footsteps. "Carter!" A small woman with a willowy frame ran up to Carter and jumped into his arms. He seemed to be used to this, as he caught her effortlessly and held her while she kissed both his cheeks, "I was worried sick! I was starting to think you would never come back."

"Hey Mox," Carter chuckled and looked at her face. "Of course I came back. Who would you mouth off to if I didn't?" His voice lowered as he spoke, but he then cleared his throat, "These guys are from Markus' place."

The small woman untangled herself from Carter's arms and turned to face us. There was a shine of tears in her eyes, but her expression had hardened into a business face. "Good. Can I assume Carter caught you up on our situation?"

Josh stepped forward and offered his hand to shake, "I believe we've met before. I'm Josh."

Moxxi blinked and did a double-take on Josh's face, "Oh...oh! Joshua! Yes, I remember! And...oh Merlin!" The serious demeanour melted away and she reached out to hug both of them. "It's so good to see you both again. Julia would have loved to see you."

Merlin smiled gently, "I know. It was sad to hear she was gone."

"Well...not gone. No proof anyway..." Moxxi amended, stepping back and twisting her hands together. "It's been weeks now. She went with a small group to regain contact with Grand Central Station and...well we haven't heard anything. We don't know if any of them are alive or if they're..." Moxxi paused and took a small breath, "Never-mind. The point is, you're here now. Food is a bit short nowadays but breakfast should be ready soon or—"

Josh put his hand up, "Thanks Moxxi, but I think the main thing we all need right now is some rest."

"O-oh! Certainly. I didn't even... of course, you would travel at night. It's the safest, after all. Right...um...well we can set you up in the Blum Lecture Room. We have some cots free, there should be enough for everyone. Alright..."

Moxxi hurried off mid-sentence. I looked over to Merlin, "She seemed...nice?"

Merlin came back to me and wrapped an arm around

my waist. "Yeah, she's always like that. A bit frazzled, but she makes a good leader," he explained with a soft chuckle.

Moxxi soon returned with a couple of helpers and led us off to a large empty room. There was more art on the walls, but the floor space had been completely cleared out. Cots, blankets, and pillows were brought in for us and we set up our beds around the room. Merlin and I picked a spot tucked away in the corner and pushed our cots together. We couldn't really snuggle, not unless one of us wanted to sleep on the hard edge of the cots, but we could at least hold hands. That would be enough.

Elleen and Ember set up theirs together in the near middle of the room. Kalle, Frank, and Arthur made a little triangle of their cots over by the far wall where the lecturer would have stood once upon a time. Josh was out talking to Moxxi for the moment, and Carter had left to find his usual room. The members of the New York Alliance had their rooms up on a higher floor. Though I wondered if his usual spot was still there for him. Everyone we had come across so far seemed surprised that he had come back at all. I couldn't imagine doing that, sending someone from our base with no idea if they would ever come back alive.

Merlin burrowed down into his blanket like a hibernating polar bear. "What's wrong, Terra?"

I leaned over to kiss his nose, as his face was the only thing showing, "Just thinking." I slipped off my shoes and got in my cot. I could see why Merlin looked so comfy, it felt like a cocoon. There was a small rustling of blankets and Merlin's hand found mine.

"Penny for your thoughts?" he asked.

I laughed lightly, "I was raised in Canada. We didn't have pennies. But..." I pulled up the blanket a little more, "I was just thinking about Carter. If you or Em or...anyone...if any of you had to leave and if I didn't know if I would ever see you again..."

Merlin nudged forward so that he could press his forehead against mine, "I'm not going anywhere," he promised. "From this day to yesterday, to whatever comes, we're in this together, right?"

"Right," I whispered back and fell asleep with his hand still in mine.

I WOKE late in the afternoon around supper time. Some of the beds were already empty by the time I begrudgingly left the comfort and warmth of my cocoon. Ember and Elleen were still in the room, sitting on their cots and talking in low voices. Merlin was gone.

"Em, where is everyone?" I asked as I pulled on my shoes.

Ember grinned a little, "The boys went to find us something to eat. I think Arthur and Kalle might have gone to talk about those planes." She explained and turned around on her cot, "There's like...a shower situation around the hall. I could show you if you like."

I got up, wondering if I should make my bed or something. It looked like everyone else mostly just left things where they were. So instead I grabbed my bag, "Sure," I agreed. "A shower would be great. Was I the last one to wake up?"

"Yup!" Ember hopped up from her bed and gave Elleen a little pat on the head. I thought I saw Elleen's cheeks turn the faintest shade of pink before she buried it in a map. "It's just over here," Ember practically skipped down the hall and I followed after her as closely as I could. I couldn't help but look around at the scattered exhibits that seemed to be everywhere. Everything was so crowded and stacked together I could only imagine how many museums worth of pieces were being kept here away from what was once the prying fingers of New Atlantis.

"How did they keep this place hidden from New Atlantis anyway?" I asked.

"Oh..." Ember looked back at me, "I don't know the full story, actually. Apparently the place like...collapsed. Or so New Atlantis was left to believe. It used to be when you walked in the front doors, only the lobby was there. The members of the New York Alliance made a little art of their own and made it look like the roof had collapsed and blocked off the rest of the museum. It was a little risky to have the base so close to the city center, but it worked out." Ember turned into a doorway that still had the old museum bathroom signs over it.

"The city center was in Central Park, right?" I asked.

"Yeah. It was on the Great Lawn. Or at least that's where it was for the last few years. When New Atlantis first started, it was in Times Square. But one of the buildings collapsed so they had to move."

We walked into a massive bathroom. It looked like the old bathrooms had been combined to make one big one, complete with shower stalls. "Collapsed? How did that happen?" It seemed odd that buildings would just collapse. It wasn't as if they were particularly decrepit. It was only a few years since the fall of the old ways, not centuries.

Ember tilted her head in thought, "No one is quite sure exactly. It was assumed to be structural damage in the building. Daddy thought someone may have accidentally triggered their Telluria in a big way."

"Right..." I murmured. "Well, thanks for showing me here. I'll meet you back in the room?"

"Sure thing!" Ember waved and skipped off back to our room. I just stood there for a second, watching her go. Why was she so chipper all of a sudden?

Half of the bathroom looked as though it was mostly untouched from the original design, the other had been redesigned into shower stalls using thin stone walls. It was obviously Tellurian made as it was clear to see it was once two bathrooms, and there would have been no reason to have showers here in the museum before. Whoever made the stalls had decorated the walls with a gorgeous filigree pattern. When I was still an earth elementalist, I never would have been able to do something so delicate.

The plumbing itself looked a bit makeshift with salvaged pipes suspended over the stalls. The stalls themselves were split in half. The first portion was a changing area with a small bench, the shower itself was in the second portion. I undressed, leaving my clothes and bag on the small bench, and stepped into the shower side of my stall. The water was instantly hot and I let it hit my shoulders and back. After the night before, my muscles were tense and sore. No doubt things were only going to get worse. As soon as it got dark we were likely going to be heading out again. Back out in the hallway, there was the soft orange glow of sunset. We probably had a couple of hours before we would be heading out again.

After the small luxury of a hot shower, I wrapped myself up in a towel and went back out to get my clothes. Except, my clothes weren't where I left them.

"Hello," Carter stepped into the entrance of my stall

with my bag in his hand and my clothes stuffed into the top of it.

"Give those back!" I yelled at him and clutched my towel closed with both hands.

He put a finger to his lips, "If you want them back you'll keep it down. I don't want your boyfriend running in here and getting the wrong idea."

My eyes flicked from my bag, then to his face, "What? That you're some kind of pervert trying to sneak a look at his girlfriend in the shower?" I knew there were seeds in my bag, I could feel them from where I stood. Would I be able to control them? Normally I needed to be a bit closer.

"Nothing like that, calm down." He dropped my bag on the floor but didn't make any move to hand it over. "I just want to ask a few questions, alright? And this is the first time I've seen you without your shadow."

"Right. A normal person would have just asked for a word. But no, you need to sneak into a shower." I wondered if I could just push past him and take my bag. I tried to mentally reach out for the seeds and see what I could wake up.

Carter looked me over and I felt his eyes stopping on each of my exposed marks. Maybe that's why he decided to corner me just out of the shower. He wanted to see the mark of my strange powers. "How many strains do you have, anyway? I see earth...fire...water..."

I wish I had another towel. I wish I had my clothes. The way his eyes moved over me made me feel naked despite having everything covered. It was almost too bad he didn't get to meet Nikolai when he was still at the base. The two would have probably gotten along fine. "I have eight marks," I growled. "Come on, just give me my clothes back and I'll answer whatever questions you want when I'm dressed."

He shook his head, "I have no guarantee of that, princess, and I haven't decided if I trust you yet." He whistled low through his teeth, "Eight, huh. I've never even heard of someone having two. Last I checked you can't have more than one. But here you are..." His hand gestured lazily to my body. "Tell me how you got them and then I want to know about your powers."

I took a small step back. A knot formed in the pit of my gut just thinking about how I got these marks. It wasn't a secret at our base, or even in our group. He could have asked anyone. Of course, he didn't know that. "The combination of all the strains changed my powers. I used to be earth. The man who did this to me...he called my power Vita, the element of life." I opted not to go into detail how I was still learning to control my power and that my endurance wasn't what it used to be. Speaking of, I was pretty sure I could feel one of my seeds starting to uncurl. Maybe I could have the bag drag itself to me. There was also the problem that we were surrounded by his element, water.

"Vita? You said some guy did this? What happened?"

A small shudder moved down my spine. I was trying to avoid talking about it. Carter took a step forward, and the words tumbled out of my mouth, "Nikolai Wolfe used me as a human experiment. He injected me with the different strains in an attempt to make Vita. And it...worked."

"Wolfe?! That—" Carter snatched up the bag again as though he might run off with it, "You're working with him?"

I gave Carter the most scathing look I could manage, "Not in any willing capacity, no." I looked down at my bag and saw the smallest leaf poking out from the zipper. Just a little longer...

I watched his face, trying to decide what he was thinking. He took two steps forwards and I scrambled backwards until my back pressed against the shower wall. "Keep this between us," he muttered and hurled my bag at me. It slipped to the floor and by the time I had scrambled to pick it up, Carter had gone. With my bag hugged to my chest, I walked out of the stall and took a cursory look around to make sure he was gone. Once I was sure I was alone again, I took a shaky breath and sank down to the floor.

Part of me wanted to curl up on the floor and cry. But I didn't. I took a few deep breaths and forced myself to pull on my usual uniform of jeans, a t-shirt, and a weathered jacket. By the time I made it back to the room, the boys were back and everyone was sitting around with small amounts of food shared between them.

"Hey Ter!" Merlin called out and patted the spot next to him on his cot. They all seemed to be eating a chunky sort of...something. "Soup," Merlin said as he offered me a bowl, "More or less anyway."

"What does that even mean?" I sat down and tasted the concoction in the bowl. Well, it was soup, but also oatmeal. Soup was a closer description of what it was, as the oats were just kind of floating in the broth. It didn't taste bad, just different.

Merlin chuckled and nodded, "Yeah, they are running low on pretty much everything so the cook has taken to some creative means of bulking up what they have."

I chased a carrot with my spoon. I wondered what they were doing for food now. Did they have a garden some-where in this building? Or were they still relying on the last of their supplies? Maybe I could help them set something up? They wouldn't be able to survive on oats and the few supplies we brought them for long. Especially when, or if, we got the rest of their group back together.

I leaned into Merlin, feeling the warmth of him through his t-shirt. Warm food and having him close helped calm me down from what happened earlier. I knew Carter said to be quiet, but I also debated what he could even do if I did talk. We would be leaving soon and he would be staying here. I likely would never see him again in my life, "Hey Merlin..."

It was at that moment that Moxxi and Carter walked into the room. I nearly dropped my soup, but caught myself in time and moved to balance my bowl on my lap.

"I hope you're all enjoying your supper," Moxxi began, standing at the head of the room. "I've already spoken to Josh, but I think it's time to catch you all up to speed on the situation as we understand it. We're also going to talk about what we'll do next."

My eyes flicked up long enough to see Carter watching me. I looked back down and took a sip of my soup. His eyes felt like spiders.

Kalle was the first to speak, "Are we going out tonight?" He asked from where he, Arthur, and Frank were sitting.

Carter nodded, "As I said before, the husks are less active at night. So long as we stay off the streets and stick to the rooftops, we should be able to avoid them."

I noted that he used the word we. "You're going, are you?" I asked, thankfully keeping my voice level.

His lips twisted into a mocking grin, "Unless you have a thorough understanding of the city, Princess, yes."

Moxxi made an audible sigh and rolled her eyes, "Carter, please don't antagonize our guests. My apologies, Terra, but yes, he is going." The small woman shrugged, "He's our best scout, and he was able to make it all the way to your base and back without too much trouble. He's your best option to guide you around the city even—"

"Is he even physically strong enough to come with us?" I pressed on, "He just travelled all the way to our base on foot and barely got a day's rest before coming back."

Carter laughed under his breath, "As much as I appreciate your concern for my well being, I'll be fine."

Apparently not noticing the sudden tension, Moxxi offered an apologetic smile, "I had similar concerns but I trust Carter and he said he's fine to go."

I could feel my face twisting in a way that I didn't particularly like and looked down to eat my soup. I said nothing back.

"If there are no other objections..." Moxxi paused for a moment to give anyone else a chance to speak. "The largest group of us were in Grand Central Station. There were plenty of places to hide and they built a rather large base within it. I'm comfortable believing that the husks wouldn't have got to them. My main concern is that they could have been locked in without any means of getting additional food or supplies. We've tried sending out scouts, but so far no one has come back. I'm thinking that will be the best place for you to start looking for them."

Josh nodded, "Mention the other places as well."

"Oh right!"

However, instead of Moxxi answering, Carter took over. I was starting to wonder who was the actual leader of this whole bloody place. "There's an old Apple store not far from here. When I was sneaking out of the city, I noticed the glass was all painted black. Bit of a weird thing for the husks to do. If we have time, I think it's worth checking out."

Ember bounced in her seat a little, "Oh is that the one that looks like a glass cube?"

"That's the one!" Carter pointed finger guns at Ember, "It's closer, but me and Mox agree it's better to check out Grand Central first. Once we get there, they might have other places that would be good to check."

Josh checked his watch and stood up. He walked over to Moxxi and Carter, "Looks like we have about an hour before full dark. Everyone start getting ready. Carter? How about you tell them all about the route we'll be taking."

Moxxi interjected before the boys got down to business. She looked over to Arthur, "Arthur was it? You're welcome to explore as much as you want. Some of the others are around and will be able to help you."

Arthur grinned, "Actually, do you have someone I could talk to about those planes?"

"Oh right!" Moxxi tapped her lips, "That would be Christopher. I'll introduce you later, kay?"

Arthur nodded, "That sounds fine," he replied and looked back at Kalle. Kalle looked, guarded, or hurt? I couldn't really read his expression. I turned my attention back to Josh and Carter.

Josh pulled out a map and held it up. With the research we did before coming here, we had a general idea of the layout of the city, but I had to begrudgingly admit that Carter knew things that we wouldn't have been able to find out through research alone. Over the next several minutes he talked out the best routes to take to Grand Central. He was able to point out what buildings were safe, what had fallen, and what ones were filled with husks.

I drank the rest of my gritty broth and Merlin tapped me on the shoulder, "Something wrong?" He whispered.

"No." I didn't look over at him, just took another sip of the broth.

"You didn't have any problem with Carter before," he

pointed out. He touched a knot in my shoulder as a silent way of letting me know he could tell how tense I was.

"It's nothing, Merlin." I looked down at the empty bowl, and then to his, "Are you done with that? I can take them back to the kitchen."

Merlin let me take the bowl out of his hands and stack it with mine, "You don't even know where the kitchen is."

"I'm sure I'll figure it out," I continued on, standing up to go.

"Ter—"

"Oh, do you think we'll need to take anything with us?" I offered a smile that didn't feel like it reached my eyes, "I'd like to travel as light as possible."

Merlin's mouth set into a hard line, "Maybe a flashlight just in case, and your seeds of course. I know Kalle is bringing the first aid bag." He reached out to take my free hand, "Are you sure nothing's wrong?"

I took a small breath and leaned over to kiss the tip of his nose, "I'm just nervous about the mission, I guess. The husks are a different kind of evil than New Atlantis, you know?"

"I know..." Merlin wrapped an arm around me and kissed the top of my head, "You'd tell me if anything was actually wrong though?"

"Of course I would." And I hoped he didn't see the lie in my eyes.

Roughly an hour later we were back on the roof of the museum and ready to go. Arthur and Moxxi were there to see us off. I was holding Merlin's hand, looking out towards the black horizon.

"Good luck to you all. And please...come back." Moxxi said with a voice that suggested she had stood on this roof one too many times saying those exact words.

Arthur stood next to her with his hands in his pockets. I noticed that he had a weathered paperback under one palm. No doubt he planned to do his usual routine of reading after he finished talking to Christopher. Arthur was watching Kalle, just Kalle. There was a tight smile on his lips. "I'm putting a pot of tea on. I'll save you some," he said in a low voice.

"Counting on it," Kalle replied, biting his lip. The two locked eyes. I felt the need to look away and give them some privacy despite them not actually doing anything. There was just something so intense right there at that moment that made my cheeks burn.

Perhaps thankfully, Josh interrupted the silence, "Alright, let's get going."

Kalle cleared his throat and turned away. He walked to the edge of the roof without looking back at Arthur. The stone of the museum started to bend itself toward the next building. We said one last goodbye and started the trek across the city.

From there on, myself and Kalle made bridges from building to building. It wasn't quite every other building, as Kalle had more stamina than me. Whenever he noticed I was getting tired, he would take over for an extra bridge or two.

It was hard to see, but I knew from our planning that we were heading down 5th avenue. Some of the more famous buildings stood silhouetted against the light of the moon. It was the only light we had, but it was enough. There was little activity from the husks. Every so often I thought I saw the shadow of one far below us or in a window. I tried to let myself think that they were all asleep for the night. I almost believed it, until a scream pierced the air.

It was the guttural broken cry of someone's life ending. "Where is that coming from?" I whispered.

Carter looked back at me, "No idea. Let's not stand around to find out, huh?" He jumped on the wooden bridge I was still growing across the expanse of air. The others were darting across and I looked back at Kalle. Except, it wasn't just Kalle.

Someone who wasn't in our group was standing there. They were little more than a dark form by the rooftop door. "Where are you going? I was just making supper. Won't you come for supper?" The woman called out in a perfectly pleasant voice. Something round was dangling from her hand. Something that had hair—

"Terra go!" Kalle yelled. I scrambled ahead of him and we both hit the bridge running. The woman was still calling out to us and she wasn't getting any further away. By the time we made it over to the other side, I looked back to see that she was making her way across my bridge.

"Take it down now!" Carter shouted.

The bridge started to dismantle itself and the husk slipped through the floor of the wood, catching herself on a single branch. Maybe if I just grew the branch enough to reach the other side, she would be able to climb back.

"Pl-please! Help! I have a family! Please!" The husk cried as she scrambled and clung to the branch. Her feet swung wildly in the open air.

Carter marched up to me and shoved me in the shoulder, "It's it or us. It wouldn't hesitate to kill any of us."

"She's a person too!" I countered and tried to catch her with the branches. Her screaming was attracting more husks from nearby. Several were walking out onto the roof of her building. I could hear sneering and the husks were shoving each other like it was some great spectacle. Someone picked up the head the husk-woman had been holding and hurled it at her. The head bounced off her foot and tumbled towards the streets far below.

Suddenly a jet of water shot from over my shoulder. It hit the woman in the hands and she lost her grip on the branch. I couldn't tear my eyes away as her limbs flailed and her screaming grew further and further away until it stopped.

"Don't try to play hero for a monster, Princess," Carter hissed, then looked up at the crowd of husks on the opposite roof. My branch was still there and husks were either jumping or throwing their neighbour from the roof to try and reach it. Carter gripped my arm and pushed me back.

"You're going to get us killed if you keep hesitating. When I say take it down, you take it down!"

I struggled and tried to pull out of his grip. The others were coming closer with Merlin in the lead, "Let her go. Now." His eyes sparked with the deep grey of the sea during a storm.

"I don't want to die today. Do you, pretty boy?" Nonetheless, Carter let go.

I could still feel where his fingers gripped me. I took a step towards Merlin where he was still glaring at Carter. Just as I did, we heard a rattle and a muffled shout from somewhere on our roof.

Kalle immediately went to work on creating the next bridge. Merlin took my hand, "Come on, we can't stay here." he whispered.

Everyone else was already moving forward. I let Merlin pull me along while I could still hear the woman's screams despite that she had been silenced for minutes now. We stepped onto the next roof and Merlin looked back at me. I didn't know what he saw in my face, "Terra?"

"That was a person—" My voice felt tight like I hadn't used it in years. "That was a person and we just—"

Kalle looked over from where he had already created the next bridge, "Hey, you guys coming?" he called to me and Merlin.

"How are you all so calm?" I blinked and looked over at Kalle, "How are you so calm? How are you just...didn't you just see what happened? We killed someone!"

Merlin started pulling me again, not letting me stop. Kalle stayed with us and sighed softly in the dark, "We all knew this would happen eventually. It's just part of the job now."

"Murder is not a part of our job, Kalle!" I wanted to

scream but it came out as a forced whisper. "How are you still going like nothing happened?"

The expression in Kalle's eyes turned hollow and he fell back behind us to take the bridge down. I didn't think he was going to answer, "Because it's not my first. I've had to— the first one is always the hardest. You learn to compartmentalize, Terra. Arthur helps too, he talks it out with me." Kalle stepped onto the next roof, and without even needing to ask, started the next bridge, "War makes murderers of us all."

"Pick up the pace you three! One close call is enough for the night, thanks." Carter ordered back at us.

I took a small shaky breath, stuck between wanting to cry, and wanting to murder Carter. I was tempted to do both but started walking again instead. I held onto Merlin's hand as we darted from bridge to bridge. I started growing bridges again to give Kalle a break. If we just kept moving, I didn't need to think. This wasn't the place or the time to lose it, I knew that. I just needed to keep moving. I would deal with it later. I just needed to keep moving.

Despite all the noise we made on the other roof, we didn't have another run-in with a husk. Grand Central station was a low stone building, or at least lower than the skyscrapers, and being so close to the ground would put us at a greater risk. While we doubted the husks would be able to just climb up to the roof in any fast sense, one husk could bring a horde of them upon us.

"Where do we go?" Josh asked Carter with the assumption that he had been here before.

Carter put his hands in his pockets, "There used to be a way around the side. I don't think we should attempt it now, though. I say we make a path through the roof." He waved over Kalle, "Hey stone boy, think you can arrange some bricks to get us in? Assuming you're not too tired from building the princess's half of the bridges."

I was prepared to ignore that comment, but Ember marched towards Carter with flames in her eyes, "One more word and the next bridge you cross will be made of fire. Got it?"

Carter put his hands up and took a step back, "Sorry, sorry. It was just a joke, jeez."

Ember narrowed her eyes, still lit by the glow of her flames, "Say sorry to her."

Carter laughed under his breath, "For what? Did I hurt her feelings?"

"Em..." I stood in front of Ember. "Forget it, okay? Let's just get this over with."

Ember was still glaring at Carter as the flames in her eyes died down. "Not another word," she hissed and stood with Elleen.

Kalle started to create a way into the building. He rearranged the stone to form a staircase descending into the darkness of the station. As Kalle led us down, there was the inescapable feeling like we were being watched as we walked downwards. It was hard to see below us. Small amounts of moonlight filtered in through the windows but it wasn't enough to see by.

I wondered, Carter kept making the point that the husks were less active at night. We had managed to get into the city without much trouble and made it from the museum to here. Aside from the incident earlier, it wasn't too hard to get around. So why did every group attempting to get to the station go missing? Did every other group just get unlucky or was it something else?

The answer came when Kalle accidentally let a piece of stone fall from the stairs and into the hall below.

"Could you be any louder?" Carter hissed. At first, there was nothing, only the answering echo of stone hitting the floor below. It was followed by an unholy scratch and the stampeding of hundreds of feet in the dark. By the limited moonlight, I could only see the endless shuffling bodies.

"Oh great. You woke them from their beauty sleep." Carter yelled over the ceaseless wails.

"Did you know about this?" Ember demanded from behind me.

Carter turned, "Do you think I would have led you this way if I did?!" He started waving for us to retreat. "You two have fire. Light 'em up!"

Flames flicked at the tips of Ember's hair, "I am not burning a room full of people!"

"They're not people!" Carter yelled back, "Or I could just drown th—"

A gunshot rang through the cacophony. My hands went to my ears and my lungs started to constrict. The screaming started to sound like the cries of someone begging me to run. I needed to run. I looked up, my eyes trying to focus on a way out. The husks were below us, people were behind me, how did I get out? I needed to get out.

There was a second shot and a scream from just behind me. The stone staircase I was standing on morphed into a small walled platform that shut out the husks below. The wails were dimmed, but only just. Merlin appeared in my line of sight as soon as we were sheltered, his hands on my face. "Terra, look at me. Terra, can you tell me where we are?"

At first, I didn't know why he was asking me this. We should be running. Everything in me screamed to run, but I looked up into his eyes that were the colour of the sea after a storm and took a deep breath. "Grand Central Station?" I whispered, uncertain.

"Stay with me, okay?" He asked, moving his hands from my face, down to hold my hand.

I gave a shaky nod and looked back at the others. Ember was holding up a hand of fire while she knelt by Elleen. Elleen was huddled on the floor with her hands pressed against her thigh. Blood was seeping between her fingers. "What happened, Elly!?" Ember asked, pale as a ghost as she kept looking from Elleen's leg to her face.

I took out my flashlight and shone it down at them. Frank kelt down with the two girls, the first aid bag open on the floor in front of him. "Keep pressure on that, Elleen. Terra, shine that light here would you?" Frank asked, indicating the bag. I moved closer, shining the light down in the bag so that Frank could find what he needed. Blood continued to drip to the floor as Frank tied a strip of cloth above Elleen's wound.

"Is she going to be alright?" Ember asked, her voice sounding tight while Frank cut Elleen's pants away from the wound.

"She should be fine," Frank replied without looking up, a pillar of calm. He inspected the wound and nodded, "Good, it looks like it went through. We're going to have to cauterize it though. Ember, could you?"

Elleen fidgeted backwards, "I could—"

Frank shook his head at once, "You need to save your energy. Ember will be able to do it more controlled."

Elleen looked up at Ember with pleading eyes. Ember simply flipped her hair over her shoulder and knelt down. "I'll be quick, I promise." She said tenderly as her fingers started to glow a bright orange.

I didn't consider until Ember touched Elleen's leg, just

how hot Ember would need to keep her flames. If it were any of us, Ember would have been able to just use normal heat, but as Elleen was fire like Ember, Ember needed to combat Elleen's fire to even start feeling warm. I winced and turned away at the sizzle and smell of burned flesh. Elleen let out a high muffled cry as the wound was cauterized. After it was done, I heard her let out a sharp breath.

"That's great Ember, thanks." Frank's calm voice spoke over the chaos, "I'm going to just stitch this up and wrap it, okay, Elleen?"

Elleen just nodded her head and leaned back against the wall. Ember knelt down next to her and squeezed her hand. She was whispering something to Elleen, but I couldn't hear it.

I stood over Frank as he got a thread and needle ready, "You should stay off it too. Someone is going to have to carry you."

Josh stepped forward, "I will." he offered.

Carter huffed, "Yes, yes, this is all great and touching but can we look at the bigger picture for a second? The husks have weapons now?"

Josh nodded, "Evidently. At first, they didn't bother with such things, but it seems they are getting more ruthless by the day. Or some at least."

I remembered my parents and how they had come at us with a kitchen knife. I knew Dad used to keep a shotgun under the stairs at our house. Part of me hoped they just never thought to use it, while the other part feared that they were simply out of bullets.

In the small room that Kalle made, we waited for Frank to finish patching up Elleen. Josh motioned for Carter to come closer, "How do you think we should proceed?" The husks were still wailing just outside the stone walls. There would be no sneaking past them now. Something thumped against the walls from the outside.

"The base is beneath the station. There were unused maintenance rooms just off the tracks the Alliance decided to use." Carter paused and listened to the wailing for a few seconds, "We need to go down, one way or another. Stone boy, can you make a tunnel or something?"

"His name is Kalle." I corrected Carter through gritted teeth.

"It's fine, Terra." Kalle put a hand up, "How far down is it? I might be able to manage."

"Two floors," Carter walked up to Kalle. "I used to have a buddy who would make windows out of diamond. Think that's doable so we can see where we're going?"

Kalle bit his lip and I could see he wasn't sure. A tunnel was easy, but a winding staircase with diamond windows was something else. Just pulling together the right minerals was going to be exhausting. "I'll give it a try but it might be slow going."

"Whatever," Carter agreed while the rest of us got ready to follow. Merlin took a hold of my hand again as if he knew that instinct to run was still trying to pull me in the opposite direction.

Kalle started the tunnel again, creating a walled staircase that led us blindly downward. I heard him make a small groan and the ever-moving wall in front of him shifted from grey stone to opaque brown, to cloudy diamond glass. It wasn't perfect, but it was enough for my flashlight to shine through and let us see our slow descent into the horde.

The moment we started moving again, the husks heightened their screaming with new fervour. Those closest to us jumped, scraping their fingertips against the tunnel as we got closer. Soon they were shoving their bodies against the glass and gnashing their teeth. One of the husks picked up another and hurled it at our little window. Another husk pointed a gun and shot at the glass. The sound was muffled but it was still far too loud for my liking. I was shaking down to my core, so much that I was worried I would drop the flashlight.

Kalle dragged sharp and ragged breaths through his teeth the further we went. He wasn't showing it yet, but his mark must have been hurting him. We pushed through the floor and the screaming finally subsided a little.

"Where?" Kalle asked between breaths.

Carter pointed through the glass. We appeared to be on an empty station platform, "See that wall over there? Get through that."

Kalle nodded and started making a straight set of stairs descending towards the wall Carter indicated. At first, the platform was empty, but soon we heard a stampede of husks coming down to meet us. They swarmed around the tunnel, doing everything they possibly could to stop us.

Kalle stumbled with still several feet to go. The tunnel rattled and shook and small cracks started to appear in the glass. If it broke now, we would be dead. The husks would tear us limb from bloody limb. I looked behind me to Merlin, he was moving his hand in such a way that I knew he was pulling water near the surface just in case.

The tunnel started to collapse around us while Kalle made the final push towards the wall. The tunnel shot forward and made an opening. With stone raining down around us, we tumbled through the entrance. Once the last person was through, Kalle slammed down a wall just as the husks were forcing their way in. I winced at the snapping echo of shattering bone from the husks who were pushing their way in when Kalle brought down the wall.

Kalle fell to his knees, gasping for breath and clutching his left calf. I knelt down next to him, putting a hand on his shoulder, "You okay, Kalle?"

"Hey Ter..." Merlin said from behind me, and something in his tone made me look up. "Shine your light over here."

Slowly I stood up and shined my flashlight around the room in which we found ourselves. All the air rushed out of my lungs.

Every surface was covered in blood.

Everything was silent. I stood frozen, the numbness starting to claw its way into my brain. You couldn't say there were bodies. There were no bodies. A single hand lay in the middle of the room, the fingers bent at impossible angles. There were a few other pieces of unidentifiable flesh scattered across the floor, but mostly it was just blood. I gagged as soon as my senses started to return. The smell of rot clung to the single dark room like a miasma.

"No...No!" Carter was the first one to speak, his voice rising until it cracked. "Open the wall!" He turned on Kalle, grabbing him by the shoulder and hauling him up.

"I can't," Kalle breathed, only just starting to catch his breath, "I don't have anything left. If I open that wall up, I won't be able to close it again."

"I'll kill them!" Carter screamed and fisted his hands in Kalle's shirt, "Open the fucking wall, or I'll bust it open. I'll flood this whole god damned subway if I have to."

Josh had just finished getting Elleen off his back, "Carter!" He got in between Carter and Kalle. Carter jerked away, letting go of Kalle and letting the man slump

Merlin. Merlin rolled Carter onto his stomach and tied his hands.

Since Merlin wasn't ready to talk, Ember decided to take over, "We only got as far as the cafeteria. It's as...cheerful as this room." She looked down at the single dismembered hand that no one had moved yet, "Carter was talking about the people who lived here and then it was just...water."

Merlin stood up, his eyes still on Carter, "He was forcing a wave towards this room. He was going to break through that wall. He would have killed us all."

Ember crossed her arms and tossed her red curls over her shoulder, "So, what's the plan now?"

Josh shook his head, "It looks like we'll be here for a few hours at least. We need to wait for Kalle to recover, and for Carter to wake up. For now, let's see if we can find out what happened here. Terra, Merlin, Ember, did you see anything?"

Ember shook her head, "More bodies, more blood." She nibbled her bottom lip, "We can keep looking though."

Josh nodded, "I'll come with you three. Frank, Elleen, Kalle? Will you be fine here alone?"

Elleen created a ball of fire and had it hover in the middle of the room. "We'll be fine. Won't we, Frank?"

Frank lifted his hand in a salute, "Have fun."

Merlin stepped back towards the door, "Right...oodles." He murmured, not sounding too enthusiastic about seeing more limbs and random bits of flesh.

"We shouldn't be long." Josh assured everyone, "According to Moxxi, the base should still be quite small. They weren't here long enough to really expand a lot."

Merlin shoved his hands in his pockets, "I remember Carter saying there are some areas you can only access by going out on the tracks. But I guess we won't be able to go there right now."

"No...probably not," Josh agreed, knowing that the tracks were likely as swarmed with husks as everywhere else. Or they would be if we went out there. "Okay...let's go."

We walked back out to the cafeteria and the only difference from earlier was the sound of dripping water. The stone floor was slick and red. Josh stopped and fell silent as his eyes drifted upwards. "How could this have happened?"

I didn't want to look up, I didn't want to shine my flashlight up. I already knew some of the things I saw earlier. "Let's just keep going. There's nothing here." I whispered.

There was a silent agreement and we kept moving. Somehow it just kept getting worse. We found a wing of bedrooms and nearly every room was plastered in the same mix of blood and bits of flesh. My stomach started to turn as the smell of rot got stronger and stronger.

"Gods..." Josh whispered under his breath when we stopped outside the last bedroom of that wing. "It must have happened so fast. There's barely any sign they fought back." Josh looked up at the scorch marks on the ceiling. There was an attempt, which made me wonder how much of the blood and corpses belonged to the people who lived here, and how much belonged to husks who were killed in the crossfire.

"Do you think at night?" Ember asked, averting her eyes from the bedroom and hastening to go back the way we came.

I bit my lip, stepping over a small spire of rock that had only just started to break through the stone floor when it's creator was stopped, "There certainly seems to be more...

just more here. Maybe that's why they didn't fight back. Everyone was asleep..."

I wasn't sure what I hated more. The idea that a whole base had been just taken out like it was nothing, or that they didn't even have the chance to fight. Everything we saw suggested that it had been brutally quick and bloody. We walked down the endless bloody hallways a little more until we came to a dead-end in the form of a heavy metal door. It was the type of door you might expect to see in a fallout shelter.

Merlin pulled on the wheel-like handle at the centre of the door and it didn't budge. There was a handle to the side of the wheel that was pushed into the locked position. "Well, I guess the husks didn't come in this way. Not unless they locked up behind them."

"Hmm." Josh frowned at the door, trying to figure out the puzzle in front of him, "We should try to find the offices." Josh eventually said. "There might be some clue there to how the husks got in."

"And hopefully the breaker panel." Ember added, "It's a little too Resident Evil in here with just a flashlight and some fire."

"I think Moxxi said the main office was near the kitchen." Josh murmured, turning to head back towards the cafeteria.

The kitchen was toward the back of the cafeteria. Food was spilled across the floor as if it had been thrown through the air. We pushed past into the small hallway, and there we found the office.

There was a small table and a couple of chairs, all knocked over and partially shattered. Papers were scattered everywhere, on the floors, the walls, and across the shelves that lined one wall. I moved to the shelves and started to look through what remained. There was blood streaked across every surface.

"Inventory, letters, it looks like they were starting to redesign," Josh turned a page in a notebook. "They were trying to figure out how long they could stretch their food. When this was written they had...a couple of weeks left, maybe?"

Merlin was studying a map pinned up on the wall that had several areas crossed out and notes written along the edges, "It looks like a map of their base. I think they were starting to seal off areas and bring everyone into this main hub."

"But how did the husks get in...?" I whispered, looking at the map. The people who had been here were preparing for the husks, that was clear. "That's the only thing I can't figure out. How did they get in?"

Josh shut the notebook he was looking at, "My best guess is they tried to send people out for help once they started to run out of food, and the husks forced their way in as soon as there was an opening."

That thought instantly made me feel like a fly in a web. Is that why the husks calmed down so quickly once we got in here? Were they waiting?

"We'll bring some of this out for Elleen, Frank, and Kalle to look at." Josh decided, gathering up a stack of papers and the notebook, "It'll give them something to work on while we search the rest of the base."

Ember studied the map while the rest of us gathered up what we could carry, "Oh hold up. The panel should be... just next door. Let's get the lights on too."

"Okay, Ember, wait for us," Josh warned. We finished picking up what we could, including the map, and walked out to the next room. It was a small utility closet and seemed to be about the only area in the base so far that wasn't covered in blood. Ember lifted her flames as she opened up the breaker box and flicked the main switch. With the hum of power, the lights flickered on around us.

"Much better!" Ember grinned.

Personally, I wasn't sure it was an improvement. The bright fluorescent lights made it almost impossible to ignore the carnage all around us. But...at least we could see without watching for every movement in the shadows. I pushed my flashlight back in my pocket. "Well, I guess we—"

Every thought I had stopped as Elleen's screams echoed in the air.

WE BOLTED FROM THE OFFICE, through the cafeteria, back to the room where we left the others. However, once we got there, someone was standing in our way. It was a girl, not much older than ten. She wore a red sundress, or maybe it was once white. Her blonde hair hung in limp high pigtails that still managed to reach her waist. As she turned to us, I could see that her cheeks were hollowed and her eyes were dark with hunger, "What did you do to Carter?" she asked in a high yet perfectly calm voice, as if she were simply asking about her favourite doll.

Josh didn't answer her right away and instead looked past her to where Elleen, Frank, and Kalle were huddled together in the corner. Elleen had fire in her hands. "You three okay?" Josh asked.

"She just came out of nowhere!" Elleen squeaked, still not putting away her fire. While we were gone, Frank must have made some attempt to clean up the room. The bits of flesh were piled neatly in the corner and there was an attempt made at washing the blood-coated walls.

The girl gave no expression, only hugging a raggedy

stuffed animal closer to her chest. It had blond fur and was round like a ball. She turned her back on us and knelt down by Carter. She took one arm off her furry ball to poke him in the shoulder, "Carter? Did you go away too?"

"Go away? Like..." I started.

The girl looked over to the single dismembered hand that now sat in the corner, "Alyssa never liked a mess. Thanks for cleaning her up. She went away too. They all did. But me and Dimitri stayed."

Josh carefully approached the girl. Being down here all alone, after having seen what she saw, it was little wonder she seemed a little...off. "Do you have a name?"

"Lulu," she went back to poking Carter in the shoulder until he started to groan.

Josh knelt down next to her as Carter started to wake, "Lulu, can you tell me what happened here?" he asked very gently.

Lulu looked up at Josh as if she were only just noticing him there. She pointed at the wall where the husks were making faint groaning noises on the other side. I guess they must have heard Elleen screaming. "They came in," she then pointed at the small pile of flesh in the corner, "And they left."

"Left like..." Josh pressed, "They were attacked?"

Lulu nodded, "They left. Me and Dimitri have been here alone since then. Well, mostly. They come back sometimes."

"They?"

Lulu pointed again at the wall, "There are ways in. But I know how to hide, and Dimitri keeps me safe. He's a knight you know." She said it so matter-of-fact, I couldn't comprehend the shock she must have experienced. "They'll be here soon. You should leave before they come."

Kalle pushed himself up from where he was sitting and walked over to Lulu, "Hey, they won't get in here right now, okay? We're here right now, we'll keep you safe."

"They all say that," Lulu shrugged, "After the first group came, then the second. And then...well...they all say it," Lulu sighed heavily and hugged her furry ball close, "And then they all go away. Oh! Did James send you? Did you bring food? James promised food."

Kalle looked over at Josh with an expression that could only be described as desperation, before shifting back to Lulu with a gentle smile for the child, "Who's James? Was he from here too?"

Lulu shook her head, "Not at first, he came here with the second group. He was silly," she stopped to giggle. "He survived the first night. After everyone was gone he left through the tunnels. He said he would come back, but he didn't."

Outside the husks were starting to quiet down again. I didn't want to know what they were doing out there. I pictured them like a thousand crawling spiders, just waiting for us on the other side of that wall. I still didn't know how they got in. The door out in the hallway was locked. Would they knock down the wall just to get to us?

Josh took off his bag and opened it in front of Lulu, "Hey, Lulu? Do you want something to eat? We have a little food with us, we could share. Once Carter is awake we'll start working on a plan to leave, okay?" Carter was still making small groaning noises and was just starting to move a little.

Lulu nodded, "Yes please."

Josh pulled out a hearty loaf of seed bread and tore off a sizable piece for Lulu. At the sight of food, she shifted the furry ball under one arm and snatched the bread out of

Josh's hands. "How long has it been since you ate?" Josh asked.

Beside me, Ember was making small panicked noises. Her eyes were wide and she was looking down at the furry ball under Lulu's arm.

Lulu didn't answer Josh until she finished the piece of bread, "A few days. They don't send as many people as they used to. So I ran out."

"Well, we're here now." Josh promised, "We're going to bring you somewhere safe, okay?"

Lulu didn't answer, she just pointed down at Josh's bag again, "Can I have more?"

"Oh! Right..."

While Josh was taking out more of the bread, Ember cleared her throat enough to get his attention. "U-um Josh..." She said in barely a squeak.

"What is it Ember?" Josh paused midway through getting the bread. In his hesitation, Lulu snatched it out of his hands again. This time, she lost the balance she had on the fuzzy ball and it thumped to the floor with more weight then I was expecting.

Ember took a quick step back and flames licked her fingertips. "Josh it's..."

"Dimitri!" Lulu cried as the ball rolled over just enough to reveal a face. It was a head. What I thought was fur, was matted blond hair. Lulu sat down cross-legged on the ground and gingerly put 'Dimitri' in her lap. "I'm sorry I dropped you Dimi. You got heavy. Did you want some bread too?" She asked, offering a piece of the bread to the head, before eating it herself.

"It's a head!" Ember practically screamed. "She's holding a head and—"

Josh quickly stood and moved back, "Calm down

Ember, please. She's been through a traumatic experience. She...found a way to cope."

"Joshua. It's. A. Head!"

Lulu shot Ember a glare, "Don't talk about Dimi like that. He has feelings, you know! The ones out there took the rest of him, but he promised he would always protect me. Where I go, he goes."

Carter chose that exact moment to finally wake up. He struggled to sit up with his hands still tied behind his back, bleary-eyed and angry "Jesus, for a small guy you can throw a punch." He muttered to no one in particular.

Lulu was watching him with wide, curious eyes. The piece of bread was held forgotten in her hands. "You came back."

Carter's eyes fell on her and his face immediately twisted into a smile, "Lulu..." He whispered, almost a question, "Lulu! Come on kid, give me a hug!" He struggled against the rope and Josh stepped forward to untie him.

Lulu picked up Dimitri and held him carefully under her arm, "You're late." She stated without expression and took another bite of bread.

Carter's arms dropped at his sides as he looked at Lulu confused and rejected. "Yeah, I know. I'm sorry. It took me a while to find these guys to help. But we're here now. Is there—?"

Josh put a hand on Carter's shoulder, "She's the only survivor, Carter." He whispered.

"And Dimi!" Lulu added, lifting up the head again. I got a better look at it this time. Whoever Dimitri was, he was young like Lulu. Maybe a little older than she was, though it was hard to say for sure given the...circumstances.

Carter's face paled as he looked down at the head and he covered his mouth with his hand. His body hunched and for a moment I thought he was going to be sick. But after a moment he righted himself and managed a weaker smile. "Th-that's right. You and Dimi. Still thick as thieves, I see." He reached out and patted Lulu on the head.

"He promised he would always always keep me safe." She said, hugging Dimitri to her chest again so that he looked like a fuzzy ball. Now that I knew what it was, I couldn't unsee the shape of the skull, the curve of the ear just poking out from Lulu's arm.

"And he's done a very good job," Carter said, softer this time. "Why don't you sit down again. You can tell me what you've been up to...okay?"

No one really relaxed with Lulu and her friend Dimitri there. It was as unnerving as it was heartbreaking. Ember stayed close to the wall as she moved all the way around the room to Elleen and huddled down with her. Lulu started to tell Carter more or less what she already told us, about the other groups that had come before, and how one man had escaped down the tunnels.

Carter whistled low under his breath, "James, huh? If anyone can survive out there, it's that crazy bastard." he said, though I wasn't sure how much he believed it.

Lulu took another piece of bread from Josh's bag, and gnawed on it thoughtfully, "When do we go back? Do you think Julia left my old room?"

Carter bit his lip, not wanting to answer most of that. Kalle answered instead, "Do we still have time to make it back tonight? I could be ready to go in a half-hour maybe."

Josh turned to look over at Kalle, "Just a half-hour? You barely got us here on a full night's rest."

"Not the way we came, no." Kalle corrected, "But if Carter or Lulu know a different way, maybe through the tunnels like in London?" He leaned back against the stone wall, "I doubt I'll get much sleep here anyway."

I doubted any of us would. Maybe it was better to leave while we still had some energy, rather than after a sleepless night inside a nightmare-scape.

Josh looked at his watch and was silent in thought for several seconds, "We would be cutting it close, but it should be fine. Kalle, eat something and get some rest. Lulu? Can you tell us how you've avoided them?"

Lulu was holding a piece of bread in two hands with Dimitri in her lap, "In the crawlspace. You won't fit. You shouldn't take the tunnels either."

Carter handed her some dried fruit, "Do you know what way James went?"

"He ran out the door and powered through." Lulu giggled, "He did a lot of screaming, it was silly."

A chill went up my spine listening to her talk. While it was good to see that someone survived, I wasn't sure that she did survive, not really. Something inside of her was so totally broken, I didn't know if she would ever be the little girl that Carter clearly remembered again.

"Okay..." Carter said, sounding a little disconcerted, "We probably won't go that way since we have you this time. We'll leave all sneaky-like, okay?"

Lulu smiled and ate a dried apple slice, "Stay off the platforms then, they sleep there. It keeps them out of the rain." She took Josh's bag from Carter and started rummaging through it, eating whatever she found, "Up."

"Up?" Carter repeated.

"Yeah, up. That's how everyone gets here. That's how you should leave."

The only problem with simply going up was that it meant going through the husk heavy areas again. "Is there...a version of 'Up' that puts us out on the street instead of inside Grand Central Station?" I asked. "If Kalle can get us that far, I can get us to the roof."

"Did we bring the map?" Josh started to look through the few papers we managed not to drop in our rush to get back here.

Ember shook her head, "I don't think so. We'll have to go back for it."

Lulu stuffed Dimitri's head in Josh's bag and jumped to her feet, "I know where the map is. It's near my crawlspace." Without another word, she darted out of the room.

"Wait! Lulu!" Carter called and got up to follow her, "Don't run off!"

"Bring her back here, Carter." Josh ordered, "Terra, Merlin, go with them."

I only nodded and turned to hurry after Lulu with Merlin and Carter. By the time we reached the cafeteria, she was standing by the kitchen and darted into the hallway the moment she saw us coming after her. The pile of papers was right where we left them, scattered around the floor outside the utility room. Lulu reached the map first and held it up with one hand. "This map is wrong. All the other doors they blocked with stone. There's just one now." She stated, then handed the map to Carter. "Want to see my crawlspace?"

Carter let the map fall to the floor as Lulu went to a small vent in the wall. She popped off the vent cover and pushed Josh's bag inside. "Don't go in there, Lulu. We're leaving soon."

"They're coming soon." Lulu said, looking up at Carter with a small tilt of her head, "I warned you they would be coming soon."

"Hey, Lulu," I asked softly, "Do you know how the husks have been getting in?"

"The door." She said simply.

Merlin almost looked relieved, "Oh good. We found that door earlier, it's locked good and tight. We'll be safe here for the night."

I heard a soft rattle. Like a rat knocking over a stone. I looked over my shoulder just as Lulu said, "I unlocked it."

The rattle became a roar.

In the panic, Lulu scuttled into the vent before any of us could stop her. As her leg disappeared, I noticed something on her ankle. It was a somewhat transparent patch of skin, just enough that I could see a few veins and an outline of bone, but more opaque then Merlin's transparent patch over his heart.

I pulled a seed out of my pocket and let the branches start to grow up my arm as we took off at a sprint back towards the others. There were already husks in the cafeteria by then, being kept back by gusts of wind and fire. I threw down my sapling, and branches exploded throughout the room, giving Carter, Merlin and I a path back to where the others were waiting. Once we arrived, Josh and Ember dropped the fire and wind. At once I felt the chaotic force of hundreds of husks at the wall of branches. Inside the room, everyone was already on their feet, with Elleen leaning against the wall for support.

"You have got to be fucking kidding me." Carter cursed under his breath as we made it back into the room.

"She was cured!" I screamed over the roar, "She's been a

husk this whole time. I saw the mark on her leg!" I spotted the look of horror and confusion on Elleen's face.

Carter growled, "That was nothing like the Lulu I knew. I thought it was just the shock of being in this little corner of hell. She was always a hugger. I called her Squid sometimes because of that and her hair." He paused, something slowly dawning on him. "Her and Dimitri went missing for a week once, just before the husks appeared. We all thought they were on one of their adventures, they did that, playing knights and stuff in the other parts of the subway."

"But New Atlantis had them." I finished.

The husks were so loud I could barely hear the string of curses. Beside me, Ember had fire in her hands, "Well what do we do now? Kalle can you tunnel out?"

"I'm going to have to," he said, sounding doubtful. "I should be able to get us up on the road if we go blindly. I don't know how much I'll be able to do after that."

Josh took a breath, "Alright Kalle, get us out. Everyone else, if they get past those branches, push them back.

I winced as I felt the branches starting to shatter as the husks continued beating. I didn't want to know what they were doing to get through the branches without tools. After that explosion of power at one time, my marks were already starting to throb. I willed the tree to grow more branches as others broke. "Kalle...hurry."

Kalle started forming a new set of stairs straight up through the ceiling. Everyone scrambled to race up after him, except for Merlin who stopped to get Elleen on his back. I went last and stopped growing out the tree. The feeling of shattering intensified even after Kalle sealed off the way behind me. He built straight up, not bothering to fix anything behind him to the way it was.

The smell of fresh air hit me like bricks when we broke out onto the New York street. We were on the ground and exposed. We had precious minutes at best before the husks realized we were here. The sky was already starting to get lighter with dawn in a couple of hours. We were running out of time.

"This way!" Carter started running to the next building over. Kalle was gasping for breath but was able to keep up. Merlin still carried Elleen on his back. "Kalle, do you have another bridge in you?"

Kalle looked up at the towering buildings and immediately winced, "I can't. Terra?"

I had no idea how we were all going to be able to scale the building on little more than a trunk and some branches, but it was worth a try. I threw down a seed and a tree trunk grew tilted up a building with branches coming out of the sides for support. It was better than nothing, even if it wasn't as supportive or easy to climb as Kalle's bridges.

Just as we were starting to make our way up, husks started coming out of Grand Central Station. Some of the husks started to climb up the bridge and I felt the panic rise in my throat. I couldn't just pull up the base of the bridge like Kalle could, not without sacrificing most of the stability.

Merlin reached back and water burst from the nearest fire hydrant. A spray of water rose up and started pushing husks from the tree bridge. As I got us up to the roof, Ember set the first bridge on fire, rather than me wasting energy taking it down to start another one. I blinked, feeling the searing heat in my fingertips from the burning tree below us. I lost my focus, and couldn't seem to concentrate on the new seed in my hand. Below us, Husks were starting to work on other ways to get up to the roof.

"Any day now, Princess," Carter growled as he helped

Merlin push off husks that were trying to scale the building itself.

I bore down through the sickening sensation of fire and grew the second bridge. Long roots shattered windows and anchored deep within the core of the building as a long trunk reached towards the taller glass-covered building across the street. By the time we made it to the next roof, Josh signalled for us to stop. It was high enough and the glass walls slick enough that we were likely safe from climbing husks now.

Josh pointed towards the roof entrance for the building below us, "Ember, melt that door closed. Terra, take down that tree." He ordered.

Ember walked over to the door and ran her finger around the perimeter of the door frame. It glowed hot molten orange, and I knew the moment she walked away, the door would not be opening except without brute force. With any luck, we wouldn't be staying here long enough to experience anyone using brute force. I turned back to my tree bridge and the trunk slowly receded back to the other side. A small oak was left growing on the other roof, too far away for me to manipulate further.

Kalle all but collapsed on the roof. Frank knelt over him. "Hey Kalle, how are you doing?" He murmured as he rubbed Kalle's back.

"Everything hurts and I'm dying," Kalle muttered sardonically. "You think I would have watched enough horror movies by now to know not to trust a cute little girl in a blood bath, huh?"

Frank laughed under his breath, "Yeah. I am totally disappointed in you. Arthur would be telling you off if he were here. It would be like him forgetting the words of Mr. Darcy's speech in Pride and Prejudice."

Kalle bit out a laugh that turned into a hacking gasping cough. "God, don't make me laugh, Frank. Ow."

"If you boys are done—" Carter started but Josh put his hand up.

"I think it's safe to say that Grand Central is done," Josh said, motioning for everyone to come within hearing distance, "I don't know if we'll be able to get all the way back tonight. It's awfully close to dawn now, and we are not in good shape. I think our main focus should be finding shelter."

Carter stuffed his hands in his pockets, "Back in the day we had safe houses all over the city. Places where we could hide if New Atlantis was chasing us. The closest one is Rockefeller. We could try there. And if that doesn't work, well, I guess we could just make something up."

I noted that all his earlier antagonism was gone from his voice. Mostly, he just sounded tired.

Josh nodded, "Excellent. If I remember correctly, that's close to here, isn't it?"

"Yeah..." Carter pointed off towards the north. "Just over there. There's a lego store on the corner that we turned into a safe house. Probably one of my favourites. You can spend hours building lego in there if you're bored."

Josh motioned to me to make the next bridge. "No doubt the husks are trying to get up here. We should get going. Terra?"

I pulled a seed out of my pocket and tossed it at the ledge of the roof. Slower than before, branches started to grow across the expanse towards the next building. The ache in my marks was starting to grow, but hopefully, I would have enough in me to get us to Rockefeller Center.

It was slow, and it hurt. The branches creaked with movement as we made our way down to the street at Rockefeller Center. We were on a small side street with an overgrown garden. In front of us, was a sunken square with a golden statue of Prometheus at the far end and flag poles all around the edge. The flags were all ripped and tattered New Atlantis flags. There were no husks here yet, but I knew they weren't far behind. As the sky got lighter, the husks were able to watch us from the ground and follow us as we went. I often saw them on the streets. Thankfully not the full horde, just the ones who weren't bored of chasing us yet.

"Over here," Carter whispered and led the way over to a shop on the corner. In the window over the door, there was a lego version of the Prometheus statue and a curling tail of a dragon coming out of the ceiling. A small amount of lego littered the floor of the shop but all in all, it didn't look that bad. It looked like it was just ignored all these years since the Fall.

"Ah, guys..." Frank had a panicked tone in his voice as he directed our attention down the street. About a hundred husks were roaming down the street like a pack of dogs. At first, it looked like they didn't see us, but then they started running.

Carter pushed on the revolving door, only to find it locked. He started to curse under his breath, "Why. The hell. Is this. Locked." He muttered, not noticing someone else approaching the glass from the other side.

"Someone's in th—"

Before I could even get the words out, a small burst of water must have hit the lock in just the right way, and a man came bursting out. Carter got trapped by the door as it spun around, and went tumbling into the shop. "Oh sorry, Carter. Didn't see you there." The man said as he lit something I hadn't seen since the fall of the old world, a cigarette.

Carter pushed his way back out, "James! Is the safe house still in there?" Carter called after the man.

"Yeah. Don't touch my whiskey!" James called back as a tommy gun made of water formed in his hands.

Carter waved at us to hurry, "Come on, right in here." He headed back inside the shop. There were more lego statues inside the shop as well, but they weren't exactly what I would have expected. I would have thought that they would have been normal things, like the Chrysler building or a mummy, but for some reason, every lego model was of guns, swords, and one red-haired lego woman holding a real handgun. I blinked but didn't have much time to think on it as I heard shouting from outside.

"SAY HELLO TO MY LITTLE FRIENDS!" James screamed. He was standing in the centre of the sunken square near the Prometheus statue and the husks were swarming towards him. At his scream, he released a spray of water bullets from his 'gun.' I had no idea if water bullets would have the same effect as real bullets, but the husks were falling and starting to scramble. With unlimited ammo, James continued to fire at the husks while he made a lazy retreat back towards us.

Once James was inside, he shot another water bullet at the lock of the revolving door, and strolled on past us like nothing ever happened. "You going to just stand there, or what?" He asked, and walked over to a large pillar decorated with small clear bubbles filled with lego pieces. James reached for a bubble that had green, yellow, blue, and red blocks, and pushed. The pillar swung open like a door, and a spiral staircase led down into a room below. I blinked once we all were inside the safe house. It was certainly unique.

"Jesus, James how long have you been here?" Carter asked as he looked at the lego...everything. There were several more lego people, lego furniture, a lego kitchen, a tv with a lego picture of a teddy bear on the 'screen.' There was even lego art on the walls. Probably the only things in the room not made of lego were a few books, supplies, and a few weapons.

"About as long since I last saw you," James answered and took the previously lit cigarette out of his mouth. Seriously, how did this guy find those? "Were you visiting the station?"

"Yup," Carter said, finding James' bottle of whiskey in the lego kitchen and taking a long swig before James took it out of his hands.

"Hey! I said not to drink my whiskey!" He grabbed a glass out of the lego cupboard. It was an actual glass, not lego, shockingly. "Ran into Lulu?"

"Yup."

"She still carrying around Dimi?"

"Yup."

James handed the glass of whiskey to Carter, "Cheers." He took a long drink, effectively emptying the bottle just as Carter emptied the glass.

Josh coughed lightly, "James is it? We haven't met, I'm Josh." He put out his hand to shake.

James merely looked at it then nodded at Josh, "Carter made it to Markus' place then. Damn, I owe May lunch then."

"You bet against me? You ass." Carter muttered with a laugh.

"Right..." Josh took his hand back, "Well, we came to help with finding other members of the New York Alliance but, well, you already understand how things are going so far."

James looked us over, "One injured. Those two look

about ready to keel over." James pointed at me and Kalle, "Yeah. I'd say you're doing a great job."

Ember flipped her hair over her shoulder, "Better than being plastered on the station walls."

"The hot redhead does make a point," James observed. "Well, chill here for a bit. Any longer than that and I'll start charging rent." James flopped down in a lego chair and pulled a box of loose lego pieces towards him.

"Come back with us." Carter said, "Moxxi will even let you bring some lego if you're good."

"Convince pretty boss lady to let me recreate the solar system in the planetarium completely out of lego and we have a deal. And pay off my debt with May."

"I think that can be arranged," Carter laughed and sat down in one of the other chairs. He then waved at the rest of us. It was easy to see that some of us weren't quite sure what to make of this guy who had just saved our collective asses. "Make yourselves comfy. I guess we'll head back tomorrow night? That alright with you boss man?" Carter asked Josh.

Josh grinned and slid to the floor to sit, "I think that's fine. Thank you, James, for taking us in."

James slid another box of lego towards us, "Here make me a flower vase."

WE SPENT THE NIGHT, or day rather, in the safe house that was James' makeshift lego paradise. Even though James had been staying there for ages without any problem, we opted to take shifts watching the door while everyone else slept. It was generally agreed that Kalle should get to skip guard duty, as he needed rest the most. Me and Elleen took the first and last shift so that we could get as much uninterrupted sleep as possible. It was the first real rest Elleen was able to get since getting shot in the leg.

However, by the time Merlin shook me awake that evening, it was clear that no one really got a good rest. Everything we saw in Grand Central Station was still so raw. Despite my bone-deep exhaustion, I had nightmares of walking through endless tunnels while hearing Lulu's voice just ahead of me saying that everything would be fine. Behind me was the horde of husks, but it wasn't just the faceless swarm of the city. I saw my parents there, I saw Grey...

James was pouring himself a glass of whiskey while we packed up and got ready to leave. Aside from our own supplies, James had a few things he insisted we couldn't leave behind. Namely, whiskey, cigarettes, and as much lego we could take. James took most of this himself, stuffing as much as he could in a large bag. Despite the clinking weight of the bottles, he didn't have any trouble hefting around the bulk.

Kalle started making a staircase up the closest building the moment we were outside. From the rooftops, we started our slow way from roof to roof. Me and Kalle took turns building bridges, perhaps a little slower than we did the night before. It was nice, for the moment, to not be chased and we didn't have far to go.

As we headed north, I could feel the trees of Central Park getting closer. "Why can't we just go through the park?" I murmured, not really meaning it, just yearning for the familiar comfort of the trees.

"I mean you could," James remarked as he paused to light a cigarette. "Though it makes Grand Central look positively sparse."

"Even this late in the year?"

James shrugged, "I guess we'll find out when winter comes. So far, they got about as much self-preservation as a lemming."

We kept going and at first, it seemed like we would go right back to the base, but Carter stopped to look down at a couple of buildings at the corner of Central Park. One looked like an old hotel. The other was a glass cube with the walls painted black.

Ember followed his gaze, "Hey isn't that the Apple Store Moxxi mentioned?"

James looked over to the glass cube and blew out a puff of smoke, "Oh yeah, the Andersons. They keep taking my cookies. Never come over for drinks."

I blinked, "Wh-what?"

Carter sighed, "I think what James means is, there are people in there? The normal kind?"

James tapped off some ashes, "Did I stutter?"

"Should we check it out then?" Ember asked, tilting her head, "We still have lots of time. Maybe we could shine a flashlight in or something. If we hear screaming, then we know it's husks. They're not exactly subtle."

Kalle finished taking down the last bridge and looked at Ember like she had grown a few heads, "You're kidding right? After Grand Central, you want to walk into more? I don't think Cyrus would like this, Ember."

That was probably the worst thing to say to Ember. She put her hands on her hips, "I think we should go. Who wants to give me a lift down? Terra, you coming?"

"Guys wait," Josh called out. Ember looked back at him with a face that just screamed he had better not bring her brother into this too. But instead, Josh said, "If you want to go check it out we need to make a plan first. We've seen firsthand how things work here. Plus we have Elleen to think about."

"We could split up." Ember suggested, "A few people can stay here. And those who want to go check out the cube can come with us. We're just going to shine a light in and see if they're human or not. We won't like, do anything."

Josh nodded slowly, "I don't want you taking any unnecessary risks. Merlin? Will you lead a small group down there."

Merlin saluted Josh, "I can do that. So Terra and Ember, who else?"

"I'll go with. I want to find out why they never came to visit." James finished his cigarette and flicked the butt off the side of the building.

"Me too." Carter agreed, "In case it's anyone I know."

I almost wanted to roll my eyes knowing Carter would be coming with us, but at the same time, I understood. I just knew the more time I spent with him, the more I just wanted this whole nightmare to be over.

Frank crossed his arms, "I'll stay here with these three." Meaning Josh, Kalle, and Elleen. "We'll keep an eye out and come to your rescue if anything happens."

"Ember, send up a flare if you guys need backup," Josh said, "We may be splitting up temporarily, but I still don't want to take any chances."

"Okay." Ember nodded then looked to me, "Whenever you're ready, Terra."

I didn't waste much time creating a series of branches for us to climb down to the street.

There was no one on the street when we crossed over to the black painted cube. It was obvious once we got up to it that it was painted from the inside. It wasn't a perfect job, as streaks of black paint left little windows through the glass. Still, it was nearly impossible to actually see anything. It was pitch black inside, and when I tried to shine in a flashlight, the angles made it impossible. The most I could see was that the entrance of the cube lowered down into a wide-open room.

"Come on, there has to be a spot here somewhere to see through" Ember mused, and started walking around the walls of the cube. All four walls were the same, mostly painted with just shreds of places to peek through. There was one bright side to this, however, as much as I was trying to shine in the flashlight, we weren't hearing any of the shrieking that the husks normally made when they spotted something they wanted to hunt. James seemed to think whoever was down there was human after all.

We came around the front of the building. There were, well, there used to be two curling staircases that went down into the open room below. Those were now blocked off with piles of debris.

In the middle of the two staircases was an elevator. The doors were once closed but now stood broken. The outer glass was also painted black but I realized that the inner glass was not. When I tried to shine my light in through the painted glass, I still wasn't able to see anything in the room below.

"One second." I murmured and started to squeeze through the broken door.

"Terra what are you doing?" Merlin asked, concern coating his voice.

"I'm just going to see if I can look down. The glass in here isn't painted," I explained, and squeezed into the elevator. I went up to the back wall of the elevator and shined my flashlight down. I didn't really see anything, just some upturned tables and maybe some plants. I thought I saw movement at the edge of my light. "I think someone is—" before I could finish my sentence, the elevator glowed to life and started its descent.

"Terra!" Merlin reached in through the doorway but had to pull his hand back as I went below him. I could hear them scrambling above me, and I could hear my heart starting to pound in my ears. I pulled a seed from my pocket and clutched the flashlight to my chest. A small sapling started to grow in my hand just in time for the elevator to ding open.

I was instantly blinded by lights directly in my face. Hands were on me, and I was pushed to the ground. There wasn't time to react, to even think. The sapling exploded into a mass of branches and roots that pushed the unseen people off of me, and cocooned me in a wooden cage.

There was a mix of sharp gasps and stifled screams from my attackers. The lights lowered and I looked out from the branches to see several people watching me. They looked battle-scarred and weary. One was pointing a gun, while others were holding more primitive weapons. "The hell is this?!" One of them asked.

Above me, I could hear Ember and Merlin calling my name through the glass.

"Shut up your friends before they wake up the whole street." A gruff voice threatened.

I scanned their bodies, looking for marks. I didn't see any. Not even the faded scars of them. "Are you cured? Or are you normal?"

The man with the gruff voice, who had nearly every visible surface of skin covered in tattoos, turned and pointed at the back of his neck. No scar from the implant, "You next girl."

"Lower your gun first."

"Come out from your tree and we'll lower our gun."

As I didn't want to be mobbed again, I would just have to trust that they wouldn't shoot me while my back was turned. I turned and lifted up the back of my curls. When I turned back, the small group in front of me seemed more relaxed.

"We didn't think there were any other survivors. Where have you been hiding?" An older woman asked, then motioned to the branches, "Though, that might have something to do with it."

I blinked, not sure what to make of them. The looks of shock on their faces suggested they weren't familiar with the powers of Telluria, but they weren't husks? "N-none of you are Tellurians? How is that even possible?"

The older woman just looked at me like I had five heads, "You're asking us how things are possible? After this...magic?"

"It's not magic, it's Telluria." I pushed up the sleeve of my jacket and pushed my arm between the branches so they could see my original mark, the quartz lines on my right forearm. "It's not faded see, I was never cured. Using the powers keeps it from spreading." I looked back just as Ember decided to try setting fire to the barricade. It would be impossible for these people to not see the flames she was conjuring from nowhere.

The group exchanged silent looks with each other. It was hard to read from my position between the branches of my protective cage. "How long have you had it?" The man with the tattoos asked.

"Yes!" I quickly said, "I've had it over a year. Most of them, for longer."

"We have a couple who are in the later stages," The man with all the tattoos explained. "We're trying to make them as comfortable as possible but—"

"We can help! We can show them how," I bit my lip and looked back where Ember was still trying to burn her way in. Just let me get my friends first? I'm afraid Ember might melt something if she keeps going."

The few people looked at each other then nodded, "Go on."

The branches pulled themselves back into the seed as I made a slow retreat back to the elevator. When I got in, one of the men in the back flicked a switch which activated it again and lifted me up. Merlin and Ember were already at the door when I came up, with Carter and James standing not far behind them, keeping watch.

I crawled out of the hole in the door and was immediately pulled into Merlin's arms, "Are you okay? We saw your branches."

I hugged him back tightly but nodded into his shoulder. "You won't believe it. There are people down there."

"Well duh, I told you that." James said, "Did you ask them if they got my pie?"

"I...did not...?" Turning back to Merlin, I looked up into his face, "They don't know about the powers, and they have a couple of people who are close to dying from Telluria. Can you come down and help?"

Carter crossed his arms, "How do you know it's not more of the husks?" He demanded, "This could be Lulu all over again and I am not going to walk into another trap today."

James patted Carter on the shoulder, "Naw, they're cool. They're just horrible neighbours." James bent down to squeeze into the elevator. Carter sighed and followed after him.

Merlin looked at me, "Are you sure, Terra? They're safe?"

I nodded, "They do this thing, they show their neck to show they were never cured. They made me show my neck as well. They're just scared. But we can help them."

Merlin nodded, and we went into the elevator. Once we were all in, I knocked on the glass and whoever was controlling the elevator lifted us down into the makeshift base.

They didn't attack us this time. Instead, the lights were kept low and the man with all the tattoos made a spinning motion with his finger, "We need to check everyone's necks first," he explained, "We don't take any chances here."

Ember, Merlin, James, and Carter all showed their necks and no one had the scar from the implant. James dropped his bag on the floor next to him which rattled with thousands of lego pieces and several bottles. "Hey, I was living down the street. Did you get my pie?"

"Pie?" The man with all the tattoos looked confused, "You don't mean that lego one that showed up in the elevator do you...?"

"You did get it! Why didn't you ever come to visit! I was trying to invite you over for drinks but noooooo."

The older woman with grey streaks through her hair said, "We assumed at the time that the note was a trick from the husks. The children enjoyed the lego, however."

Merlin stepped forward and lit his face with one of his calm smiles, "Terra told us that you have sick here. Could we see them?"

"Yeah, she said you guys know a way to treat it." The man with the tattoos said, eyes flicking once again to my marks, then to Ember's flame-filled eyes. "A couple of them don't have much time left."

"Oh, we'll see about that." Merlin said cheerfully enough, "We all have Telluria here. I'm on to five years now. I'm Merlin by the way."

"Joe." The man with the tattoos grunted and nodded his head for us to follow him. The main area was large, and not totally empty. Once upon a time, it was an electronic store so there were plenty of tables and chairs around the room. Many of the tables were set up with plants. The roof of the cube was not painted so they would likely get enough light in the day to grow some food. It was probably why they picked here over what might have been some more obvious choices. Other places around the room were work areas for other activities. It was a little of everything, kitchen, play area, workshop. No one else was out in that room, however, except for the few people with us.

"We spend most of our time out in this room, but we sleep here at night." Joe explained and gestured to an old storage room with the door ajar. There were at least two dozen people of every age in various states of sleep inside. Sheets were put up to section off 'rooms.' Joe kept walking to another room further off.

We followed him into a bathroom where a bed had been made up on the floor. The blankets were soaking wet, as was the person under them. The little I could see of their face, it was beaded with water.

"This is Alan. We're trying to make him as comfortable as possible but as you can see..." Joe began. It was clear that Alan wouldn't make it another week at his current state, not unless he took to the powers. I looked to Merlin with a question in my eyes. He nodded once, it was still possible for him. Perhaps not a big chance, but a chance.

"There's one more..." Joe led us to the end of a hallway where someone was sleeping standing up if you could call it that. Their entire body from the neck down was made of stone. They were completely locked in. The same way I would have been if things had turned out different. "This is Georgette." Joe's voice got tight before he turned around, "Come on."

Joe brought us out to the main room, "No one else has got it since those things started attacking everyone. Maybe Telluria is done, not that it matters. Once the winter comes I'm not sure we'll last much longer unless we find another source of food."

A few of the others were still in the room, waiting to hear what we had to say. Merlin had the look of someone who held onto hope, "There's still a chance." A couple of

people from the Apple store looked dubious as he continued, "Alan, for sure. The woman, well it's harder if you
can't move but there's still a chance."

Joe indicated a couple of seats in the corner of the large
main room, "Explain."

MERLIN and I stayed in the cube while Ember, James, and Carter went back to get Josh, Kalle, Elleen, and Frank. Back in the water-slicked bathroom, Merlin knelt at Alan's side and the man looked up at him through bleary eyes, "Hey Alan, I'm here to help you," Merlin said with that gentle calm voice that he was so good at.

"You're going to kill me, aren't you?" Alan whispered, his voice coming in and out like the gentle waves of the sea, "Put me out of my misery."

"No," Merlin put his hand on Alan's shoulder, "We're going to get you better."

Alan immediately stiffened, "You're from New Atlantis?"

Merlin quickly shook his head, "No. We're from somewhere else."

I stood in the doorway as Merlin explained the powers to Alan. It never ceased to amaze me how well he could deliver that explanation. He said he could count on one hand that number of times he had someone freak out on him. I didn't know if I should count myself lucky or not that

I stood out as one of those people. I watched while Alan's eyes widened in wonder at the small water otter jumping around the tiled floor that Merlin conjured as a demonstration.

"Now it's your turn," Merlin said softly. "You feel it, don't you, sort of a pull. Even if you weren't being kept in a bathroom for practicality sake, you probably feel more at peace in here, huh?"

Alan slowly nodded, "I do. When I first got it I used to dream of the sea. I grew up on a river. I just keep thinking about what it would be like to become one with the water. I guess I am now but..."

"You are. Since you're one with the water, you can control it, right? Feel the current..." Merlin manipulated the water on the floor to flow in slow circles around Alan. "Reach out to it with your mind. Or actually reach out to it. Whatever works for you, really. It's an extension of you. It came from you after all."

Alan shifted and inched a slow finger towards the ever-flowing water. He gazed at it, half in curiosity, half in tired dread. It was clear that if this didn't work, he would be giving up. His hands were so transparent, if this didn't work he would likely burst into nothingness right here and now. I looked over my shoulder towards the door and realized that if Alan did die, Joe was likely to never forgive us.

I heard a sigh and looked back to Alan who had a placid smile on his face. He was still reaching out to the stream of water. Where he pointed, the water was diverting into slow circles around his hand.

Merlin grinned brighter, "That's it. Just keep that up," he encouraged, "See if you can make that bigger."

Alan kept his focus on the swirling water. The small whirlpool steadily got bigger, taking more of Merlin's stream. Focusing on his work, Alan shrugged off his blankets and started to slowly sit up. A brightness was returning to his eyes.

Joe was open-mouthed and staring, "Alan! You're sitting up."

"Looks like I am!" A hearty laugh rippled in Alan's chest like a brook, "Can you believe it, Joe?"

Merlin hopped to his feet, "Keep that up for as long as you comfortably can, okay? You'll notice your mark will start to hurt eventually, if it's not already. When that happens, take a break for a bit." Merlin moved back to me and slid his arm around my back, "You should start seeing your skin turn solid as you practice more. Look, you're already starting to dry off on the outside."

Sure enough, Alan's face wasn't beaded with moisture anymore.

We walked back out into the main room to give Alan a little privacy. The others were just coming out of the elevator and were walking towards us. Merlin turned to Joe, "Kalle can talk Georgette through the process. It might be a little more difficult for her, given she can't move, but if she has a strong mind..."

"Oh, she does," Joe answered, "She's my daughter. More stubborn than a whole pack of—what did you call them—Husks?" He glanced at Alan "How long before they're healed?"

"Healed? Well never, technically. They'll have to keep using their powers a little every day to keep the mark under control. But aside from that? Give it a week, maybe two."

If Joe had been drinking anything, I think he might have spit it out, "A week or two? That's it? How did more people not know about this?"

Merlin paused, "Well..."

Carter walked up and wasted no time to scoff, "Yeah, like Old Nik would let anyone use a cure that didn't give him a brainwashed army and unlimited power." Again I found myself glad that Carter never knew that Nikolai was at our base, and walking mostly free.

Josh stepped forward, "As much as that sounds like the rantings of a conspiracy theorist, unfortunately, it is more or less true. Along with some other factors. I'm Josh, by the way." Josh extended his hand to shake with Joe's.

"Joe." Joe said, and shook Josh's hand, "How many of you are there, anyway?"

Josh tapped his chin in thought, "I'm not sure about the current numbers, but the last headcount of current members was well over tens of thousands. Those are just the ones we know about. There are organizations like ours all over the world. Speaking of..." he looked back at our small group, "We really should be getting back while the streets are still clear. Ember made quite the spectacle earlier and it is honestly a miracle the husks didn't come."

"I thought Terra was being lowered into some husk infested trap! I nearly burned this whole cube down." Ember said, looking up at the glass walls as if she were still thinking about it.

"Again, we're sorry about that," Joe said, "We set up the elevator that way for husks. They like to wander in, and we steal whatever they have on them." I didn't want to ask what they did with the husks afterwards. "But you're not going anywhere until you help Georgette as well. Which one of you is Kalle?"

Kalle raised his hand and pushed up from the back, "That would be me."

Joe had the look of a man that wasn't quite used to having to look up at anyone. "Merlin said you were Type E.

My daughter has an advanced case of Telluria and he said you could talk her through your magic...cure..."

With a soft chuckle, Kalle nodded, "Yeah, sure."

Merlin waved over Kalle to follow him back to where Georgette was still sleeping, "Come on, I'll show you."

We had about an hour left until sunrise. Alan was doing well and was resting again for the moment. Georgette was having slower progress but anything was better than nothing. She had managed to start moving her fingers before she needed to stop. Merlin suspected that it had already started to touch her organs and it would take her longer to come back to normal. For now, however, we needed to get back to Moxxi.

Joe decided to come with us to meet Moxxi and see the base. No decisions were being made yet, but he was exploring the option of moving his people to the museum. There was plenty of room after all, and safety in numbers.

We left the glass cube through the elevator and stepped out onto the street. Kalle started the first bridge that climbed up onto the hotel across from the cube.

"Wasn't this place in a movie or something?" I asked Merlin as we moved across the roof and I started to make the next bridge.

"Home Alone? The second one?" Merlin suggested, "It was my sister's favourite Christmas movie."

I grinned and nodded, "Yeah, that one."

Despite Joe's biker look, he kept looking bewildered and somewhat lost every time a new bridge was created and subsequently destroyed. It must have been a bit of a shock for him to see this.

It didn't take long to make it up to the museum roof. James was practically skipping as he went over to where the hidden door was and knocked on the small mirrored window. The wall opened up a little slower this time, as the same young boy looked from Carter to James, "You found them?" he asked.

Carter just shook his head and ruffled the boy's hair, "Go get Mox."

The boy hesitated, and I could see the shine of tears in his eyes even in the dark. He ran off before he could say anything, leaving us to get Moxxi.

Joe kept looking around as we moved further into the museum. We weren't sure where we should go exactly but Carter just led us back to our old room. Our beds were still set up. It looked like Arthur had tried to wait up for us, but fell asleep at some point during the night. He was slumped over in his cot, a book dangling from his hand. Kalle made his way over to Arthur and knelt down by him. He gently shook his shoulder, "Hey, Arty."

Arthur groaned and opened his eyes, "Kalle?" the book dropped from his hand and he tackled Kalle in a hug. Arthur's hands fisted on Kalle's shirt, "I thought you were gone. Everyone was saying—I thought you were gone!"

Kalle laughed hollow in his throat, "We almost were," he whispered back, "But I'm not. I'm back now."

Arthur made a noise that sounded somewhere between a laugh and a cry. Kalle shifted up so he could sit next to him on the cot, putting his hand on the back of Arthur's neck, the two touched foreheads.

I felt an arm slink around my waist and I looked up to see Merlin. "Wow, Arthur doing PDA. He really must have been worried."

I lightly punched Merlin in the ribs, "Leave them alone," I hissed and snuggled in closer to Merlin.

The sound of light footsteps was heard and Moxxi came running in the door. There was the look of elation on her face, and then as she counted the heads in the room, pain. "You didn't find them..."

Carter walked over to her and shook his head, "No." he admitted. "We got James. And, well, it's a long story. But I don't think we should look for the others anymore."

"Oh..." Moxxi's shoulders started to shake, "I can't do this. I can't. Julia was the leader. I..."

Carter hushed her and wrapped his arms around her, "I know, but you're a great leader, Mox. Everyone thinks so. You're not alone, remember."

I could see the top of her head bobbing in a small nod. She sniffled and pushed Carter away just a little. Her eyes found Joe "I...I'm sorry. Who are you?"

Joe had his hands in his pockets, "I'm Joe. There's a crew of us living in the Apple store down the road."

Moxxi's eyes widened, "Oh...oh! Well, that's wonderful!"

Carter kept a hand on the small of her back and rubbed it in little circles, "They are normal. They didn't know about Telluria. They had a couple of people dying from it but Merlin and Kalle gave them the talk."

"How—wow, I am so glad you found so many survivors. Even if it couldn't be—" Moxxi sighed, "You're welcome to move everyone here if you like. We have plenty of room. Or we could set something up."

"I came to see you about just that, ma'am," Joe said, "But take your time."

Behind us all, James coughed, "I was promised to get to rebuild the planetarium in Lego?"

Moxxi looked at James for a long second, her eyes getting wider and wider, "Oh my...James! I can't believe—how did you survive?!"

"Lego." He stated, "Hey, is my room still up there? I want to move it anyway. Dibs on the planetarium!" Without another word, James ran off.

Moxxi stared after him, then her shoulders started to shake again. I thought she might have been starting to cry, but instead, laughter tumbled from her lips, "I see he's just the same."

"Yup," Carter said, and he started to laugh with her.

We took a little time to decompress and Moxxi went to find us something to eat. Joe stayed in our room for the time being, but Moxxi promised to take him upstairs later to find a place for him and his group to stay, assuming they would want to be close together.

James had presumably gone off to set up a new room in the planetarium. He came at some point, just long enough to take the rest of the lego that was in everyone's bags. I wondered if he was going to recreate the whole kitchen and everything he had in his other hideout eventually, or if he would do something else. He did say he wanted to make the solar system.

After we ate, pure exhaustion took over and we fell asleep for a few hours. It wasn't until late afternoon that mostly everyone woke up and Moxxi came back with another man and Carter in tow. Her eyes were bloodshot and her face was red and splotchy as though she had been crying, but she attempted a small smile.

"You helped us, so it is time for us to uphold our half of

the bargain," she said simply, then gestured to the man next to her that we hadn't met yet, "This is Christopher. He used to work with New Atlantis and was one of their pilots. He knows all the ins and outs of what equipment they have available."

Arthur gave a little wave, as he already talked to Christopher while we were gone, but aside from that he mainly stayed silent. I was sitting on Merlin's cot with my legs folded beneath me, "Where's the nearest airport?" I asked. After all, the one where we left our plane was a small private airport, not one of the international ones that New Atlantis would have commandeered.

"That would be La Guardia," Christopher answered, "That was where I was working anyway. When I left, most of the craft were still locked in the hangers, they should still be there. As I told Arthur, my security pass should still work. The airport had an essence powered generator with a full tank. So it should still have power for years yet."

Josh stood up, "Arthur? Have you decided what we should take."

Arthur nodded, "I was thinking a helicopter if we can find one. They're more agile than our plane. I can fly that back to base, and Kalle can take the plane."

I looked around at the number of people in the room. Merlin seemed to be thinking the same thing as me as he said, "How many people can go in the helicopter?"

Christopher shrugged, "It all depends what you find. Some hold four. Some hold more."

Josh hummed under his breath, "After what we've been through, I don't want us splitting up if we can help it. We'll all go to La Guardia. Once we get there and secure a working craft, we'll hide out while Arthur takes Kalle and a couple of others back to get our plane." Josh looked back to Arthur, "Will that work?"

Arthur nodded, "Yup."

"Okay. Then that's our plan. Terra? Kalle? When will you be ready to go?"

We looked at each other. It was late afternoon. We had the rest of the evening to fuel up and settle things with the base here, and then we could go. "Tonight?" I ventured, looking over at Kalle.

He nodded, "Tonight. That should be fine. In which case, I'm going to have another nap."

"We don't need to hurry. There is absolutely no problem in waiting another day or two if you both need it."

I shook my head, "Josh, I think we all just want to go home."

At that Josh smiled, understanding, "Fair enough."

Moxxi also nodded, "And once you have a helicopter, it'll be easy for you to come back. Plenty of the rooftops here have helicopter pads. We could set something up for you."

"Actually, before we go," I started, "Is there a place in the museum that gets a lot of sun? I was thinking I could get a garden set up for you. I have some seeds that could get you started."

Moxxi clapped her hands together, "Oh that would be wonderful! Thank you so much!" They were going to need some other form of food. We wouldn't be able to keep bringing what we had forever.

"It's no problem." I said and scooted off the cot, "Do you have a place in mind?"

"Hmmm...oh! Yes, come with me." Moxxi said, and I followed her out to see about a garden.

I SPENT the rest of that evening setting up a garden for the New York Alliance. Moxxi was able to pull together some planter boxes from old exhibits and the soil was still mostly usable. I warned her though that they were probably going to want to start a small compost somewhere to add some nutrients back to the soil. After that, I got to work. I used whatever seeds I brought with me, along with a few kitchen scraps to get a wide variety of vegetables and herbs started. Among other things, there were carrots, potatoes, cucumber, peppers, squash, and several types of salad greens. I grew the plants up to various stages so that they would be able to start harvesting some immediately, while the rest would take time to grow.

Once I had that done, Moxxi introduced me to a couple of the Alliance members. They used to be avid gardeners, and one even worked in a plant nursery before the Fall. They offered to take care of the plants once I was gone. I promised to come back eventually, if they needed any help, but part of me hoped that I wouldn't need to.

Joe was no longer in the room with us when I came

back. It turned out that he had found a wing that his group could take over. He was currently moving some of the art that was stored there and finding a new home for it.

Kalle was just waking up from another nap and everyone was eating the last of the little food we had. Merlin handed me a piece of sourdough bread that the cook had dropped off, "Excited to go back?"

"More then ever," I murmured and bit into the bread. "Let's not spend any more time in subways, please. Something always seems to go wrong."

"Understatement of the century," Merlin agreed. Not only Lulu, but we both remembered when New Atlantis found us in the London Underground. "Are you sure everything is okay with you?"

I nodded, "I mean at least we're not running from husks anymore, for the moment."

Merlin frowned, "We will be in a second. Are you ready?"

I knelt up and kissed him on the nose, "You worry too much. We'll get out of here soon, and then we'll be home."

Josh walked in and clapped his hands together to get our attention, "The sun is setting. Everyone should start getting ready. Carter said it should only take a few hours to get to the airport, but I want to give us plenty of time just in case."

I stood up and grabbed my bag. The cots and blankets were still left around the room but Moxxi said her team would clean those up later. They would likely be taken by Joe and his group.

We met Moxxi, Christopher, Carter, and Joe by the stairs that would lead up to the roof. Christopher unclipped a keycard from his pocket and handed it over to Josh, "This will get you past any security locks."

"Is there anything we should worry about?" Josh asked.

"Hmmm..." Christoper scratched the back of his balding head, "There were a couple of machina hounds, but the card gives off a signal to say you're a worker. So if they come close, just get close together. You should have enough radius to avoid them."

Elleen leaned over to look past Josh's shoulder, "Is there any way to just turn them off?"

"In the control tower probably. But that wasn't my department."

Elleen looked up to Josh, "Do you think...if we have enough time..."

"You want to kidnap a couple of machina dogs and bring them back to our base?" Josh guessed with an amused grin.

"Just think of it! If we can get them working, they could guard the base. Or help at least."

Josh shook his head, "I don't think we should go out of our way for them. But if they get close and the opportunity presents itself..." he suggested, then turned back to Moxxi, "Thank you for your hospitality. And I'm sorry for your losses."

Moxxi gave a little shrug, "It's not so much of a shock, but still, I do wish more had survived," she said with a soft sigh, "You should get going."

We went outside onto the rooftop. Christopher stayed behind, but Moxxi, Carter, Joe, and someone I didn't recognize came out with us.

"We're heading back to the cube to check on Alan and Georgette." Joe explained, "I'll discuss our options with my group, but I think it's best we move over here."

Moxxi nodded, "I'm so glad you decided to join us. Be careful on the way back. Will you come back tonight?"

Joe looked off in the direction of the cube, "It will probably be a while before Alan and Georgette can be moved. But if everyone agrees, we could start moving people tonight."

Merlin waved, "Good luck to Alan and Georgette! Moxxi will have people who can help them along with their training. So long as they do just a tiny bit every day, soon they'll be good as new."

Josh looked off towards the distant horizon. It was full dark now, "We should be going..."

"Thank you so much again!" Moxxi said, "Come back sometime!"

"Yeah, thanks Moxxi. We'll see you soon, okay?" Josh said.

"Oh! And make sure you fly over when you get the helicopter so that we know you did it," she added.

Arthur chuckled, "Of course."

Kalle also nodded, "Shall I then?"

"Yup." Josh gestured out towards the buildings, and Kalle started the first bridge.

Once again Kalle and I took turns building the bridges from building to building. Since we were warned to stay out of Central Park, we decided to go north and take the long way around. La Guardia was east of the Museum with more closely stacked buildings. The further we got from Manhattan however, the lower the buildings started to get. It made it easier to see any active husks that were roaming the streets below. For the most part, everything was silent. We did see a husk or two but opted to move far out of their way to avoid being seen. Every so often there would be a scream in the dark, but no one came out onto the rooftops for us.

As Carter predicted, it took a few hours to reach the edges of the airport. It felt both better, and eerier, to be on the empty cracked field of concrete. It was soothing to feel the grass that was pushing through the cracks, feeling the life just beneath the surface trying to push through. But at the same time, we were out in the open and if any husks were at the airport, there would be no hiding anymore. It was a New Atlantis airport after all, and many of the employees were cured. Christopher said that most employees left when the husks arrived, we just had to hope they didn't come back since then. Luckily, our plan was just to get to a hangar, get a helicopter, and get out.

As we walked towards the hangars, it made me realize, if a cure wasn't found, we would be doing this sort of thing for the rest of our lives. We would always be hiding, fighting, watching our every step as the husks would always be there. They would always be lurking and waiting to tear us apart like boogiemen. This wasn't a life I wanted to live forever. Everything I did was with the hope of change in mind. But what if that hope was gone?

In the dark, I felt the two marks on my arms. Nikolai thought that my power would lead to a true cure. I hated the idea of listening to him, as the husks were his creation in the first place. But there were moments like this when I wondered, what if there was a true cure? What if the husks could be saved? What if there was a way to go back? There was no going back to the way things were in my childhood. We'd come too far since then. Telluria changed everything.

We jogged across the cracked runways to the central hub of the airport. There was less and less grass the closer we got. It was easy to see how suddenly the husks appeared.

The airport showed every sign of having been abandoned on what, otherwise, was just an average day. There was an airplane left open, with half of its engine spilled out over the tarmac. There were pallets of crates left out, ready to be loaded somewhere. One of the pallets was tipped out and was clearly raided long ago. Josh motioned with his hand for us to pick up the pace as we made our way to the hangers. Christopher had given Josh a rough description of where to find things, hoping that nothing had moved too much since the husks appeared.

Despite the airport being abandoned for the last year, most of the lights were still on. That was the thing with Essence. It was so efficient, the airport would likely be powered for years before it ran out. Especially since a few lights wouldn't take up too much power.

It was eerily quiet as we slowed to a stop at a hanger and slid up the door. Arthur let out a low whistle as his eyes gazed over the selection of aircraft, "Well I'll be, Chris wasn't kidding." He walked a little into the hanger. This seemed to be mostly a collection of smaller craft, helicopters and propeller planes.

"So what one are we taking?" Kalle asked, looking in the windows of a small two-person helicopter.

"Give me a minute," Arthur muttered and started looking. I didn't know what exactly he was looking for in a helicopter, but I trusted him to make a good choice.

I sat down on the pavement for a rest, and Merlin joined me. My mind was still where I was thinking in the field. "Merlin..."

"Yeah?" He asked, leaning forward slightly to look me in the eyes.

"Do you think...do you believe what Nik says about Vita is true?" I whispered. The others were also talking amongst themselves. They all knew about Nikolai's suspicions, but I wasn't sure I wanted them to hear me questioning.

Merlin sighed and summoned up just enough water to draw on the pavement, "I don't know. Cy says that Nikolai has been obsessed with finding a cure ever since his mother fell sick. The extraction, according to Markus, was supposed to be a temporary measure. Nikolai was always looking for a true cure." Merlin slowly drew a smiley face, then a frown on the ground, "Markus didn't agree with mind-controlling people in the meantime."

"Why didn't you ever tell me this before?" I asked him. I didn't like the feeling of being in the dark. Especially when it was my power that Cyrus and Merlin had been talking about, behind my back.

Merlin turned his stormy grey eyes back up to face me, "We were going to. But you hate Nikolai. I guess we were just giving you time. The only reason Cyrus agreed to start letting Nikolai out was so he could continue his research. As best he can anyway. Nikolai says he needs human trials. He needs his old research. He needs...well, you." He gave me an apologetic look, "He's constantly complaining about it to Cyrus."

My heart clenched. I thought of Cyrus, back at the base trying to hold everything together. I thought of him having to take the brunt of running the base, of dealing with Nikolai, of keeping everyone safe. I didn't know how he did it for so long. It was little wonder that he was starting to unravel. "Merlin, I think...maybe...I don't know..."

Merlin put his finger under my chin so that I would look him in the eyes, "Whatever it is, you can tell me. Okay?" he whispered, "But if you're not ready, then we can wait," he told me in a way that suggested that he knew what I wanted to talk about. He said it with the eternal patience of water slowly making its way down a stream. Even though we might meander, he knew we would get there eventually.

"When we get back to the base..." I promised and leaned against him.

"This one!"

I sat up as Arthur was stepping out of the cockpit of a helicopter, "This one is perfect for us. A Bell 430. It seats up to seven. But it can be used to bring a good amount of supplies to the other bases if we need it. In the preliminary walk around all looked good. I'm just going to bring it outside to start it up. I'll know pretty fast if something is wrong."

"Alright." Josh waved at the rest of us, "Who's going to go with Arthur to get our plane? Kalle obviously. Frank, I assume you too?"

Frank nodded, "Yeah."

Ember stood up, "I'll go too," she agreed, "Can't leave the poor boys all alone after all."

"Four should be enough then. The rest of us will wait here. How long do you think it'll take, Arthur?"

"Give it an hour. Probably less. Give or take."

"We'll be here when you get back then. Perhaps if things stay quiet we'll look around a little. It wouldn't be so bad to get our hands on some New Atlantis equipment to bring home."

Elleen's face lit up at that. "Yes!"

Ember giggled, "Well don't have too much fun without us."

Josh, Elleen, Merlin, and I waited until the lights of the helicopter were lost among the starry sky before we turned back to the hangar. Elleen was practically vibrating at the chance to look around. It was rare to see her this excited about anything, as she was normally shyer and reserved.

In the little time we had to explore, we agreed to try and find the control room. I had to admit that it would be helpful to have a few machina around our base to help with patrols. Braxton, the head of the new guard team, would be ecstatic.

With Christopher's card, we were easily able to slip inside the terminal. There were signs that it once had been a public airport, what with all the chairs and empty restaurants that lined the endless halls. There were also plenty of signs to show us where to go.

"Didn't Christopher say that there were some husks around when he left?" I said as we walked through the completely empty airport. "Shouldn't there be at least a couple around?" It seemed like a perfectly good place for husks to spend time.

"No idea," Josh replied, "We should be thankful for it at least."

I hummed in agreement as Josh took out Christopher's card and scanned his way through a door. We were now walking through an area that seemed more utilitarian. According to the signs, there were warehouses straight ahead somewhere, likely filled with a wide array of supplies that New Atlantis would have given out to the citizens of this area. Down a corridor to the left, was the way to the control tower.

I guessed we used about half the time we had just walked to the control tower in the maze of corridors and stairs. Windows lined the round room, cramped with equipment. Most of the computers were silent, probably in some kind of sleep mode after going unused for so long. There were enough blinking lights throughout the room to suggest everything was still powered on. Elleen was ecstatic. She dashed around the room, flicking on the screens to see what they all controlled. I imagined most of them were for the planes, but that wasn't what Elleen was looking for.

Elleen sat down in front of one of the computers off to the side. If it were monitoring the air traffic, it would have been in one of the worst places to see the runways. She typed away, clearly looking for something. "Josh, could you scan that card over here?" Elleen asked, indicating a card reader to the side of her computer.

Josh did as asked and Elleen went back to typing again. Eventually, she stopped and sat back in the chair, "Darn, nearly all of the airport machina are offline." Elleen murmured, "There are a couple cleaning machina still doing their rounds, but none of the really useful ones."

Josh looked over her shoulder, "Did they just run out of power?"

"Doubt it," Elleen spun around, "Machina all had an internal Essence tank. But they were also programmed to go back to their refuelling dock as needed. If they are offline, it's more likely that they were damaged."

"Are you able to see what happened to them?" Josh asked, "Or where they are now?"

Elleen nodded and turned back to the computer, "Most have a GPS tracker, that would be easy. The models with cameras might have had a live feed." She hit a few more keys and a new screen came up. "This is the last thing this one recorded before it went offline. I think it was one of the hounds Christopher mentioned."

In the video, it was raining. The machina was walking around one of the buildings. Everything was quiet except for the sound of rain. Then there was the clang of metal on concrete somewhere off-camera. The sound got closer, and the camera gave a sudden jolt. It was tossed around and all we were able to see were blurs of colour and hear the crush of ripping metal before the camera went black.

I blinked, "It...was attacked?" I asked, not entirely sure what I was seeing.

"It looks like it," Ellen agreed. "That explains why we didn't come across the hounds. But I don't think husks could take out a machina that easily. They are built to take a beating."

"But then what...?" I murmured, looking back out the window towards the dark tarmac. I just hoped whatever was out there, was gone now.

Josh sighed and looked down at his watch, "We should be heading back. Arthur shouldn't be much longer if all went well."

"Right..." Elleen got up from the chair, "Do you think

we could come back here sometime? We didn't even get a chance to check the warehouse."

Josh nodded as he headed back towards the exit, "Hopefully."

It didn't take as long to get back out on the tarmac. We didn't come across anything in the long empty hallways, not even the cleaning machina that was supposed to be wandering around somewhere. I could see my breath in the cold night air as we made our way back to where we started.

The four of us watched the starry sky in search of Arthur. It was starting to get lighter, so it would be easier to see him now against the sky.

"There he is!" Elleen called, pointing towards a set of moving dots in the sky.

I sat down on the pavement, as there was nothing to do but wait. I thought I might be able to hear the faint hum of the helicopter and I was just looking forward to being home again.

Merlin, meanwhile, was looking off into the darkness. I knew from the maps we studied that there was a body of water nearby. "Hey, Merlin?" I asked, reaching up to tug on his hand.

"Oh...hey..." He blinked and looked back at me, then back out into the distance, "Elleen, you said all the machina were offline, right?" He asked, still looking toward the darkness.

"Unfortunately, yes. As I said before, there were a couple of maintenance ones left, but they—"

"What's that then?"

My eyes followed where Merlin was pointing at two

small dots in the darkness across the tarmac. "Could the computer be wrong?" I asked, moving to my feet.

"Possibly..." Elleen said, "Though if the machina isn't receiving orders from the computer, there's no guarantee that Christopher's card will work."

Arthur slowly came to land some twenty feet away from us. Not wanting to meet whatever machina was out on the runway with us, we hurried to get on the helicopter.

"How did it go?" Josh yelled over the whirl of the helicopter blades.

"Perfect. Come on, let's see if we can beat them back." Arthur called out.

I got in first, then Merlin behind me. Josh got in next and turned to help Elleen, who was having some trouble with her injured leg.

As I buckled myself in, I looked over at the dots of light in the distance. The longer I looked, the less convinced I was it was the two hounds Christopher warned us about. The dots weren't moving like two sets of eyes, but rather like two eyes on one machina.

A machina lion leapt out from the shadows. It was at least the size of an elephant, and its metal teeth glinted in the light of the airport. There was barely any time to register it's sudden appearance when it pounced. Josh caught the creature with a strong gust of wind. It tumbled and made loud mechanical whirring noises as it started to get back on its feet. I threw a sapling on the ground and let the whip-like branches of a willow tree reach up and wrap around the lion's legs, anchoring it to the ground. The lion started to struggle at once and I winced as one by one the branches started to break.

In the precious seconds we had before the lion broke free, Josh hauled Elleen into the helicopter and Arthur started lifting into the air. In our wake, a wave of water swept across the ground to help keep the lion down.

But a lion wasn't a husk, and this lion was made of metal and wheels. It wasn't affected by the water at all as it broke free from the last of the branches and jumped.

I felt like I was watching it in slow motion. The lion opened it's mechanical mouth and a three-fingered claw like you might find in an old vending machine whipped out and caught Elleen by the bad leg before pulling her from the helicopter.

All I could hear was Elleen's screaming and the roar of the helicopter blades. The helicopter started to rock dangerously at sudden gusting winds.

"Josh! You're going to bring us down!" Arthur warned as he fought to keep us in the air.

"Terra! Root it! Merlin, try to keep it from escaping!" Josh yelled.

I pulled another seed from my pocket. The lion had Elleen in its mouth now and started running with her into the darkness. Arthur directed the helicopter to start chasing them. I threw down the seed, but by the time it reached the ground, the roots and branches couldn't reach. Water gushed across the pavement, but like before the lion was barely slowing down.

"I can't do much more without risking drowning her," Merlin called over to Josh.

Arthur flicked a few switches and flood lights came on from the helicopter. We caught the flick of a tail running around a building. We chased it, leading us towards the city buildings. Arthur was forced to pull up, trying to keep up from above the rooftops. The lion kept running, moving between tight alleys and sheltered entrances before we lost sight of it altogether.

WE SEARCHED until well after dawn. We searched until the husks started to wake and they stood out in the streets watching us fly over again and again. We searched until, between the husks and the machina lion, we were quickly losing hope that she would still be alive even if we did find her.

No one talked the entire way back. We couldn't. I kept looking over to the empty seat across from Josh. I kept thinking of Ember, and of Elleen's sister. I kept thinking of Elleen's screams as she was pulled from the helicopter and the world seemed to shut off. That numb feeling sunk into my veins again. It always seemed to be there when I saw death. I hated it. I hated all of this.

It was nearly noon by the time we reached the base. The others were waiting in the hanger for us with Cyrus, no doubt worried because we came back so late. Ember ran up to the helicopter the moment it was safe to and looked at our faces. I watched as the blood drained from her face. "Where's Elleen?"

Josh merely looked up, shook his head, and walked away.

"Where...where's Elleen?!" Ember asked again, looking at me. "Why isn't she with you? Where is she?"

"There was..."

"**Where is she?**"

Merlin grabbed Ember and wrapped her up in a hug, "I'm sorry Em. I'm sorry. It was so quick..."

Ember pushed Merlin off her and turned back to me. The fire burned dangerously in her eyes amidst a pool of tears, "Husks?"

I shook my head, "No...not them. It was a machina. It just...it just came out of nowhere and it just grabbed her and ran off and we looked as long as we could. We searched for ages but..."

"No..." Ember turned to Arthur who was climbing out of the cockpit. "Take me back. I'll find her then. Just drop me off or whatever or..."

"Ember...we..."

Cyrus touched his sister's arm. He looked so much like his father in that moment, just so very tired, "They would have searched as much as they could. Josh would have never given up on her if he knew there was another chance."

"You don't even care!" Ember faced her brother, flames starting to flicker through her hair. I could feel the heat coming off her, "She was nothing to you! Just another soldier. Just like when Daddy lost someone. Don't..." Ember wiped at the tears that were starting to fall, "Don't tell me they did everything they could. Don't tell me...don't treat me like I'm a child, Cyrus! You have no idea what we've seen in the last few days. You have no idea...what she...I'm going back. I don't care. I'll walk back if I have to. Carter did and he was fine."

"You're not going, Ember," Cyrus said firm, "Please Em...we need to accept—"

Ember pushed away from her brother and started walking in the direction of the forest. The grass under her feet burned with every step. I could feel the crackle of it through my core. I could taste the ash in my mouth.

Cyrus let her walk for a little bit. She wasn't even halfway to the forest when he flicked his hand, and I felt the air move. Ember made it three more steps before she fell to the ground. Cyrus walked over to her and picked her up in his arms. "She'll be fine..." he whispered, sounding exhausted, "She just passed out...I promised to never do that again."

Merlin just took a breath, but he said nothing.

I felt like my heart was being squeezed in my chest, "Did you need to knock her out?" I pleaded with Cyrus as he started to walk back inside, "She's not a child."

Cyrus just stopped, but he didn't look back, "She would have burned everything in her wake trying to find Elleen. And in doing so, the husks would have found us. I love my sister, but I can't risk the lives of everyone under my charge."

I took a step back. He sounded so hollow. This wasn't the Cyrus that I had come to know. He was so defeated, like in the few days we had been gone, everything had come crashing down. "But what about Elleen? Isn't there anything...?"

"I'm going to put Ember in the fire training room with a guard until she's calmed down," He started, "I want everyone to meet in the recruitment office for a debriefing, immediately. As soon as he's well enough to fly, I'll send Arthur back to tell the New York Alliance about Elleen." Cyrus looked down at his sister, "Did you see her die?"

"N-no...but..."

"If she survived, she may try to get back to the New York base then." He murmured as if he was saying it to Ember. He then walked back into the base.

We all met in the recruitment office for debriefing. Despite the fact that we were all exhausted and wanted nothing more than to sleep and grieve, it was better to do it while everything was still fresh.

Josh finished explaining what happened at the airport. His voice broke explaining how Elleen was so excited about the control tower and getting machina for the base. He explained what happened when we went outside. How the lion had appeared and Christopher's card hadn't repelled it as it should have. Cyrus made a note to ask Nikolai how that worked, perhaps his uncle could make something that would repel all machina, not just the ones it was programmed for. There were still warehouses that we never had the chance to search, it was too good an opportunity to pass up. In this new world we were making, we would need everything we could get.

We hoped, perhaps naively, that Elleen would find a way back to the New York Alliance. However, she was alone, and she was fighting off a machina that was designed to tear her apart. There were also the husks, who would swarm on her in a heartbeat.

Ember wasn't at the debriefing with us. Cyrus had sent her to the fire training room and she was under guard for the time being. Perhaps that was for the best, as much as I didn't like it. I didn't like the person that Cyrus was becoming under the stress of running the base on his own. I wondered if he recognized how he was acting. That he was doing just as his father would. Worse perhaps, as I never saw Markus even suggest using his powers to control his children. But perhaps I didn't see them interact enough.

The room was heavy and silent as everyone parted ways for the morning and went back to their rooms. I doubted there would be a lot of sleep happening. Between Elleen, and the nightmare we lived for the past few days, I doubted even my sheer exhaustion would guarantee sleep.

Merlin didn't say anything as we walked to our rooms. I stopped at his door, "Goodnight..." I murmured, "Or good morning..."

A half-hearted grin pulled on his lips that didn't quite meet his eyes, "Are you sure you don't want me to walk you to your room?" he asked, pushing open his door.

I looked down the hall to where my empty room was waiting. Ember wouldn't be there. Even if she was, how many times did I come back for the night and find her and Elleen sitting on the bed and talking about cars or stars or anything else that got them so excited that sparks were literally flying in the room? I looked back at Merlin, "Can I stay with you?" I whispered. Cyrus wouldn't be there after all, not in the middle of the day.

Merlin offered a small tired smile and put an arm around my shoulders. He led me inside and we collapsed on his small bed together. Merlin's arms wrapped around me, and I buried my face in his chest. "She's really gone, isn't she?" I whispered, my voice muffled by the warm sweater he was wearing.

"I think so..." He answered back, and I could feel the rumble of his voice in his chest. "I keep thinking about it, trying to think of what I could have done differently..."

"I keep hearing her screaming..." I admitted as well. "My

branches couldn't reach her. I couldn't reach her. She was so close..."

Merlin gently smoothed down my hair, "Try to rest a little. Even if you don't sleep. Just close your eyes for a little while, okay? I'll be here if you wake up."

I just nodded, my face still buried in his chest. I knew he was worried I was going to get nightmares again, after so long having them under control. I closed my eyes to the sound of him breathing. I could hear his heart beating like a rhythmic sea. It was just enough to lull me into an uneasy sleep.

It was well past midnight and I was still awake. Between the nightmares and only being active at night for several days, it was going to take a few days for my sleep schedule to get back to normal. Merlin had managed to fall back to sleep that evening, so I left him to get some rest without worrying about me. Instead, I went up to my solarium. The plants seemed to breathe and stretch to life when I walked in. Many of the vines reached for me, but I didn't let them pull me up into their embrace. Instead, I walked forward to the only other person in the room.

Ember stood with one hand on the cooled glass wall with her face turned to the sky. It was a clear night and all the stars were shivering in the obsidian sky. "She loved the stars, you know." Ember whispered after I walked up to her, "She could have talked about them for hours. Not just the science, though that was her favourite part, but she used to write horoscopes. She said she didn't really believe it and it was just for fun, but sometimes I wondered."

I reached out and took Ember's hand. It was warm, like

someone running a deadly fever, but that was normal for Ember. "I'm sorry..." was all I could think to say. "If I was quicker. If my branches could have grabbed her..."

Ember shook her head, "I don't want to talk about that." She kept her eyes up and searched the stars. I wondered what she was looking for up there, "Every time I try to imagine how she died, I burn. So I'm thinking about how she lived."

"Did you know her for a long time?" I asked as I had only known Elleen for the last year.

"She came here maybe a month after Daddy opened the base. She already figured out the powers on her own." There was a soft dreamy smile on her lips, "Of course she did. She was always so smart. She helped train me, you know..."

"You?" I was surprised, "I thought Markus taught you."

"He tried. But each element has its nuances and...well, after losing Mama and running away from our home, I was having a hard time controlling mine. Daddy didn't know what to do, so I slept in the fire training room where at least if I lost control, it was contained." Ember looked at me briefly, then turned her face back towards the stars, "When Elleen came, she started staying in there with me. She didn't really need to, but she kept me company and helped me contain the fire when it got out of hand."

I turned back towards the room and closed my eyes. Elleen's screams ricocheted through my brain, "She didn't need to die." I whispered.

"Terra..." Ember started.

I turned back and shook my head, "I don't mean like I could have stopped it. I wish I could have if things had been different. But no, I mean she shouldn't have been in that position to begin with."

"What do you mean?"

"I mean..." I flung my hands in the air as I looked for the words, "I mean look at our life right now. All the hiding and running from the husks. If we hadn't blown up New Atlantis, she never would have even been there. If we found a way to stop the husks..."

Ember tilted her head, "You would want to turn the compulsion back on?"

"Yes, no, I don't know," I stopped and for several long seconds I didn't say anything, "It would make it easier maybe, even if it was just temporary before we could find something more permanent."

"You mean a true cure." Ember said, "Like Uncle wants."

I bristled but reluctantly nodded.

"It's a lovely dream." Ember went back to watching her beloved stars, "But Elleen won't come back with 'what ifs.' What if the cure was found. What if the compulsion could be turned back on. What if I..."

I watched as her fingers reached out to the sky as if she might pull down a star. "I loved her. I love her. I was going to ask her out once we got back from New York. I don't know why I waited now. I wanted it to be special, I guess. I wanted to be a little extra like that." She pulled her hand back to her chest and I saw her body start to tremble. "And now she'll never know."

The plants in front of her were giving me the feeling of rain and salt. I reached out to Ember, sliding a hand along her back until she turned in to me and sobbed. While I held her, I watched the shivering stars above us and thought of Elleen.

WINTER TRULY ARRIVED at the base. The grounds outside were draped in fluffy white snow and all gardening was left to the mansion room gardens. Between the new lights, the careful monitoring, and my walking through the rooms from time to time, the indoor gardens were flourishing. Hopefully, it would stay that way even without my help and other bases could build similar gardens.

Despite the losses we endured, joy still managed to drift through the base. Christmas was coming and the hallways were soon festooned with holly and pine. I grew a Christmas tree in the middle of the cafeteria for everyone to enjoy and decorate as they wanted.

Ember was still in mourning and threw herself into her work. Most nights she didn't come back to our room and, as time went on, I was spending fewer nights there myself. More often than not, I found myself sneaking into Merlin's bed late in the night. If Cyrus minded the extra person in their room, he never said anything. Sometimes he wouldn't come back at all and would sleep in the small room that was closer to his office instead.

I woke up in Merlin's arms on Christmas day with him already awake and smiling. It was just the two of us in the room again and I shuffled up to kiss him on the nose, "Merry Christmas." I whispered, my voice still thick with sleep.

"Merry Christmas!" Merlin reached behind him and handed me a small box wrapped in plain brown paper. I took the paper off carefully, setting it aside and opening the box. Inside were a pair of earrings of tumbled jade stones. "Elleen helped make them ages ago," he murmured, "I had the stones for a while, I was just saving them for something special."

I slid them in my ears, feeling the gentle weight of them when I moved. They would match the necklace that he gave me when I first joined the resistance. "They're beautiful," I said and kissed the tip of his nose, then rolled forward to fetch his gift from under the foot of the bed. It was wrapped in sheets of newspaper that I found when we were walking through La Guardia. The gift itself was hefty and rectangular and most obviously a book.

"Oh I wonder what this is," Merlin chuckled and sat up in bed. The blankets pooled around his waist as he tore at the paper and revealed the cover. "'Guns, Germs, and Steel.' Wow, Terra... where did you find this?" he asked, even while he was cracking open the book gingerly.

"Remember in New York I went to bring our dishes back to the kitchen?" I asked,

"Yeah, despite having no idea where the kitchen was," he said, the mirth growing in his eyes as if he knew where I was going with this.

"Yeah well...I got lost."

"Of course you did," he continued as if that sounded like a very reasonable thing.

"Well, I found the library, and I looked around for a little bit. They had so many books. But I found this one and I remember you talked about it once."

"But...you didn't come back with a book. When did you manage to get this?"

"I asked Moxxi once we got back from....well, back. I snuck it into my bag later when you were gone to the bathroom."

Merlin chuckled and put the book down to hug me, "I love it. I love you."

Despite that we had been together for over a year now, I still felt filled with light whenever he said it, "I love you too."

We met Cyrus and Ember in the mansion's music room for a small Christmas morning together. Cyrus had swung by the cafeteria first and brought up a breakfast of tea and toast for us to share. Ember and Cyrus took turns on the piano, playing a mix of carols and everything else. Everything else included a very lively rendition of Bohemian Rhapsody. There was still something sombre about Ember, but for the day it seemed she was trying to enjoy herself.

The whole base came to the cafeteria at supper time and the cooks outdid themselves with a feast. We all dressed in whatever we had that was best, which led to a wide variety of outfits. I swapped out my regular jeans for a skirt, and Merlin put on a flannel shirt. Ember somehow had a red sequin dress and Cyrus tossed on a suit jacket. I wondered if it was things they brought from their old life, or if they just happened to luck out.

The supper was beautiful and carols would burst out spontaneously from different tables. I spotted Mrs.

McNair laughing with some new friends during a raucous rendition of "God Rest Ye Merry Gentlemen". A few times the songs would be taken up by the rest of the room. I kept watching the Christmas tree, someone had strung it with lights and popcorn and paper stars. From time to time I saw little flickers of fire hovering off the branches like candlelight.

It was lovely, or was, until Nikolai approached our table. He must have seen the general dislike on our faces as he put out his hands in an offering of peace, "I won't darken your doorstep for very long. I merely wanted to wish you a happy Christmas, and to give you this." Nikolai handed over a piece of paper, face down, to Cyrus. When he flipped it up, it was a charcoal drawing of a woman with Markus, and two small children.

"Uncle it's..." Ember reached out to the drawing.

"That portrait used to hang over the fireplace in your home. It's probably still there," Nikolai explained, "As much as we disagreed, I still respected him, and I would always love you and your mother." Nikolai took a step back, "I thought you might like a picture of your mother, as I do not know if Markus was able to take one with him.

Cyrus slowly stood up. I could see a muscle working in his jaw, but slowly he put out his hand and shook Nikolai's, "Thank you. Merry Christmas."

"Merry Christmas..." Without another word, Nikolai walked away and returned to his table in the centre of the room.

Ember bit her lip, and stood up, "I need...I need to get some air." She whispered, taking her cider with her. "If anyone cares for a walk..."

"I'll come, and Emmy, here." Cyrus took off his jacket and put it over her shoulders, "Terra? Merlin? Did you want to come?" He asked as he was already standing. The room around us was breaking into a chorus of jingle bells.

I stood up as well, "Yeah, I think so." I agreed, and with Merlin's silence assent, the four of us left.

The grounds were as silent as the falling snow. The star-strewn sky was clear, and the air was frostbitten. Our breath rose white as we walked around the gardens, actively avoiding the graveyard. Perhaps we had too much death. Perhaps it was that we knew more would be coming.

"Daddy would have really liked the carols, don't you think, Cy?" Ember asked as we walked. She was shivering, I could hear the chatter in her voice.

"Yeah...he would have. He would have sat down with his coffee and pretended to hate every second of it though," Cyrus agreed, "Hey Em, are you sure you don't want to go inside?"

Ember shook her head and kept on walking. "Mama was always able to get him to smile though. She would have gotten him to dance." She looked wistfully up at the stars, "We haven't done that in a long time, huh? Held a dance."

"You know we can't have all those lights on in the ballroom," Cyrus murmured.

"Maybe we should build something underground," Ember continued, "Elleen said that the base could go on for miles if we ever bothered to do it. We don't need to be cooped up as we are..."

I stuffed my hands in the pockets of my skirt to keep them warm, "I wish we could build up instead. Under the sun and stars and amongst the trees."

"When we can, sure..." Ember mused, "All those

skyscrapers, imagine what we could do if everything could just...start over. When we start to rebuild the world." She sighed and looked up again, "I don't know. Sometimes wiping the slate clean seems like the only way to go. And other times...would it be such a bad thing to live underground? We could be like those little men in the Time Machine?"

"Morlocks?" Merlin asked, "I'm pretty sure they were the bad guys of that story."

Ember went silent as she played with a wire-wrapped ring she wore on her left hand. There was a pale stone in the middle, like snow, or starlight. "Hey Ember, I never saw that ring before," I said, meaning to start a conversation. "It's pretty."

"O-oh! Yes...it's...well you can look if you want." Ember stopped and turned to me. She held out her hand so I could look at the intricate whorls of the wires wrapping round and round the stone-like filigree. It reminded me a little of the work Elleen did on the earrings that Merlin ask her to make.

Oh.

"Hey Em—" I started and then was stopped at the feeling of something crashing through the trees. It was an off-putting feeling of being startled awake again and again and again. "Guy's, something is coming. And it's big." I warned.

"Is it husks?" Cyrus demanded.

I shook my head, "I don't think so. It feels too big."

"Could be a vehicle," Cyrus said, "Ready..."

There would be no time to get anyone else, so we stood our ground while I tried to feel how close it was. I pulled a seed out of my pocket and it burst into a wall of branches and roots. The limbs wrapped themselves around neighbouring trees to anchor itself down. I tried to expand it more, unable to tell how long we had before the thing came.

Then I felt it. Something massive crashing through the woods nearest us. Ember's hands lit with flame and she put a firewall behind my wooden one. Beside us, snow gathered up around Merlin, and a small blizzard swirled in front of Cyrus.

The something massive came and jumped straight over the wall I made. It's glowing red eyes bore down at us as it stocked forward. It had branches in its teeth that were lit with fire as if it needed light to see by. A lion. A machina lion. The, machina lion.

"That...is that the thing?" Ember demanded, the fire growing in her eyes with such ferocity that I didn't have time to confirm or deny when she shot fire at it with everything she had. But something very interesting happened when she did. The fire stopped. It reached the lion, and simply hovered in mid-air before sparking out. The lion slowed to a stop in front of us and laid down on the ground while something on it's back slid down. The small figure put up her flame-lit hands, "This wasn't exactly the greeting I was expecting..." Elleen said.

"Ell? Elleen? It can't—" Ember started running.

"Ember wait!" Cyrus called in panic and took off behind her. Merlin and I gave each-other a single look before we too ran after Ember.

Ember ran right into Elleen and pounced. The two fell into the snow with Elleen on her back. "Ooof. H-hey Em...could you watch the leg?" Elleen asked, her voice tight with pain.

"What?" Ember scrambled off and held a fire above us so she could look down. In the dim flickering light, we could see that Elleen's leg, the same one that had been shot in

Grand Central Station, was even more mangled now. She had bandaged it in what was once fresh medical-grade bandages but were now spotted red with old blood. There was also a jagged cut across her face that was an angry red, but healing. "Oh, my days...what happened? How did you...how are you...?"

Cyrus and Merlin moved to help her up. I watched, my mouth forgetting how to talk for the longest time, "We...we thought you were dead." I whispered. "We saw it take you. You stopped screaming..."

Elleen offered a bashful smile, "Well I...passed out."

I reached forward, touching her arm as I couldn't quite believe she was here. "How?"

Elleen looked from me to Ember. She was leaning heavily on Merlin. "Could we go inside first? It's kinda cold out here."

Cyrus nodded quickly and secured one of Elleen's arms around his neck. Merlin did the same. "Medbay? Almost everyone is in the cafeteria right now if you want to avoid a swarm."

Elleen nodded slightly, going quiet with the cold and fatigue.

I meanwhile looked back at the lion that was still lying perfectly still in the snow, "Ah...what about that?" I asked.

"Helios," Elleen said, and it stood up, "Patrol the perimeter of this building. Alert only." As the lion walked off, Elleen started to move her legs gingerly towards the mansion with Cyrus' and Merlin's help.

In the med bay, the nurse on duty cleaned and wrapped Elleen's leg. We stood around the edges of the room while the nurse worked, all except Ember. Ember stayed next to Elleen and wouldn't let go of her hand. No one said a word until the nurse left.

"Elly...how?" Ember asked again, a soft pleading tone in her voice.

Elleen looked down at her lap, "It's a long story," She admitted, "But you remember how I told you I used to work with research and development for...well not quite New Atlantis, but they funded our lab?"

"Yeah..." Ember started, letting the question in her voice linger.

"Well...I did a lot of work with robotics. A lot of stuff like the machina and Helios," She explained. "We weren't like, manufacturing them. We were doing the base work, like design, engineering, coding."

I knew Elleen had that kind of skill, we all did. Last year when New Atlantis found a way to detect active cases of Telluria, Elleen was the one to find a way to jam their signal.

"Machina like Helios were designed to be guards and could kill, so there were safety switches all over the place. I was able to hit the switch on the side of its mouth." Elleen explained.

"And...then what?" Ember was practically bouncing. She was a bundle of nervous energy and I could tell she just wanted to know exactly how Elleen had come back to her. Back to all of us.

"Well, it makes the machina shut down. So it dropped me. We were in the middle of the city and there were some husks down the street so I climbed up on his back and pulled open the control panel. There were some manual controls there so I was able to at least start it back up and get back to the airport."

"You started it back up? In a husk infested city? And you're still alive?!" Ember's voice was rising slightly in pitch. Merlin, on the other hand, just gave a low whistle.

"Well, I went back to the airport and camped out there. I was bleeding really bad and I needed to get patched up first. I found a first aid kit. Then—"

"But if you were just at the airport, what took you so long? It only took Carter a month, and he was on foot! You've been almost two!"

"Ember calm...maybe you should sit," Cyrus warned, however, Ember stayed on her feet.

Elleen gave Ember's hand a small squeeze, "I needed to rest for a few days, I wouldn't have made it at all if I left right away. Plus I needed to reprogram Helios first."

"But why didn't you try to contact anyone? Surely you could have used the radio or something. Arthur could have picked it up maybe."

At that Elleen bit her lip, "I...I assumed you all thought I was dead and that you wouldn't be listening for a radio transmission."

"Well, you assumed right!" Ember was on the verge of screaming. Her free hand came up to wipe away the angry tears that were starting to roll down her cheeks.

"I don't blame you," Elleen said softly and gave Ember's hand a little tug so that she would sit down on the edge of the bed. Ember laid down, curling up next to Elleen.

"I thought you were dead...they all kept saying you were dead," Ember whispered.

Merlin spoke up from where he was standing by the wall, "What happened next, Elleen?"

"Oh...well once I could hobble a bit, I looked around the warehouses and found some things I needed to reprogram Helios. That itself took me another week. I made a couple of changes to his defence protocol and his focus area so that he would actually be able to leave the area. Then...well we left."

"We..." Ember sat up a little and curled her legs under her, "So you rode that thing all the way here?"

Elleen gave a bit of a bashful laugh, "I could barely walk. Um...and well I had a general idea of where to go. I watched the take-off from here enough times. So we just, wandered around until we found it."

"But how did you avoid the husks?" Ember asked, "And where did you get food?"

"There's lots of food at the airport. And I programmed Helios to guard me in my sleep. That's why the airport was empty because he was keeping away the husks. I was thinking I could program him to guard the base. I would make sure he can recognize us from the husks first, of course. And..."

Ember moved in to hug Elleen tightly around the neck, "I missed you so much. You're not allowed to leave me ever again."

Elleen tilted her head to lean against Ember's, "I promise."

BRAXTON WAS OVERJOYED with having a machina lion to help with guard duty. Once she was feeling better, Elleen had Helios come down to the hanger so that she could work on it.

The news trickled out fairly quickly that Elleen was back. Less then a week after her return, a surprise party was held in her honour in the cafeteria. She was shocked and bashful and hid her reddened face behind Ember as Cyrus told her story. Elleen also started sitting with the four of us at our table. As often as they could, Elleen and Ember were inseparable.

One dull grey morning, I was walking through the mansion gardens to give them a little boost. Under the head gardener's guidance, the plants were thriving. I was starting to feel comfortable that if something happened to my powers, the base would be able to survive without them.

I was getting close to the back rooms of the mansion, where the generator and the Essence extraction pod were located when I heard Nikolai's voice rising beyond the bubbling chatter of the plants.

"Yes. The origin of our species," Nikolai's voice was as fevered as his burning flesh. "The beginning. Where Vita must go to end it all."

"Okay, yes, Uncle, but what are you expecting to find at one of these zones?" Cyrus asked, sounding ever patient.

I moved to the door, not bothering to hide that I was there. Nikolai's burning eyes landed on me the moment I appeared. He was standing near the pod, facing Ember and Cyrus with his hands waving as he spoke.

"Gaia, of course!" Nikolai looked at me like I obviously knew what the hell he was talking about. I did not. "She is there for us. Waiting. Our sins will be forgiven once we have visited the heart of the mother."

"..." That was it. Nikolai was a lunatic. A raving lunatic.

"Uncle. Maybe...you could use more words? We're not really following." Ember said tentatively. "Father spoke a little of Gaia, but he didn't keep up with the research after we left so we're a little out of the loop."

Nikolai looked at the faces around him as if noticing for the first time we were there at all. I wondered what it must be like, to live in your head so much. "Oh. Right. You are aware of the Earth Mother, yes?" He started, adopting a tone as if he were speaking to children. "Every culture has had one going back millennia. She created us to be stewards of this world, and in all our years we have forgotten her. We have moved on and forgotten our path. We have forgotten and now our world is dying. We are killing her. And in all her wisdom she is making sure that we do not succeed." Nikolai looked down at his hand. The flames that burned just beneath the skin. After all this time, he still refused to use his powers. He would rather power the entire base with his Essence at the price of her charred flesh. He did not believe it was right to use the Telluria as a gift. It was our punishment. Or at least that was what he babbled constantly. "She is the cure."

"Surely she's not real," I asked, looking over to Cyrus and Ember. They both had similar expressions that said the same thing. What Nikolai was saying was real to them.

"I doubt she will be there in some petty human form. But she is out there." Nikolai assured us.

"Okay, so what are we actually looking for?" I asked, trying very hard not to sound sarcastic and failing miserably, "Since we're not looking for some 'petty human form' as you put it? And where is she?"

"That, I do not know. As we have not seen the earth mother since the time of our creation, there are no records of what she actually looks like." Nikolai looked regretful, "There are places though, where I think she might be. Places the Telluria never touched."

"And your proof of this is...?"

"Everything! The sickness maps, weather changes before Telluria took place, migration patterns, they all point to half a dozen places around the globe." Nikolai shook his head, "But my dear nephew will not allow me to continue my research. He would rather we wallow away in this bunker until we turn to dust."

Cyrus pinched the bridge of his nose, "We've been over this, Uncle. You can research all you want, I have given you all of father's notes and free reign of—"

"Of everything but the one thing I requested." Nikolai cut in. He stepped towards Cyrus, getting inches from his face, "You deny me the one thing my research was missing." As Nikolai's face turned towards me once again, I felt a vice constrict around my lungs, as if I wanted to scream yet couldn't get enough air to do so.

"Terra is not research, Uncle," Cyrus said, his voice

sharp and hard like sheer winds eroding away stone. "She is my friend, and I will not allow you to torture her again."

"Do it." I didn't know what made me say it. I wasn't sure I even registered saying it until the words were already out of my mouth. "I'll help." But just as Nikolai started to smile, I raised my hand, "But I get to call the shots. If I want to stop, I stop. If there is something I don't want to do, I'm not doing it. Also, I want someone else to be with me at all times."

Nikolai's crocodile grin pulled at his lips, "At least someone here has an ounce of logic then. Thank you, Miss Chase, for being the voice of reason."

My stomach was churning and I already regretted agreeing. Cyrus and Ember both approached me. Cyrus put a hand on my shoulder, "Terra, are you sure?" He asked in a whisper, "You don't have to."

"I'm sure." I agreed, "We need a cure, we can't keep living like this Cyrus, and you know it."

"She's right Cy, this isn't a life," Ember whispered.

I nodded and reached out my shaking hands to take theirs, "It won't be like last time. I'm in charge now."

I hated every second I had to work with Nikolai. The only mercy perhaps, was that he didn't usually want me around for very long. For perhaps an hour a day, myself and one other person would go to the research space Cyrus set aside for him. First, he had me demonstrate the power of Vita, by growing and shrinking plants at will. There were blood tests, examinations of my marks, and notes on my dreams when I cared to share them. He wanted a sample of Essence of Vita but I refused. He begged and pleaded like a petulant child after a new toy for days but getting in that pod under his watch was where I drew the line.

I always preferred it when Merlin came with me. He would bring books and try to distract me with facts about the world. One day, he was reading a history of humans.

"Did you know that the oldest skeleton ever found was named Lucy?" Merlin said, looking over the book. "She was an *Australopithecus afarensis* and was 3.2 million years old.

"Oldest as of that publication. There were others." Nikolai scoffed as he walked over to me, "Hold out your hand." Nikolai said, holding a small lancet. "I'm taking a blood sample."

I gave him the most withering look I could manage. "Right. Well, at least you're asking permission now." I muttered. I held out my hand, and he pressed the small lancet to the side of my finger. With a small click, the needle popped out and a bead of blood immediately began to bubble at the surface. As quickly as he could, Nikolai grabbed several glass microscope slides and pressed my finger against them. "You can go back to your reading now." He waved me off and went back to talk with his microscope.

I crossed my arms and looked over to Merlin, "You know, the last day I ever have to interact with him, will be a good day."

"I know," Merlin looked at me and gave a little half-grin, "But for the greater good and all that, right?" he chuckled, "Someday there will be gold statues of you on every corner. The woman who cured Telluria." Merlin swept his hands across the air as if he were reading a marquee.

"More like I'll be forgotten to history." In spite of myself, I smiled slightly.

"There you go." Merlin reached over and poked my cheek, "I haven't seen that in a while."

"You can leave now," Nikolai called from his microscope, not even looking over at us.

I just rolled my eyes as Merlin and I left before he changed his mind.

This went on for weeks. Winter turned to nearly spring. The powdered snow turned wet and heavy with the milder days. Winter was clinging to us, refusing to leave despite multiple attempts. Day after day Nikolai continued his tests, but every time I asked him if he was getting anywhere, he either didn't answer me, or spoke in vague riddles. On one particularly frustrating morning, I marched out of Nikolai's lab with Cyrus in tow.

"Has he found anything yet? It's been weeks." I demanded, tired of waiting for Nikolai to give us any idea of how researching was going.

"As far as I know, not yet. Since you started working with him, he barely talks, he barely eats. He keeps himself cooped up there all day, playing with his data. I'm not sure what he's looking for, exactly. A cure, I know but..."

I gave an exasperated sigh, "When I agreed to help, I thought it might get somewhere, Cy. I thought we would have had some progress by now."

"Remember your terms, you can stop at any time."

"Okay fine." I started again, backtracking. "But how long do we need to wait? We should be doing something. Anything. The husks won't stay away from the base forever. Isn't there more we can do? What if we reached out to the other bases, make sure they are okay. Do we know who's still alive? What if there are more like New York, who got split up and lost."

There was a long silence and I realize, for one horrifying second, that there was something that Cyrus wasn't telling me. Something he hadn't told anyone. "How many bases are left...?"

Cyrus turned, making his way back towards his office. I chased to follow him, grabbing onto his arm, "How many, Cy?!"

"Not out here, Terra," He whispered, leading me back to his office.

"Cy?" I paused and looked at him. He was dragging his hands through his hair like he did when he was stressed out."

"We don't know, Terra..." He nearly whispered. He slumped down in the chair behind the desk, "Arthur and Kalle have been going out. They have been trying to reach out to every other group we know of. But...they don't always come back with good news. New York was just the beginning. Florida. England. Germany. Japan. Everywhere we go, there are groups missing, or worse." He opened up a bottom drawer in his desk and shuffled through it until he brought out a map. He laid it flat across the desk surface. It was a map of the world, with circles and x's and numbers dotted everywhere in an angry red marker.

"Is this...?" I pulled the map towards me and my mouth went dry. The number of places that were simply crossed out was staggering.

"This is the general overview, yes," Cyrus admitted. "It's not everything, of course, but it's what we could find.

I took the seat across from him. "Who else knows?"

"Just Arthur and Kalle. Probably Frank. And now you." He gave a little shrug. The action was nonchalant but I could see the weight of this knowledge had been pressing on Cyrus for so long. I couldn't imagine having to hold that burden himself. I understood why he didn't tell anyone. To do so would have been to incite chaos and to destroy our hope. The only thing keeping everyone going was the belief that we would make it through this. That people were out there surviving alongside us. That someday, we would be able to walk free outside once again, with our families and friends, without the fear of the husks. Aside from that, there was the hope for a cure. A true cure that could stop the husks. It was the only reason Nikolai was let out of his cage.

I realized with a sort of dim horror mixed with respect, that Cyrus was using Nikolai. It wasn't about family ties at all. It was that Nikolai could do so much for the morale of the base, just by being his crazy, cure-obsessed self.

The silence stretched between us as this all dawned on me. "I don't know how you do it, Cyrus."

He gave a half-hearted chuckle, "I don't know either."

"How very touching."

I bristled as I heard Nikolai's voice from the doorway. "What do you want? You said we were done for the day."

"I need another blood sample." He said simply, "It is the least you can do, Miss Chase, as you insist on keeping my resources so limited."

I rolled my eyes and looked back at Cyrus. "She already told you, as I have told you, that she will not go in the pod. After what you did to her, I feel she has reason to draw that particular boundary."

Nikolai's hands flew up, "Well this thread of cooperation isn't enough. Unless you want your people to be like all those x's on your map, then I need more to work with."

Cyrus said nothing as he folded up the map and placed it back in the drawer, "Aside from the essence of Vita, what else would you suggest?"

"For starters?" Nikolai asked, watching Cyrus' face as if

to gauge if it were a genuine offer, "I need my original research."

"I gave you everything father had." Cyrus countered.

"It's not enough!" The flames beneath Nikolai's skin flared and parts of his shirt started to smoke, "Ember said herself that your father stopped his research when you three fled. I kept going. I have much more, more than he ever dreamed of. I need it."

"That's impossible—"

"Why?" I looked to Cyrus, "Why can't we get the research? Shouldn't we be putting everything we have into this?"

Cyrus stood up and gestured to Nikolai, "You're siding with him?"

"I'm siding with the right thing to do." I corrected, "I don't want us to be another x on the map. I don't want to live the rest of my life like this, Cy. Please..."

Cyrus tugged on the ends of his hair then pulled a scrap piece of paper towards him and scribbled a quick note, "Give this to Josh please."

"What is it?"

"An extra helicopter is fine, but if we need anything further out, we'll need a second plane." Cyrus explained, "I don't want to leave the base without one if we're to be gone for an extended time."

"You mean—"

"A week." Cyrus clarified. "New Atlantis was in ruins when we left. The research might not have even survived. We can go and look for one week. After that, we come back and find some other way. We'll take a small group, the three of us, Ember, Merlin, and Arthur. Agreed?"

"Good to see you finally coming to reason, nephew."

Nikolai said cooly, "Thank you, Miss Chase, for your assistance."

"I am not doing this for you." I bit out, then moved around the desk to hug Cyrus, "Thank you."

Cyrus patted the top of my head, "Ember has been nagging me too. I guess you were the straw that broke the camel's back. Now go give Josh that note. He'll get everything arranged."

"So let me get this straight." Merlin started. It was about an hour later and I just finished telling him everything. I hadn't yet found Ember, "So Josh is going to arrange a mission to get another plane, and then we're going back to the Azores to find Nik's research?"

"Yup." We were walking through the later winter snow around the mansion.

"Are you going to be okay?" He asked, "You know you don't need to go."

"Yes, I do." I didn't want to hide from Nikolai anymore. "Besides, it'll be harder on Cyrus and Ember. Ember especially."

"Yeah..."

Ember lived on high emotions. She was all passion and fury. I didn't know how she was going to react to going back to the beach where her father died. Part of me wondered if it was wise for her to go at all, but Cyrus was right about Nikolai. He wouldn't be able to handle the man himself, and Nikolai doted on Ember, even if she spent most of her time these days ignoring him.

Merlin kicked at the snow, "There's really no way around it. Nikolai needs to go, obviously. So Cyrus and

Ember need to go. And since you've decided you're going, therefore I'm going. Even if Cyrus ordered you not to, I know you would just hide in the cargo or something."

I giggled softly and fluttered my lashes at Merlin, "I would never..."

Merlin snorted out a laugh, "Right." Clearly not believing a word I was saying, he instead directed his attention to the trees, "How do they feel now, by the way?"

I followed his gaze towards the nearby forest, "Like sleep. Everything feels like it's asleep." It was the closest I could describe it. It felt deeper than just sleep, like the silence that ran to your bones. It felt like the sound of falling snow. "How does the snow feel to you?"

"Like...swimming. Just fluffier?" Merlin grinned, "I guess it's similar to the summer for you. It's...loud? If I could give water a voice, it's like old men chatting on a park bench. It makes me wonder what a desert would be like if I ever went to one."

"Maybe once all this is over, we can find out."

Merlin put his arm around me and I stopped to turn into him. He placed a kiss on the tip of my nose, "When all this is over. That's a thought, huh? Would you go back to Toronto...if you didn't need to hide anymore?"

Once upon a time, I thought I might, but after a moment of thought I shook my head, "Maybe for a visit, but I don't think it would feel like home now. It was once, but I'm not that person anymore. I wouldn't be able to just step back into that life." My eyes met his, and his eyes were the colour of sunlight just behind the clouds, "I think I would stay here."

"Mansion life for you, huh?" Merlin chuckled, "Or perhaps..." he put his chin on the top of my head, "Well, I don't really have anywhere else to go. I was thinking I wouldn't mind building a house here in the woods. The base is great and all but I kind of want my own space, you know?" He pulled back just enough to look down at me again and winked, "I'll find a way not to piss off the trees, of course."

I never thought of it before, but I could see it. I could see a little cabin in the woods, just me and Merlin. "I could probably pull some strings," I whispered, and yet it still sounded so loud in the falling snow.

"So long as you're there." Merlin tilted his head down, "After all this is over, we could live anywhere. I just want to be with you."

I shifted up on my toes, "That I can do," I promised, and met his lips with mine.

THE TIME HAD FINALLY COME. We would be leaving for the Azores in three days' time. Nearly everything was ready to go. Josh sent Ember, Elleen, Arthur, and Kalle to get another plane. They came back with that and then some as Elleen knew where lots of supplies and food were hidden in La Guardia. Josh agreed to keep an eye on things in the base while we were gone. Now we were just waiting on the kitchen to finish making us some bread and other things to bring with us. The rest of our little group were down in the hanger packing up the plane while Elleen and I were picking some apples in the solarium. It was a stormy day in early spring, the kind of storm that makes you question if it's spring at all. The windows rattled in their frames and wet sheets of snow brought visibility outside to a near zero. From the solarium, it was near impossible to see the trees beyond the base. At best we could see them for seconds at a time when the wind dropped out.

Elleen paused to look out the window and tilted her head, "I didn't think Braxton and the others were scouting today."

"They're not. I saw them at breakfast an hour ago." I murmured and glanced out the window. I caught a glimpse of three people walking out of the woods before the wind picked up again. "Huh, maybe they headed out after-all." I went back to pick more apples.

"T-terra..." Elleen took a step back from the window.

"Yeah?" I asked, and saw that Elleen was transfixed by something out the window. I looked again and the apples I was holding tumbled to the floor. There were at least twenty people now, all stumbling out of the woods. More husks were coming as the wind picked up again, "Shit!"

I grabbed Elleen's hand and we bolted for the door. The nearest emergency alarm was at the entrance of the bunker. We sprinted downstairs to the alarm and I reached out and pulled it. The entire base, mansion and bunker included, screamed with sirens.

"Do you think everyone else is still in the hanger?" Elleen asked.

"They were. We'll go there first." The rest of the base would be meeting in the cafeteria as the alarms sounded. At the very least we would meet them on the way and make sure the hanger doors were closed.

The hallways were chaotic with activity as everyone came out of their rooms and migrated towards the cafeteria. Thankfully, we didn't need to go far to reach one of the entrances of the hanger. I was partially surprised to see everyone still there, and the hanger door wide open. What remained of the supplies were being thrown in with wild abandon. Cyrus all but ran towards me, "Terra, we're leaving now. Kalle saw the husks. If they surround the base, it'll be impossible to leave. You were right, we need to end this."

"Now?!" I could see in his eyes that something about our

situation just became real to him. The base felt like the only secure place before, but that sense of security was gone now. There was no choice but to go. I ran and grabbed the first piece of gear my hands landed on, a coil of rope, and tossed it to Merlin to put in the plane.

It was chaos. Utter chaos. Everything was getting thrown on the plane, half packed and loose items. I looked out to the stormy sky and had no idea how Arthur was going to manage to take off in this. Merlin and Cyrus were going to have to help somehow if they could even do something like that.

Elleen pulled a small tablet out of her pocket, "I'll call in Helios to keep them off the runway. We can cover your escape."

"Alone?" Ember stopped and looked back at Elleen, "You need to get to safety!"

"I'll only stay long enough to make sure you guys are gone," Elleen promised.

"Come with us." Ember pleaded, "You'll be safer."

Elleen shook her head again, "You need someone to lock the door behind you, and to tell Josh what happened," she said. "Go..."

Before Elleen could finish, Ember pulled her into her. Their lips met in a blindingly passionate kiss. It was hard and quick, and more than enough heat to make me look away.

In less than two seconds, Elleen had pushed Ember back, "Go save us all." Elleen said, barely audible over the wind and snow.

Ember ran to the plane just as the last of the gear was thrown in. Everyone got aboard with Cyrus closing the door to the plane. I looked out the window to see Elleen waving as we started to move down the runway. Helios ran past towards the end of the runway to keep it clear of husks. Kalle and Arthur were both up in the cockpit, starting the take-off sequence. Cyrus was up there with them, trying his best to tame the stormy winds around us. Merlin was in his seat next to me with his eyes closed and his hand over the mark on his heart. Ember was towards the back of the plane, her head held in her hands as flames burned around her fingertips. Both were clearing the runway of the thick slushy snow as we started to move forward. There was nothing I could do but sit and hope. I buckled myself in just as the jets propelled us forward and up into the air. I looked down for a last glimpse of the base, only to see what was now hundreds of husks surrounding it, with more still coming out of the woods. The last thing I saw before the storm blocked my sight completely, was a glint of Helios, keeping them safe.

<hr />

We weren't able to fly for very long in that storm. Arthur certainly didn't want to chance going across the Atlantic in our tiny plane. So instead, he brought us to a small island that was the furthest east one could go in North America. He didn't even bother bringing us down in an airport, instead he picked a spot where he knew we would have the least chance of coming across another soul. Kalle made a smooth runway on top of some low mountains near the shore. The mountains were flat on top with wind-swept snow clinging to the barren orange rocks. It didn't look real. It looked like something out of a martian movie. Only the stormy grey sky and the tumbling pine hills below verified that it was still on earth.

"Where are we?" Merlin asked once we landed, his

voice pinched with exhaustion and pain from the couple hours of keeping snow off the wings and helping with the landing.

"Home," Arthur said, staring straight ahead at the grey ocean beyond the expanse of snowy nothing. "Newfoundland. This plane wasn't going to get over the ocean today, and back in the day international flights used to stop here before crossing over anyway. Well...not right here..."

Merlin started to get up, winced, and sat back down with a hand on his chest.

"Merlin! Are you okay?" I asked, leaning over him.

"I'm fine..." he whispered, closing his eyes, "Everything hurts and I need a nap. Maybe food. Food would be nice."

"You kids didn't exactly prepare for a mountain top in the middle of a storm, but we'll make due," Arthur murmured, "There's a hot plate around here somewhere."

I looked down at the mess on the plane floor. Everything was in here, with no rhyme or reason. "Ah...right." I climbed over Merlin's lap to wade into the mess, "I guess we have some time to figure all this out."

Ember hadn't moved since we landed. She was still curled in her seat, her knees hugged up to her chest, "The base...do you think everyone will be okay? If they get in..."

Nikolai simply looked out the window, "If the husks get in, then Markus' little resistance will simply need to keep them out. Isn't that what all your training was for?"

Ember's eyes widened slowly, and I could see Grand Central Station in them. Cyrus thankfully came to the rescue, "We're not an army, but yes, they are well capable of defending the bunker. I had protocols in place for such an attack and Josh knows them. They will be safe."

"But—" Ember started, looking up at her brother, "If they get overpowered. If..."

Cyrus waded to the back of the plane and knelt in front of Ember. He took her hand, "Josh told me what happened in New York. We used that to make sure we wouldn't make the same mistakes. They can hold out for months."

There was a long silence in the plane, until Nikolai chuckled, "Months...I've been searching for the cure for years." His burning eyes looked towards me, "You had better hope Miss Chase is willing to do what is necessary."

I started towards Nikolai without thinking. All the pressure I had felt for months was starting to break and bubble to the surface. I didn't know what I was doing, only that I wanted to see him hurt, "Stop putting this all on me! I don't know anything about this Vita or whatever it is that you did to me!" I picked up the closest item, which happened to be a frying pan, and got ready to hurl it at him when I felt a pair of arms loop around me and stop me from moving.

"Terra. Please." Kalle asked.

I simply dropped the frying pan. The ringing echoed through the plane and Kalle slowly let me go. Merlin shuffled over to my window seat, and I slumped down where he was sitting previously. I could feel the heat rise in my cheeks and I had very vivid daydreams of punching Nikolai in his smug face.

Cyrus gave an audible sigh, "Uncle, please don't. We're all worried about the base, and we have no choice now but to find the cure. I know you are convinced that Terra's power might be the key to finding it, but please do not provoke her," he asked very calmly.

"This is why you should have let me continue my research when we were still safe. You left it too late, nephew," Nikolai replied just as calmly, but there was the edge of flame in his voice. "If your people die, it will be because you hesitated. You're just like your father."

"Then at least it means I'm a good man," Cyrus retorted softly and came back towards the front of the plane. "Everyone, we'll rest up for now and try to wait out the storm. We'll be going as soon as Arthur says we can." Cyrus looked to Arthur, "Is that fine with you?"

Arthur nodded, "I'm willing to bet we'll be waiting out the night. Best get comfy you lot."

THE STORM DIDN'T DIE down until the next afternoon. By then, we were able to completely pack everything away, and Nikolai was able to refuel the plane with a mobile essence extraction unit. For the moment, I was playing nice. Everyone seemed to be going through the motions, trying to spend the hours as best they could to not worry. Merlin and I tried to put together a puzzle once everything else was finished, but I found my mind wandering back to the base.

Somehow the waiting felt easier once we were in the air again. It was clear skies into the night and everyone aside from Arthur and Kalle tried to get a little sleep. By dawn, we were landing in the Azores. The snow was gone, and the warm sun beamed in through the small plane windows as we landed on the former Islet of Vila Franca. It was a tiny islet formed from an ancient volcano and was right next to the New Atlantis ruins. There were tall cliffs and an almost perfectly round saltwater inlet. Nikolai assured us that the islet was uninhabited. Or at least it was when he was still overseeing his empire from there. The islet would act as our camp while we were here. With any luck, very few people from the nearby island would have even noticed us landing there.

It was surreal to be back in the Azores. I stood on the beach, looking out to the twisted wreck that was the New Atlantis base. I had no idea how we were going to find Nikolai's research. He claimed it was in a black-box-type setup, deep within the frame of the building itself. But I had forgotten just how extensive the damage was.

"Well, I guess Arthur and I will get some breakfast started while you guys go take a look?" Kalle suggested as he stepped out onto the beach, "Terra, you should make one of your boats."

"I wouldn't say my boats are exactly seaworthy, but if that's the only option we have..." I muttered. If there were another boat around that we could borrow, I likely would have gone with that instead. Since that wasn't an option, I just hoped that the design would be improved from the last time I made one.

With a small sigh, I took a seed out of my pocket and threw it at the water. Branches and roots started to spread across the water and I aimed for something a little more raft-like. It was only a short distance that we needed to go, maybe a hundred feet at most.

There was still a trunk for a seat, but this one looked a little more sturdy than the one from New York. Ember and Cyrus climbed on without question while Merlin walked out onto the open water waiting to glide us along. Nikolai was the only one to hesitate, looking at the boat with an incredulous look on his charred face, "You have got to be kidding me," he said, "That hardly looks seaworthy."

"You're welcome to swim," I said cooly and climbed on after Ember.

Just as Merlin started to push the boat away from the

shore, Nikolai scoffed, "Wait...wait." He climbed on, and I immediately wished I got on first rather than having to sit next to him. "Just as well. We might end up swimming anyway."

"Oh, I doubt that." Merlin hummed and pushed the little craft across the water with his own powers. Kalle and Arthur gave us a brief wave before they turned back to their own work of starting up a campfire.

It only took a few minutes to reach the twisted mess that was once the New Atlantis base. I pulled another seed out of my pocket once we were close enough and newly sprouting branches anchored in the ruins and climbed up the side of the building to what was now the roof.

Water pooled in bits of metal on the top of the ruins. My tree continued to stretch out, making us a solid platform to stand on and scaffolding that stretched downwards to work from. Ember went first, attaching a rope to the scaffolding and lowering herself onto the jagged structure beneath it. She started to melt a path down into the building. Nikolai found a spot on my wooden platform and simply watched his niece work. Until we got inside, it was all he could do since he still refused to use his powers.

After about an hour, Ember was working her way down through what we started referring to as the top floor. I stretched the scaffolding further down, giving Ember a stable place to work from and creating a structure for the shattered building.

"It's getting worse the further down I go," Ember said as she climbed back up to the main platform, "Uncle, I hope you made that black box truly indestructible."

"Of course I did. Nothing short of a cataclysm could have broken it," He assured us, and not for the first time, "The research will be there."

Arthur and Kalle had a feast waiting for us back on the islet. It was a welcomed breakfast of eggs, toast, and various fruits and vegetables. Arthur put his hands on his hips with a proud grin on his face, "I know we agreed to ration what we have, as we very well may be longer than a week now, but I figured we could use a pickup. Consider this your boost before we really get down to business."

While we ate, I picked the seeds out of the fruit. At least if we needed to, I could always grow more. We wouldn't go hungry while we searched for the cure, we might just have to be mostly vegetarian for a bit.

"How is it going so far?" Kalle asked.

Ember looked up from her piece of toast and gave a half-hearted chuckle, "You know that pile of scrap metal in the hangar?"

"Yeah..." Kalle started, taking a bite of an apple.

"Imagine that all melted together, and make a building out of it."

Kalle gave a low whistle, "Looks like we're going to be here for a bit then. Maybe I could help, it's a lot of metal, yeah?"

Ember nodded, "That would be great, Kalle, thank you."

As soon as we finished eating, we climbed back up to the top of New Atlantis and started anew. It was weird being inside again. I grew more roots and vines around us as Kalle and Ember carved a path through the rubble. While the further down we went, the more melted everything was, the upper floors were still somewhat recognizable. Tilted hall-ways were littered with glass and equipment, some of which Nikolai wanted us to take back with us. There were more tests he could run, more data he could collect, and the idea of handing over that power made me sick.

Much to my dismay, we dropped directly through the room where I first received Vita. It was mostly intact, aside from the broken window and a massive shard of steel cutting through the floor under my pod. Just being there made my marks burn with memory.

"Hey Terra, can you build a platform down here? It's getting a bit shaky." Ember called from where she was still melting her way down. Kalle shifted some of the larger loose rubble out of her way while Merlin and Cyrus cooled down the metal Ember previously touched with her burning hands.

"Oh. Sure." I murmured, tearing my eyes away from the room and going back to grow a wooden platform between the floors.

Nikolai was busy ruffling around the skewered pod when Ember called out, "Uncle? Are you almost done up there? I think we're getting close. This looks like one of the server rooms."

Nikolai tucked something under his arm and came over to the hole, "Yes, it will be around there somewhere."

"What's that?" I pointed at the notebook that he had tucked under his arm.

"My notes."

"Of...?"

He just looked at me with those burning eyes and I suddenly didn't want an answer to that question, "I suspect they might be useful."

I started to feel nauseous. Thankfully this was only the

first day and we were almost there. If we found the research today, then maybe it wouldn't take so long to find the cure. Maybe we wouldn't have to try out less desirable means of finding the cure.

The clanging and banging from deep within the New Atlantis base suddenly went silent. "Guys..."

A chill ran up my spine at Ember's tone. I scurried down behind Ember and Kalle, with Nikolai behind me, then Merlin and Cyrus. We were standing on a charred and melted slab of steel wedged between what was probably two former floors. Everything was so crushed together down here it was difficult to really tell the difference between floors or rooms anymore. All I knew for sure, was welded to a beam at Ember's feet, was a black box. Or at least, it was once a black box. Half of it was as charred and melted as everything else around us, the rest was pierced through with a steel rod. Ember looked up at Nikolai with pleading eyes, "Uncle...this isn't..."

"That's just a case. It is likely only damaged on the outside." Nikolai said, sounding calm, but I heard the pinched note at the back of his voice. "Dig it out carefully."

"Let me," Kalle said, gently nudging Ember aside so that he could try to extract the box without using heat. First, he removed the rod going through it, then carefully disconnected the box from the wall. I winced at the clattering noise the box made when Kalle lifted it out of the hole as if something on the inside was broken.

"Get the lid off," Nikolai ordered, his molten skin glowing with his impatience, like a volcano getting ready to erupt.

Kalle put his hands on the lid of the box and rolled it back like a sheet of paper. He took one look inside and took a step back, his hand on his mouth.

"What is it?" Ember asked, pushing forward and looking down. Her face paled as her eyes remained locked on the box, "Oh."

"What is it?" I asked, and came up to look. As soon as my eyes fell on the contents inside the box, I felt tears sting my eyes. Everything inside was melted or shattered. I didn't know if it would even be possible to get data off of the hard drives in that case. Just as I started to bend to touch the contents, Nikolai grabbed my wrist. Like being touched by a snake, I wrenched my hand away.

"Don't touch anything. There may still be a chance to retrieve the data," he chastised as if I were a child.

"You were sure it would still be here! You said it couldn't be damaged!" I argued, letting my voice rise, "Look at it. It's half-melted! You failed!" The branches of my scaffolding tree started to grow wild with my agitation, crawling through the crevices of the tiny space we were in.

Nikolai fixed his burning eyes on me, "That box was built to withstand hurricanes, fires, earthquakes.... It was built to withstand anything that nature could throw at it. It was not built to contain an explosion started by one of the very men who helped design it."

"Uncle." Cyrus spoke up with a deadly calm in his voice, "I have asked you once, and I will tell you again, do not, speak of our father that way." I noted that Cyrus did not say 'please.'

"Your father was a traitor and a misguided fool. He gave up on the true cure for his little treatment. The only one who failed here was—"

Ember's hand swung out and slapped Nikolai across the face. If I wasn't so shocked, I might have been impressed. "Daddy did everything, *everything*, he could to help people with Telluria."

Nikolai took his hand off his cheek and towered over Ember, "Your father turned his back on what needed to be done in favour of what was easy. We could have found Gaia by now if he hadn't betrayed me!"

"You killed our mother," Cyrus said, like the stillness before a tornado.

"Oh is that what he told you? He didn't tell you who started the fire that night?"

"Uncle—" Cyrus started, his eyes starting to fill with panic.

"There were only three people on that compound with Type F. Your mother was incapable of performing such a feat, I wasn't sick yet, that only left—"

The realization hit me just as I began to feel the scaffolding tree start to catch fire. I had the sensation of fire crawling just off the surface of my skin. Ember's eyes were ablaze, with fire in her hair, in her hands, licking across her entire body. Fire started to fill the chamber we were in until it wasn't just the fire on my tree that felt suffocating.

"Ember!" Cyrus screamed over the growing roar of the flames, "Ember stop!" The wind started to pick up around her with Cyrus trying to contain her fire.

"Is it true?!" She screamed, not taking her eyes off Nikolai. The open case between them started to burn along with everything else.

Nikolai fell to his knees and put his hand right in the flame to try and stop the hard drives from burning. They started to melt in his hands, "You stupid, STUPID girl! You're just like your father! Selfish and emotional. Look what you've done!"

"Is it true?!" Ember screamed again, and I felt the base start to rumble.

"Ember, please! You need to stop!" I cried, looking up at our way out and the burning tree.

"Yes, destroy us all. We have no hope left. Put us out of our misery." Nikolai replied and I realized he was fading. I took a step back, right into Merlin. Nikolai's body was joining the fire, becoming one with it. All his years of cheating Telluria were catching up with him at this moment and it was finally claiming him.

"Merlin! Kalle! Get down now! I'll follow with Ember!" Cyrus ordered as I saw he was starting to struggle to keep the flames off us.

Kalle just nodded once and opened up a chasm beneath us that went right to the ocean, while Merlin brought up the water. I had just enough time to take a breath before I was dragged into the cool darkness of the ocean beneath the base.

I GASPED for breath as we came to the surface near the islet beach. After Kalle carved a way out of the building, Merlin took hold of the currents and pushed us away from the New Atlantis base.

"Start swimming!" Merlin called, gasping as the ocean was the hardest place for him to control. It was so vast and so connected.

I started swimming towards the shore, stopping to look back at New Atlantis constantly. Smoke was coming out from where our hole was. I could hear a deep rumble from somewhere over there again.

I paused only for a moment, long enough to feel a shudder through the water. I looked back in time to see a flash of fire blasting from the middle of the building. At the same time, two figures came flying out of the top.

Smaller explosions rocked the base, making chunks of it fall into the sea. Above us, Cyrus was soaring through the air, holding tight to his sister as they made a controlled fall towards the beach. From our spot in the water, we could see the pair of them tumble on to the sand.

My feet found ground and I waded out of the water as fast as I could before running across the beach to them. Cyrus was lying on his stomach in the sand with Ember kneeling over him, "Cy! Cy! Please say something! Move! Anything!"

I fell to my knees next to them, "What happened?!" Merlin and Kalle were just behind me.

"He flew us out!" Ember cried with tears in her eyes and soot on her face. "Cyrus, please just say something."

I understood her panic. While Cyrus had been making attempts at flying for as long as I knew him, he could barely hover for a couple of seconds without starting to feel pain in his lower back where his mark was. Any longer could leave him temporarily paralyzed if he wasn't careful.

There was a soft groan from Cyrus and he shifted his head to look at Ember, "I can't feel my legs."

"You...you dummy!" Ember cried and stood up, "You had better hope feeling comes back or I'm going to kill you. Do you understand me?!"

Cyrus just groaned again, "Merlin, Kalle, I'm going to need a lift back to the plane. Do you think you could pull me over?"

"Merlin give me a hand. I'll carry him." Kalle said as he bent to pick Cyrus up.

I watched as Merlin helped get Cyrus on Kalle's back. There were some minor burns that I could see once he wasn't lying on his stomach. He must have grabbed Ember while she was still on fire. I bit my lip, reminding myself that, more than likely, Cyrus would be fine. "What about Nikolai and the research?"

"Gone..." Ember whispered, handing me Nikolai's notebook.

Cyrus was brought into the plane where he could rest and recover. There was no telling how long it would take him to regain his ability to walk. We sat around the fire that night, barely saying anything. The research was gone, Nikolai was gone, no one knew where we could go next. We couldn't go back to the base, not until we found the cure.

By dawn I was awake. I felt adrift, now that the research was truly gone. Cyrus was still asleep in the plane, recovering from the day before. Arthur and Kalle were sitting around the campfire, drinking morning tea in the sunrise and enjoying a few quiet moments together at the beginning of a new day. I decided to climb the cliffs of the little islet just for some room to think. All we had left was Nikolai's notebook, and the notes he left on the plane. That was all we had now to direct us to Vita. I spent the night reading everything over, even the clinical notes on my torture, but nothing jumped out at me as being useful.

By the time I reached the top of the highest cliff, mostly with the help of Vita, Merlin was right there beside me. He had followed soon after I left and we had climbed in amiable silence. According to Arthur, this place used to be a famous cliff diving spot. You could see it. The sheer drops over deep water. There were signs of foot traffic once upon a time. But like everything else, it was from a different time, a different place.

Merlin and I stood looking out over the vast ocean. He couldn't seem to stop staring at it, like how I might stare at a sea of trees. "Is it uncomfortable to be here?" I asked.

"Not really...it's just distracting. But it's like you and the grass, the trees, everything. You can tune it out so it's sort of white noise." He wrapped an arm around me. "It's nice to be distracted sometimes."

I looked up at him and at once I knew what he meant. All this unknowing. No one talked about it, but the base was always on our minds. They could last ages so long as nothing got in. But what if something went wrong?

I looked down at the campsite and saw the tiny figures of everyone sitting around. No doubt they were drinking Arthur's tea. He seemed to make it no matter the weather. Maybe they were talking about what our next move could be. That was the thing, no one really knew what we could do now. The research was gone, Nikolai was gone, all we had left was a few sparse notes.

"Wait...Terra, look." Merlin pointed down at the plane and a figure coming out of it. A figure with blonde hair. Without another word, Merlin grabbed me and summoned up a gust of water from the sea. It swept us both off the rocks and down towards the beach. My stomach rushed into my throat at the sudden and thrilling leap down from the rocks as I felt the controlled swirl of the water around us. We touched down next to the camp and were totally dry as if nothing happened. I looked up to Merlin, feeling slightly dazed. He only chuckled and took my hand before leading me to the camp.

Cyrus was sitting by the campfire with Ember fussing over him. "Are you sure you're okay to walk, Cy? How are your burns?"

"Emmy, the burns weren't that bad to begin with. Calm down. And I can walk well enough," Cyrus answered, tugging on her arm to make her sit.

Merlin walked over and patted Cyrus on the shoulder, "It's good to see you up and about."

"Thanks," Cyrus accepted a cup of hot tea from Arthur

and took a small sip. He still looked weak, but at least he was walking again, "Also, I had an idea of where we could go."

My eyes widened slightly, "Where?"

He simply looked at Ember, "Home."

The Chiaro Villa was nestled on a rocky Italian shore. It already had a small private runway that was mostly in perfect shape, if not a little cracked and overgrown. The small collection of buildings were arranged in a crescent shape around a cobbled courtyard. Like the runway, everything was just slightly overgrown, but you could see that it was once a beautiful home with endless beds of flowers. This early in the year, the remaining greenery was alive with leaves and twisted weeds.

The buildings themselves were made of pale stone with clay roofs covered in climbing vines. Most of the buildings still looked like they were in perfect shape, except for one that had charred marks licking the window frames.

"Welcome home, Em." Cyrus said, walking into the courtyard.

Her eyes drifted to the burned building for just a second before she smiled lightly and nodded, "I didn't think we would see it again."

Cyrus walked over to a set of ornate wooden doors that had a very high tech lock off to the side. He placed his hand on it and there was a soft buzz and a click.

"It looks like the security system still has power at least," Cyrus said as he pushed open the door, "Em? Maybe you should check out the generator though."

"I'll go do that now," Ember said and skipped off.

Cyrus led the rest of us inside. The double doors opened up into a airy entrance hall. Everything was covered in a thick layer of dust and it looked like everyone dropped what they were doing and left in an instant. As we walked in further to a sitting room, there was a book left open on the floor as if it had been tossed aside. There was a nearby kitchen that still had dishes in the sink.

Cyrus walked over to the ceiling-high windows and pulled open the sheer white curtains. "Make yourselves at home. The first two bedrooms at the top of the stairs are mine and Embers, but you're welcome to the rest." I noticed there was a familiar painting sitting above the fireplace in the sitting room. It was a twin of the one Nikolai drew for Christmas.

"Cy? You said Nikolai's and Markus' old lab was here?" I asked, wanting to see that first above everything else.

"The lab was the building that was burned." Cyrus admitted regretfully, "However, I know Uncle had a lot of notes in his apartment."

"Show me."

———

The lab was burned. That much was clear. I kicked the small pile of sand that was spilled over what remained of the interior. "Father put out the fire. He only just discovered the powers and didn't have full control, but he did his best," Cyrus explained. It was just me and Cyrus for the moment. Everyone else stayed back in the main house to pick out some bedrooms and get something started for supper. Ember was still off working on the generator.

"Cyrus, I have to ask you...did Ember do this?" I whispered, looking back at him.

Cyrus shook his head, "We don't know," he said, moving back towards the door, "Uncle Nikolai, Ember, and our mother were all here. Ember...she wanted to see Mom. We hadn't been allowed to see her in weeks, so she snuck in. Her and Uncle Nikolai argued, and the fire started. Honestly, it could have been either one of them.

"What happened to your mother?" I asked, but as soon as I saw Cyrus' face I wish I hadn't.

He didn't look at me, and his voice was low when he said, "She died in the fire. She was the first husk before Uncle Nikolai invented the compulsion."

I gasped softly, "Cyrus, I'm so sorry."

"It would be best if Ember didn't come in here. There's no stopping her, I know, but try not to encourage her, okay?"

I bit my lip and followed Cyrus as we made our way to the building next door. It was a smaller, self-contained house. There were two floors, and it was decorated in that minimalist way that reminded me of New Atlantis buildings.

"This was Uncle Nikolai's apartment. He has a personal study over there. That's probably where most of his notes are. Wait until Ember gets the rest of the power turned on before you try turning on his computer, okay? The password will be taped to the bottom of his keyboard." Cyrus turned to walk back out. He still had a slight limp but was mostly recovered. "I'm going to check on everyone and make sure they're getting settled."

"Hey, Cyrus—"

He stopped and looked back, "I hope we find it too," he whispered, then disappeared.

I searched that apartment for hours, looking for every possible scrap of research that Nikolai might have left behind. I piled everything into boxes, and once Ember got the power working again, I used all the paper left in the printer to get everything I could find off of Nikolai's computer.

I brought it all back to the main house where everyone was just getting supper on the table.

"Terra! I was just coming to get you." Merlin said, "Did you find anything?"

I dropped a box on the floor, "I packed up everything I could find. I'll need some help bringing it all in here though."

Merlin nodded once and waved at Kalle to come with him. Together, the three of us brought everything back. I flipped through papers as we ate, not understanding most of what was written in the half-mad scribbles. Ember and Cyrus at least could decipher some of his writing and offered to transcribe it.

The days went on like that, obsessing over every inch of research we had at our disposal. Most of the research was old, things we already knew about Telluria. After all, some of this research went back to the very beginning, when the illness first started to appear.

It was almost a week later when I found myself looking at a symbol that was recurring in the notes. It was like a tree with its branches and roots spread out so it made a circle. I lifted a page up to Cyrus, who was busy transcribing some of the pages. "Cyrus, what's this symbol mean? I keep seeing it."

Cyrus rubbed his eyes and looked over, "The tree of life." He put the pen behind his ear, "It became something of a talisman for Father and Uncle Nikolai. Among other things, it represented the connection between all things."

"Like our connection to Gaia." I murmured, looking back down at the page.

"Exactly."

One sunny afternoon, Ember flopped down on the couch and pulled her scarf off of her hair that she had been using to keep her curls contained as she worked, "Merlin, do you think you could add a little Essence to the generator? Just mine keeps making it overheat."

"No problem, Em," Merlin said, looking over his book briefly, "When do you need it?"

"Oh, anytime today would be perfect."

I tilted my head, "What do you mean?"

Ember sat forward slightly, "I suppose you wouldn't know. Essence works best when it's a mixture of all four types. Pure Essence from each Telluria strain have ever so slightly different properties.

"What happens when it's not mixed?" I asked.

"Well it depends what you're using it for," Ember continued, "Like, if Merlin powered the plane, Arthur would be dealing with a slight pull downwards whenever we crossed an ocean."

"I'm used to it anyway. When it was just Markus, mountains would always be throwing my instruments off," Arthur said with a bit of a shrug from the kitchen.

"Well, yes, but as I was saying, for a plane, really Cyrus' essence would be the best choice with air. Myself or Uncle Nik would also be okay, as the closest pull from us would be the sun."

Cyrus was flipping through Nikolai's notebook, "Father showed me in the lab once that blood samples from the separate strains would be pulled towards their element. He put a drop of his blood in a petri dish and then put a rock next to it. The blood went to the rock."

I stood up. I could feel it clicking together like one of the puzzles me and Merlin would do on the plane. "Can we use my Essence? If my power is really Vita, then shouldn't it pull towards...wherever the source is, right? Gaia, if it's a thing." I looked at their faces, mixed between concern and excitement. "Just hear me out. Markus told me that Telluria is made from our connection to the earth, right? And the husks are made by breaking that connection. Meanwhile, Nikolai's research says that Vita is from the origin of our connection. All the other elements pull somewhere, then why not this?"

Cyrus and Ember looked at each other. Cyrus shrugged, "It's worth a try."

Ember tapped her chin, "I could probably add something to the plane's navigation system."

Finally, it felt like we were getting somewhere, "Okay, let's do it." I said, "Just tell me what you need me to do."

———

Ember's work was nothing short of genius. She hooked up the pod to a smaller Essence container, "I'm really sorry..." She said as I got in it.

"It's fine," I said, even though every bone in my body was screaming to get out and to run literally anywhere.

It was quick, thankfully. She only needed enough essence to calibrate the navigation system to direct them towards the source of Vita. With my Essence in hand,

Ember, Arthur, and Kalle spent two full days working on the navigation system. There was nothing the rest of us could do but wait.

Finally came the day when Ember ran in with a grin on her face, "We did it!" She screamed, "Pack your bags! We have a signal. It's weak, but we have a signal."

There was a mad rush to get everything together. Despite assuming that we would be leaving at any moment, all of our belongings seemed to be sprawled over the complex. Within the hour we were packed up again and ready to go. I hesitated as I climbed back into the plane, and felt Merlin touch my arm. "Did you forget something?"

"This is really happening, isn't it?" I asked.

"Yeah," he said, and smiled, "This is happening. Soon it will all be over and we'll be able to find a new normal."

"And build our cabin in the woods?"

"I already have the layout planned."

Everyone got on the plane and it took off. Ember looked wistfully out the window, "Bye house," she said. "Maybe we can come back sometime, fix it up."

"Yeah, maybe." Cyrus agreed. "There would be plenty of room for you and Elleen."

A small smile lit her face as we climbed further into the air.

WHILE WE WERE FLYING through the air, I walked up to the cockpit to see the navigation screen. There was now a small green dot at the top of the screen we were flying towards. "Do you have any idea where we're going?" I asked Arthur.

Arthur shook his head, "I'm personally hoping somewhere not in the middle of the ocean, or Antarctica. But so far...south." Was all that he could really say. "I'll let you kids know when the signal gets stronger."

I nodded and went back to my seat. Nikolai's notes were spread out all over the table. I was sick of looking at them by this point. It was like reading in circles. It was like reading rocket science in circles...in another language. It would have been just as good if Nikolai wrote it in Latin or something.

The page I picked up said something about how no animals had gotten the disease, it was strictly for humans. There was some scribble in the corner that read one name, "Lucy"

"Hey, Cyrus? Who's Lucy?" I asked.

Cyrus looked up from Nikolai's notebook. "No idea. Why?"

"It's written here," I explained, handing back the page, "It sounds familiar but I can't place my finger on it."

Merlin sat silently in his seat. He looked out the window to the sandy expanse below us. "That's the Nile down there," he said, his voice far away, "We're going south...in Africa...Lucy..."

My heart was starting to beat harder, "You know who it is?"

Merlin blinked, and looked over to me, "So do you. I told you about her one time in Nik's lab."

"Lucy?" I tried to think back to all those times Merlin came with me when Nikolai wanted to run some test or another. I pictured Merlin sitting in the chair across from me with a book open in his lap. I pictured Nikolai giving some snarky remark, "She was...a skeleton?"

"She was one of the oldest known human skeletons." Merlin explained, bouncing slightly in his seat, "Nikolai's notes say to go to the source of Vita. Telluria, Vita, Essence, it's all revolved around our connection to the earth, to Gaia. Right?"

"Right..." I said, feeling the conclusion speeding towards me like an oncoming train.

"We need to go where humanity started. Where our connection to the earth began. Where Lucy's skeleton was found." Merlin said, standing up. "We need to go to Ethiopia."

Merlin gave Arthur the general coordinates of where to go. My dear sweet history nerd. Of course, he would be familiar with the history of people themselves, going back to the very beginning. He had a general idea of where the cave was where Lucy was found. With that, and the navigation system Ember made, if Merlin was right, we would have no trouble finding Gaia.

It was only a couple more hours before the navigation system started to beep with the target being so close. It wasn't quite where Lucy was found, but it was close, just in her backyard. Arthur started to lower down the plane. "I'm going to have to fly over a couple of times to find the closest place to land." He called back.

I felt something tingling as we got closer. It was like walking into a forest, that same feeling of life all around me, but different somehow, more centred. I started holding onto the jade necklace that Merlin gave me as we eventually came to land.

When we stepped out of the plane, we were next to a river and surrounded by trees. I could feel the trees around me, beckoning me to climb up into their embrace. I could feel something stronger too, a tingling through my spine that felt like coming home. "It's here," I whispered. I found Merlin's hand, "I can feel it. It's here."

He looked down into my eyes, smoothed a hand through my curls, and kissed the top of my head, "Let's go find it then."

Cyrus and Ember were right behind us. Cyrus tossed a bag over his shoulder with a few basic things before looking back to Kalle and Arthur, "We'll be back by tonight. Set up a camp and watch out for husks and animals."

"I don't think we'll be seeing many husks around here," Arthur called back. "Be careful!"

Cyrus nodded and turned to me, "Lead the way, Terra."

The four of us headed out with nothing more than that

vague pulling feeling leading me. As we walked, Ember left a charred mark on the trees. It was enough to mark them but not enough to really hurt them. From what I could feel, it was barely a scratch.

We were walking for a solid hour when I started to notice something. "Guys...have any of you noticed any animals?" I asked.

We could all hear them. There was the sound of the hunt, of wings, of claws, just out of our view. But we hadn't actually seen anything. "I can't feel anything from the forest either. It's like everything that would be in the trees is just slightly far away."

Ember marked a rock with scorch as we stepped out into a clearing. "Is it like bears...where they leave people alone?" She asked.

"You would think there would still be birds or something though," Cyrus said, looking back at the trees.

I shook my head, "Let's just...keep going." It was getting stronger now. The feeling of that pull had grown from a whisper to a soft babble in the back of my mind. It didn't sound like anything, and yet it sounded like everything. "We're almost there anyway."

"Terra..." Merlin gave my hand a little squeeze, "Just don't...get your hopes up, okay? Whatever we find, it might still take a little time before we know how to use it exactly." He warned. That wasn't like him. Merlin was the type to go with the flow on everything. Caution was my job.

"I know."

A clearing led down towards some rocks. There were signs that people were here once, sometime in the time before Telluria. There were forgotten campfires, a metal bowl, a sun-faded picture of a man and a young girl, and the pieces of a rifle cut in half.

Merlin bent down to look at the picture, "Is it around here, Terra?"

"Close," I repeated again. "Not quite here. Just a little further." I looked towards the nearby hill. I could hear the distant roar of crashing water. "That way."

We walked across the forgotten camp, down a rocky hill, and around a small bank to find ourselves on the edge of a small lake. The lake had a waterfall at the far edge, where the water cascaded off the rocks and the mist gathered up in the hot air. I could feel it. All of the elements at play in this one place. "Merlin, can you move that waterfall aside?" I asked him, walking down the bank towards it.

"Well...I probably could." He said, looking up at it. He sounded a little dubious, but he lifted his arm as if he were pushing aside a curtain. The water moved with him. Behind it was slabs of rock that seemed to be layered over each other. It reminded me so much of that small cave I hid inside that first night I ran from home.

Carefully stepping over the rocks, I moved to where the slabs overlapped and slipped between them. It would have been impossible to see from outside, harder still with the waterfall beating down on whoever came here. It was little wonder that it was never found before. The other three came in behind me, and Ember lit her hands with fire.

"It's here...somewhere in here," I said as I walked forward. The walls of the cave were smooth and bare. We walked in, following a narrow passage that opened up into a small dark chamber. Once Ember's light reached the back of the cave, I made a soft gasp, "Look at this," I whispered, directing Ember to move her hands closer to the back wall.

Cave paintings, ancient and pristine. Hundreds of hands were painted on the walls in white, black, and red paint. In the very middle of all of the handprints, was a tree.

My breath caught, "This is it. Oh my god...this is it."

"This?" Merlin looked at the handprints. They spread out the entire back wall, but the chamber was a dead end. Merlin frowned and started to feel along the cracks in the walls.

Cyrus lightly touched the paint, "It's almost like the paint is part of the stone." He murmured, "Ember can you turn up the light a little?"

"I'll try...let me know if it gets hot in here." She said, and the flames in her hands grew a little more.

I kept staring at the tree. That feeling like concentrated life was the strongest I had ever felt, but what did we do now? I didn't have the earth element to move the stone out of the way anymore. Kalle did, but we would have to go back and get him. We were so close, I didn't want to leave. The heat from Ember's flames was getting sweltering in the small cave. It would be hard to stay here for very long. Merlin, for one, wouldn't be able to handle it for very long with his element, and mine was already getting uncomfortable.

I took a step back and bit my lip, "I think we should go back for now. We need Kalle...and a flashlight." I didn't want to, I wanted to follow this pulling feeling that called me beyond the stone. But without Kalle, we had no way past it.

Cyrus made a small noise in the back of his throat and crossed his arms. Ember brought her flames back down to just enough to see by. "I think you're right, Terra. It's getting late as well. We'll go back and let Arthur and Kalle know what we found. In the morning we'll try again, fresh and ready for whatever comes next."

Arthur and Kalle had a camp set up for us by the time we made it back. We were so far from any town that Arthur felt safe starting a fire. Just in case, Kalle made a cage of stone around the plane and the camp. It would be enough to keep out any large animals that thought it was a good idea to try us for lunch. Though, as before, there still weren't any animals to be seen. Not even birds. It was growing steadily eerier over time.

"How did it go?" Arthur asked, "You guys were gone for a while."

I sat down in front of the fire, crossing my legs and dropping my hands in my lap. "We found a cave, it had paintings inside."

Kalle looked up from the potatoes baking in the embers of the fire, "Did you find it?" No one needed to ask what he meant.

"It led us there. It's there...somewhere." I bit my lip again and looked up at Kalle, "Can you come with us tomorrow? The cave was a dead end, but I think the way we need to go is past that wall. Maybe if you moved some rocks, we would be able to find it."

Kalle gave a quick nod, "Of course." He then looked to Arthur, "You'll be fine here, yeah? I can tighten up the cage if you want. Plus you could hide in the plane if something happened."

Arthur clapped Kalle on the shoulder, "I'll be fine, Wifey. Go help the kids find the cure."

The campfire sparked as Ember snapped her head towards them, "Wifey? Are you—?"

Kalle made a grumbling noise and poked at the baking potatoes with a stick. His shoulder-length blonde hair came down to hide his face, but I thought for a moment that I saw the faintest hint of pink. "It's just a pet name. Shut it."

Ember flipped her hair over her shoulder and stifled a giggle. "Anything you say, Wifey."

Cyrus sat down in front of the fire with Nikolai's notebook for the millionth time and didn't even look up as he said, "Didn't I hear Elleen calling you...what was it?"

"Cy don't you dare!" Ember started, a vague look of panic in her eyes.

"Her burning queen...I think it was." Cyrus said, and glanced up at his sister with a mischievous giggle.

Ember turned on her brother, hands fisted at her sides, "Cyrus, I am going to kill you!"

Cyrus made a flicking motion and a puff of air got Ember in the face, "Eat snickers."

In spite of myself, I felt my shoulders start to shake with laughter. I meant to keep it in, and almost did until I heard Merlin making a small snorting noise next to me. It started as a giggle, then true honest laughter. It was infectious and delirious. Merlin joined in, and Cyrus after him. Soon we were all laughing, and I was holding my stomach until it hurt. It made no sense, and yet it did.

There were tears in my eyes by the time I was able to stop. I straightened up, and felt...lighter. I couldn't remember the last time I truly laughed. I don't think any of us did.

We slept on the plane that night. I woke in the middle of the night, sticky in the heavy, sweltering heat. I got up and tiptoed out the open plane door. I breathed in the sweet air, lungs filling with the hint of rain. I could feel it through my marks. I could hear it in the coming storm. Rain pattered just beyond the trees, then a little closer, and closer, until I raised my face to the pelting rain. There was fire there too, building in the clouds, not quite ready to strike. The earth was solid and familiar beneath my feet. And all around me, life.

"What are you doing out here?" Merlin stood up from the campfire and wrapped his arms around my waist. The rain was clinging to his hair, rolling off it and down his face.

"I'm scared," I admitted for the first time. "Tomorrow..."

"If it works, it's over. We can start to really live."

"But this..." I raised my hands to the sky and water caught in my palms. "Won't you miss it? Just a little? This... energy. Everything is singing."

His hand caught mine, encapsulating the little pool. "We don't know if it'll go away. But...if it does..." He kissed me. "I'll be okay, Ter. It'll be another reality is all."

I nodded, alive with that truth flowing through me. If it was a beginning, it felt like the end. I kissed him, stopping my own worries before I could let them surface again, and dragged him into darkness one last time.

I DIDN'T REMEMBER GOING BACK into the plane the night before. I woke up in Merlin's arms, our two blankets pulled over us. Sunlight streamed in through the plane windows. I could hear the sounds of the others talking outside, and the light crackle of the campfire. I groaned lightly and rolled into Merlin.

His hand brushed my hair, "Morning," he whispered, and kissed the top of my head.

"Are we back in the base? With everything fine again?" I murmured back, not wanting to open my eyes.

"Not yet," He started to untangle our limbs, "But soon."

I took my time getting dressed, mentally preparing for whatever was going to come next. For months I hated what had been done to me, I hated how my powers were different, how I was somehow special. It was all coming down to this, and it felt like the day before a big performance. When the time came, would I play my part right?

As I came outside, everyone was sitting around the fire eating breakfast. Cyrus got up and handed me a plate. It was loaded with our best food, bacon, eggs, toast, and slices of fruit, "Today's the big day. You should eat up."

Despite not feeling hungry at all, I cleaned my plate. Food was too precious to waste, and none of us knew what today would bring. I moved through the morning in silence, taking my time to get things ready. I felt the others watching me, but thankfully they were not pushing me to move faster. There was a heavy air of uncertainty around the camp as we got ready to leave. Arthur and Kalle said their goodbyes, and Kalle created a door in the stone cage for us. He looked back only once and waved at Arthur, who had settled beside the fire to wait.

We tracked back to the waterfall the same way we went the day before. Just as Merlin started to lift his hand to push the water aside, Cyrus stopped him and gathered us in a small circle on the rocks. "Guys, I want us to come out the same way we went in. Together. Deal?"

I nodded, though the gesture felt hollow. Still, I put my hands in the middle of the circle with the others as Cyrus called out, "Okay, three, two, one, let's go!"

Merlin grasped my hand tightly once we pulled away. I looked into his eyes and saw the same thought I was thinking. That hopefully staying together wouldn't mean not coming out at all. He pushed the water aside, and one by one we walked between the gaps in the rocks into the cave.

Kalle pulled out a flashlight and filled the cave with light, "Oh wow." He moved the light along the back wall where all the paintings were. "You weren't kidding. This is crazy."

I pulled out my own flashlight and looked at the paintings with fresh eyes. At once I felt my face creasing into a frown. The tree in the center seemed different now. The roots were longer, looping around the hands and down towards the floor. The branches were reaching further up, touching the ceiling. As I looked towards the middle line of the painting, I saw figures that I never saw before. Places where I could have sworn were more hands, now showed figures from different points of history. Nearest the tree were pictures of hunters and gatherers chasing antelopes across the wild savanna. A little off there were pictures of farming, pictures of grain stalks growing up in cultivated fields. There were pictures of towns, of roads, of things that ancient people shouldn't have even been able to think up. Wagons and printing presses and steam engines and cars and planes and at the very end, a building that looked like New Atlantis' head-quarters.

The whole cave felt charged with energy. It made no sense, but I felt the energy of life here as if the rock itself was alive.

Kalle tilted his head as he looked at the cave wall. "Well, what do you want me to do? It feels like a shame to ruin the paint. But maybe I could tunnel around? I think I feel a hollow further in."

Ember was looking at the wall from another end of the cave, "Guys..." There was a shake in her voice as she lifted her flames to look at the picture of the tree again. Only..it wasn't just the tree anymore. I shook my head and looked again. It was impossible, I had just looked at the tree.

The tree was still there, but on the sides of it were four figures with their hands on the trunk and one standing in the middle. The one in the middle had curly brown hair, just like mine. There was a woman with bright red hair, a tall man with long blond hair, a shorter man with short blond hair, and a man with dark, almost black hair.

"This wasn't here. I was just looking at this and it was

just a tree. This...this is us." I could feel my heartbeat starting to climb up into my neck, "This is impossible."

Cyrus reached out and touched the drawing of the tree. As he did, the part of the painting that was 'him' also started to glow. Parts of the painting that had things to do with air, planes, windmills, even the drawings of air started to glow in a pale golden light. Cyrus wrenched his hand away and the glow went away as soon as he did.

"Woah, dude..." Merlin sounded in awe as he touched it next. Once again, parts of the painting started to glow. But for Merlin it was a soft blue, streams, boats, even steam were lighting up for him. He kept his hand there longer, looking down at the paintings, across the history of humanity. Eventually, he too pulled his hand away.

"I think..." I whispered, feeling my breath catching, "I think we need to all touch the tree. And then...then...well I don't know what happens then." I looked at the picture of me, in the center of it all.

Ember got closer to the picture, "Should we try it?"

Kalle stepped forward as well, "Worth a try." He added and reached out to touch the wall.

Ember, Cyrus, and Merlin all did after him, and nearly the entire wall began to glow in the colours of their elements. Red for fire, blue for water, gold for wind, and brown for earth.

"Terra..."

Shivers moved up my spine as I heard a whisper that didn't belong to anyone with me. My hand was shaking as I reached out to the wall. I expected the stone to be cold, but it was warm.

"Terra..."

I touched the trunk of the tree and the light spread out from my hand, filling the branches, twisting through the roots, and finally, every hand on the wall glowed. The sound of cracking stone echoed through the cave, and suddenly the wall under my hand rippled like liquid.

"Come to me, Terra..."

I pushed through the stone, pulled by the voice on the other side.

"Terra!" Merlin screamed. I could feel him reaching for me but his hand slipped off of me as I walked through the stone wall. "Terra! Terra can you hear me!" His voice was muffled through the stone. Still, I could hear him pounding his fists on the stone.

"I'm okay!" I shouted back, then paused. I was in a passage that was glowing with the same soft green light that the wall had been when I touched it. "I just...I'll be right back."

"No! Terra, wait! Terra!" Merlin kept yelling, and I could hear the soft murmur of other voices, but I couldn't hear what they were saying.

"Terra, come..."

"Wait for me," I whispered, knowing that he would never hear me as I turned away from his screaming and started to walk down the empty hallway. I would have just as easily stopped myself going down that passage as I would have stopped breathing. There were more paintings on the walls here, but they told a different story. Outside had been the story of us. But here was the story of the earth. I saw a lifeless rock floating in space. I saw fire and ash as the world was created. The air became clear. Life began. Life came and went and came again.

The light seemed to be getting brighter as I reached the end of the hallway. It opened out into a massive chamber that I needed to step down into. It didn't look like it should be possible, remembering how tall the waterfall was outside.

The colours of the elements swirled on the walls, painting more pictures in light. They continued to tell a story, the story of life itself. I saw the past, the future, and this very moment. The light painted the image of a girl standing at the roots of a dying and diminutive tree.

"I am glad you came, Terra," the voice said. "I have waited."

I knelt down, reaching out to the tree. I almost touched it, but pulled my hand back at the last second. Whatever had been pulling me to this place, it was pulling me to this tree. "It's you...isn't it. You're...this?" My voice was a quavering whisper.

"Yes..."

"What are you?"

There was silence as the lights slowed and stilled, shining like stars overhead, "I am Vita. I am Gaia. I am Life." It spoke like breathing. Every breath was soft with just the whisper of meaning. Yet I could hear it, clear as the full moon on a cloudless night.

"And you're dying," I stated, hovering my hand just under one of the curled leaves. A rainbow of fallen leaves littered the ground beneath it.

There was the sound like a single breath that made my hair sway only slightly, "I have been for a very long time," it admitted, "My children could never see what they were doing, so consumed with their own survival." The voice was soft, gentle as a mother worried for her children.

Gaia. She was supposed to be a myth, nothing more than a story to explain how the earth gave birth to life, but she was here, in front of me. She was the only thing keeping humanity alive, and yet we brought her almost to the point of death. I felt tears sting my eyes, "Is this our punishment?" I lifted my arms as my marks glowed, "We're killing you, so you're killing us." Could I really blame her? It was her life, or ours.

"No, child."

"Then what is it!" Some small part of me knew that I should have been afraid. I should have had more reverence for the Mother of all life itself. "Your disease killed millions! All those people...Grey...they're all dead."

"I am sorry, Terra."

"BULLSHIT! You killed them!"

"Humanity killed them." Gaia's voice had grown firm, "Humanity has killed me. Telluria has worked the way I designed it. It is my last hope...or yours."

I swiped at my tears with the back of my hand. "And what the hell is that supposed to mean?"

"Terra. All life lost, is not lost. Everything comes back to me in the end. In all the eons that I have lived, I have been nourished by the cycle of time." The lights flared, painting images on the walls and ceiling as she spoke. They showed all the worst moments in our history, of war, industry, and consumption. "Humanity's greed has broken the cycle, and so the cycle must be restored. Either by humanity mending their ways, or ending humanity." Different images appeared of better times, of walking through the woods, of planting, of caring for our home. "You were created to be stewards of the earth, but you have only brought destruction."

I lowered my head and closed my eyes. I didn't want to see the pictures anymore. They glowed with their awful judgment, the horrible truth that we killed our only home. "'Then why a slow death? Why not just wipe us all out." I whispered, what was the point of making us suffer if she only wanted us gone.

"Child..." The voice was saddened, "Do you not see?

Telluria, it may bring death, yes, but for those who chose to help me, it was a gift. I wanted to give you a chance."

I paused, raising my eyes to the dying tree once again. Merlin said something similar the first time he showed me the power of Telluria, a curse, a gift, our fate balanced on the edge of a sword. "It's too late," my throat felt tight and I dropped my gaze again. I didn't know if she could 'see' me, but I didn't want her to watch me as my shoulders started to shake with fresh sobs. "Humanity is gone. We weren't able to save ourselves. Those of us who are left, if Telluria doesn't kill us, then the husks will."

The lights in the room pulsed with her gentle sighing breath, "Yes..." It whispered, "And no."

My gaze snapped back up, "Can...can the husks be fixed?"

"The only thing wrong with them is that they lost their connection to me. They are no longer a part of this earth. When they die, their energy will disappear forever. New Atlantis nearly ended everything with their 'cure.' With every cured and husk who dies, I grow quickly weaker."

I shifted up, starting to rise up to my feet, "But can it be fixed?" I asked again, tired of the cryptic answers and pulling at the one spark of hope I had left. I thought of my parents and the hollow monsters that they had become. I would give anything just to be able to hug them again. Even just to walk through a town and feel safe.

"Yes."

"How? Please tell me how." My heart swelled and I rose fully to my feet.

"A sacrifice, child. I need you." The lights made one last painting, of me taking the tree inside of me, "I need a vessel that can handle the pure energy of Vita. I need you to take me where I can grow again. For too long have I hidden away from my creations."

I bit my lip, and looked back towards the hallway, towards Merlin, Ember, Cyrus, and Kalle. I couldn't hear Merlin's voice anymore. "Will I die?" I whispered.

"I don't know. You will need to be strong."

I took a breath, not knowing if it would be my last. "Okay."

At my consent, a strong wind picked up in the cavern. The tree before me shrivelled to dust, and all the lights went out.

EMBER WRAPPED Merlin's bleeding hands in bandages. It was the first time since Terra disappeared that he wasn't pounding them against the walls. "They are going to hurt in the morning. You're lucky you heal fast."

Merlin was practically vibrating to get back into action. "We can still keep trying. Maybe if we got some more rocks or—"

"And what? Smash them against the wall like some kind of barbarian? You'll just hurt yourself, or one of us, in the process." Ember tied off the last bandage and crossed her arms. "For a smart guy, you can be such an idiot."

"But we have to do something! Terra, she—" Merlin tried to get up, only to be pushed back down by Cyrus' hand on his shoulder.

"Merlin, our powers aren't working against that wall," Cyrus said, trying to sound calm but there was a tightness in his voice. "If Kalle can't get through it, you beating it with a rock won't either."

"Or melting it or breaking it up with wind and waves," Ember added. She stood up and chewed on her thumbnail as she contemplated the wall. They had spent hours trying everything in imagination to get through it. Terra said she would be back, so where was she?

Cyrus nodded at his sister, "Watch him, I'm going to check on Kalle."

As Cyrus walked away, Merlin got to his feet, "So what? We're just giving up on her? On everything we worked for?"

Cyrus stopped in the doorway, "Of course not. We're not giving up, but repeating the same thing and expecting different results is the definition of insanity."

Merlin turned back to the wall, running his bandaged hands over the painted surface as if he might find a seam somewhere in the stone. Maybe like outside, he could find layers of rock he could slip through that they just missed somehow. He stood in front of the painted tree, the place where Terra disappeared. All the paintings were still glowing faintly, filling the back of the cave in soft coloured light. Merlin pressed his hand against the tree painting, wishing he could just slip through as she did. If he could just follow her.

One by one, all the lights on the wall started to go out. Merlin pulled back as the cave was left in darkness. His brain started to buzz with what this could mean when a new light appeared. Terra stepped through the wall. Her marks, the earth, air, fire, and water, were connected by vines of green light. They twisted around her arms, her legs, her neck, even her eyes were glowing with that vivid green light.

"Ter—" Merlin barely dared to breathe.

She did not look at him. She didn't look at any of them, "We must return to the base. There, we will finish it," she said in a soft voice that resonated in Merlin's head. It took him a moment to realize that she wasn't moving her mouth.

"B-but are you okay? What happened?" Merlin moved to pull her into his arms, but the moment he touched her skin, a jolt of pure energy burned his already injured hands.

Terra smiled at him in a way that made the hair on the back of his neck stand up. "It will be over soon. Soon everything will be okay."

She began to walk out of the cave with her hair moving in an unfelt breeze. Merlin hastened to follow her, lifting his arm to move the curtain of water aside. Before he could, she did it herself. Merlin froze, despite her having all the marks, she was never able to control other elements before. Just vita.

"Terra, wait!" Ember tried this time, reaching out for her friend. She too recoiled as energy surged through her fingertips.

Merlin rushed to stand in front of her, "Terra, talk to us, please. We were worried sick."

Outside, Cyrus and Kalle were coming back to the cave. Terra merely looked at them as if they were all strangers to her, "There is a task that must be completed. The world tree, replanted. The sick, healed." She walked past Merlin and he jumped back to avoid another jolt of energy, "We must hurry. Gaia will not survive long in this vessel."

Merlin remembered how scared Terra had been the night before. This wasn't her, it wasn't the way she talked, it wasn't the way she moved. This was just her body with something else puppeteering it. He couldn't get close enough to her to stop her, and he couldn't get her to say anything else. All of his questions were answered in the same way.

He stayed close to her as they returned to the plane. It was nearly nightfall and as they walked it became clear the animals were no longer keeping their distance. Birds and monkeys followed from the treetops. Antelopes, lions, rhinos, and elephants followed them on all sides from a respectable distance. Predators walked among the prey.

Once they reached the stone cage of their camp, Arthur jumped to attention to see them coming. He grabbed the rifle he had next to him by the campfire, "Behind you!" he called, "Get in, hurry!"

Terra raised her hand and the stone cage disappeared, "Do not harm the children of Gaia. They followed as my escort. They will leave in peace."

"T-terra?" Arthur lowered the rifle, "What in blessed..."

"We must return. There is work to be done," Terra said and climbed into the plane without so much as another word. As she did, all the animals turned and disappeared into the trees.

Kalle went right to Arthur, who still looked dazed at the sudden appearance, "So is anyone going to fill me in?" Arthur asked.

Cyrus pulled the air from the campfire, suffocating the flames, "Just do as she says. We'll explain on the way, what we understand anyway."

Merlin climbed in after Terra. She had gone to the back of the plane, taking a seat by the window. The moment she sat down, she closed her eyes and slumped over in her chair while her marks began to pulse like a beating heart.

"Terra!" Merlin went to her and pain be damned, he took her wrist and searched for a pulse. A current of energy moved between them as he felt a steady beat beneath her skin. It matched the soft pulsing of the light she gave off.

The same light that glowed on his fingertips for a few seconds after he pulled his hand away.

Cyrus climbed into the plane soon after, "Is she okay?" He watched Merlin sink into the seat next to her and hold his head in his hands.

"No," Merlin whispered in a strained voice. "None of this is okay. She's resting now...I think. She's still breathing."

Cyrus came to the back of the plane and put a hand on Merlin's shoulder, "It'll be alright. We'll get back home, and we'll take care of this. We'll get her back."

Mutely, Merlin nodded.

"I'll go explain everything to Arthur. You and Em get some rest."

Cyrus climbed up to the cockpit to talk to Arthur and Merlin sat back and closed his eyes, knowing perfectly well that he wasn't going to get any rest.

Arthur got them home in record time. The fuel gauge never seemed to move, and there were the most perfect winds to push them home. The entire way back, the plane was accompanied by a flock of seabirds. From time to time Merlin looked out the window to see the giant wings of an albatross. By morning, Arthur said that he kept seeing whales pop up in the ocean below.

As they approached the base, Merlin could see their home was now surrounded by a giant wall. The wall had to be ten feet thick and at least fifty feet high. Outside the wall were thousands of husks. From the air, they looked like swarming ants trying to climb up the impenetrable wall.

"Bless their hearts," Arthur said from the pilot seat. "Kalle where do you want me to land?"

"The runway. I'll lower the wall enough to squeeze in." Kalle looked down at the horde of husks, "I sure hope Terra was right about this."

Merlin looked over to Terra. It wasn't her, not really. She had stayed in her weird sleeping state for the entire trip, the marks still pulsing with her heartbeat.

Arthur flew over the base once before turning to get into position. With Kalle's help, it was a smooth landing. Cyrus got up to open the plane door, letting in the distant roar of the husks beyond the wall. The moment the door was open, Terra sat up and opened her eyes. She got to her feet and walked out.

Josh, Elleen, and Mrs. McNair were already running across the grass as Terra walked towards the gardens. Merlin, Cyrus, and Ember followed closely behind her.

"Terra dear?" Mrs. McNair reached out as Terra walked by, but pulled back as Terra didn't so much as acknowledge her.

Merlin put his hand on Mrs. McNair's wrist, "I wouldn't touch her, Clara. She's..."

"What happened?" Mrs. McNair turned on Merlin with all the savagery of an angry viper, "I told you to keep her safe. I told you—"

"I know!" Merlin sounded anguished, "I don't know what happened. It's Gaia..the earth mother...we think she possessed Terra."

"She *what*?" Mrs. McNair turned back to Terra, who was already walking away from the entire scene.

"Terra, wait!" Merlin called and broke into a run to catch up with her, "Please Terra—Gaia—whoever. Tell me what's going to happen."

Her glowing green eyes landed slowly on Merlin, "Your

duty is over now. You have delivered me here. I must finish this now, this vessel will not last much longer."

Merlin swallowed hard, "But will Terra live?"

"I do not know," She walked into the gardens where the first signs of spring were starting to appear.

His heart felt like it was being dipped in acid. Terra was off to the side of the gardens, away from the vegetables and the graveyard. There was a small patch of tulips starting to poke through the soil, "Here."

"What are you going to do?" He asked, his voice starting to break. Whatever it was, he knew that he couldn't stop it. He had felt it when he touched her, the power that coursed through her veins.

"This vessel carries the seed of the world tree. She carries Gaia itself. Before the task is done, swear that you will care for the tree, Merlin."

He didn't bloody care about the tree. All he cared about was the woman in front of him, "But will Terra be okay? Please—"

Terra smiled softly, "Swear it," she demanded again, softer this time. She reached up and cupped Merlin's cheek in her hand. Just this once, it didn't burn. It felt like a humming warmth against his skin, familiar and powerful all at once. "Swear to protect the tree. In return, I promise the damage to the earth and its people will be healed."

Merlin's hands fisted at his sides, "I don't care about everyone and everything! I care about her!" He wanted to shake her, he wanted to scream and make it leave Terra's body.

"Terra is strong. I cannot promise that she will survive, but I do promise to do everything in my power to spare her. She knew the risks when she accepted me."

"No..."

The glow in Terra's eyes dimmed. It was her eyes again, filling with tears. The marks and the vines of light that connected them were still glowing with power. "M-Merlin."

"Terra." He pulled her into his arms, "Please don't make me do this..."

She held him tight, her fingertips digging into his back as though she never wanted to let go, "This is the only way, Merlin. Once Gaia is planted, everything will be fixed. The husks, Telluria, everything. Just promise me...promise you'll watch the tree. Keep it safe. Keep us safe."

Merlin pulled back, just enough to take her face in his hands, "I don't want to lose you," he whispered, his voice breaking.

A small smile pulled on her lips before she closed the gap and kissed him. It didn't burn. It tasted like her, of nectar and light. "Please Merlin," she pressed her forehead against his, "We won't last much longer like this. It hurts. She'll try to protect me. I promise Merlin...if I can...I'll come back to you."

He looked down into her eyes, silently pleading with him to do this. He stole one last kiss, letting it linger between them, "I swear..." he said, "Come back to me..."

There was a smile in her eyes, and then Gaia's glow returned.

Terra stepped back away from Merlin. The light grew brighter, like staring into the sun. Merlin and the others who weren't far behind him were forced to look away. He could feel the heat of it, the power of life coursing through the earth. Terra's body made a small noise, like a moan, followed by the sound of creaking wood. The light faded as a tree steadily grew from the place where Terra had been standing. It reached up towards the sky, higher than any tree Merlin had ever seen in his life. Higher than the mighty oak, higher than the redwoods of his home, higher than the skyscrapers of New York. The trunk was massive, easily the width of the mansion. The roots spread out over the ground before burrowing deep within the earth. As he looked up, leaves started to bud on the branches high above them. In the sun, they looked like glittering jewels.

Most noticeable was the sudden silence. The wails of the husks outside stopped. After the blinding silence, it rose again to the babbling chatter of thousands of people.

Merlin looked up at the tree, up at the living form of Mother Nature whom he had sworn to protect. He put his hand over the transparent patch of skin over his heart and knelt before the tree. "I swear to protect you both, from this day, until my last," he whispered, hoping that somehow, somewhere, Terra could hear him.

"You do know I'm going to need a second in command now, right?" Cyrus pointed out as he and Josh walked through the campsite that had popped up around the mansion. Many of the once husks had started the trek back to their homes once they 'woke up.' However, there were still hundreds who had chosen to stay. While Cyrus had put Elleen in charge of expanding the base below, there simply weren't hundreds of rooms ready.

"Yeah yeah," Josh chuckled, "You're going to need a great many things, Cyrus Chiaro." Josh pointed out. "A bigger vegetable garden for one."

"I'm going to need a whole farm." Cyrus said with a sigh, "Have Kalle and Arthur come back yet?"

"Nope," Josh said with a grin.

Ember and Elleen rode over on Helios. The machina lion laid down, letting Ember hop off.

"How did your trip go?" Cyrus asked, greeting his sister with a hug.

"Okay. So like, that next town over, pretty much abandoned." Ember started, "Maybe give it a bit for people to finish wandering home, but after that, we could totally start moving people into the houses that are left."

"That's great, Emmy!" Cyrus said, "Were you able to check the warehouse as well?"

"Mmhmm," She nodded, "Same as the others, everything that was fresh is rotted now, but there is still a lot we could use. It should tie us over until we get into the swing of things, right?"

"It's what people do. We survive." Cyrus said as it was sort of becoming a personal motto by this point. Life had gotten both easier and harder now that Telluria was gone. But they would manage.

"Have you seen Merlin?" Ember asked, "I found a couple of things he needed."

Cyrus nudged his chin towards the tree. It towered over everything else on the grounds and it's jewel-toned leaves shimmered in the new summer sun. "Simon and Braxton are helping him put up the walls of his cabin."

The two siblings shared a look before Ember waved up at Elleen, "I'll catch up with you in a bit." she said, then started the trek up to the tree.

Near the roots of the tree, Ember could see three men building a cabin in the sun. She ran up, waving at the one with black hair, "Merlin!" She called, "It's looking great!"

It wasn't very big, just one main room with a loft to act as a bedroom. So far the three men had just about finished framing everything. Merlin jogged over to Ember as Simon and Braxton took a break. "It's coming together really fast. Braxton thinks it might take another couple weeks to finish everything."

"I'm really happy for you, Merlin! You deserve it." Ember gushed. As she did, a shadow passed over Merlin's face. "Terra will love it too." She added, softer.

The two of them looked towards the tree. They agreed, Merlin, Ember, and Cyrus, to act as though Terra was still with them. She was alive, just as the tree. None of them heard the voice of Gaia since she took root, but they knew she was listening. If she could listen, perhaps Terra could too.

"Thanks, Em," Merlin said with a soft smile. "Maybe you and Elleen could get your own place sometime too."

"Maybe. I will admit we were spying a few houses in town, but I think we're staying here for now. Until things get settled at least."

Over near the cabin, Simon added a piece of scrap wood to the small campfire he and Braxton were sitting around. Ember watched the fire, her amber eyes almost seeming to flicker like flames. "Do you miss it?" Merlin asked her.

"Every day." She tore her eyes from the fire, "I wouldn't change it though. I wouldn't change it for anything."

Merlin listened to the light babble of the campsite on the grounds, to the rustle of the forest, to the bubble of the nearby stream. No more being hunted. No more having to hide. "Me neither, Em." His eyes lifted to Gaia's jewel-toned leaves, "Me neither."

MERLIN KEPT HIS WORD. He protected the tree. Gaia's roots grew strong and Telluria was gone. In spite of the new sense of peace that had fallen over the world, he often missed his powers. He still felt a connection to the water, like it was part of him. When he watched the river that now flowed past the base towards the ocean, he felt the phantom ache over his heart. His mark was still there, and when he looked in the mirror, he could still see the shadow of his heart beating beneath semi-transparent flesh. There were times, in the dark of night when the doubts came, when he wondered if this was real. What if he was really dead, and this was some sort of strange purgatory he had dreamt up. All he knew for sure was that it wasn't heaven. If it was, Terra would have been there with him. In his dreams, he could feel her in his arms. He would see that wild brown hair that reminded him of the woods she loved so much. He would smell her, like earth and the trees. The same way Gaia smelled.

Telluria was gone, but it didn't mean life was now easy. Civilization was gone. All that remained was the shell of what they once were. The base was forced to restructure and expand. Under Cyrus' and Ember's guidance, the mansion became livable again and the endless tunnels underneath were refurbished. The base became a place where people could come and learn to rebuild their lives. It became the centre of the new world.

New Atlantis' old systems started to pick back up. Food was being given out to those who needed it most. Free classes were held to teach people how to farm and forage. Elleen and engineers all over the world were working to harness electricity from the land, sea, sky, and to make it available to everyone. Until then, there was enough Essence stored in the world to keep the essentials going for a couple of years. It would be hard, but someday there would be a semblance of a normal world again. A new world.

While the rest of the world rebuilt, Merlin stayed with the tree. He built a cabin near the roots where he could watch, and wait. A year passed and the tree went through a full cycle of the seasons. In the summer, the pale opalescence flowers fell and the tree turned out a rainbow of jewel-toned leaves. In the fall, the leaves turned and fell. In the winter, snow gathered on the branches and animals burrowed beneath the roots. At the thawing of winter, the bark split and Merlin collected the sap with buckets. It was sweet and made even the weariest feel rested. Once they discovered the sap had healing properties, Merlin started to boil it down into syrup and stored it away to last the base throughout the year.

Spring came again and the pale flowers returned. The petals shimmered in the sunlight in shifting shades of pastels and opals. Merlin walked up to the tree in the dawn light, as he did every morning before starting his work around the base. "Morning," he said with a soft grin and climbed up on the roots. "Good news, Elleen thinks she knows how the make the plane completely solar-powered. I guess Arthur will never have to worry about fuel again."

The wind moved through the branches and Merlin looked up to watch the shimmer of the budding jewel-tone leaves. It looked like there were the beginnings of fruit where the flowers once were. "Hey, Terra...Cyrus wants to send a team to Toronto. I think...I might go. I want to visit your parents. It was nice to have them here over the winter and Cyrus wants to help your dad set up his lab again. Remember those seeds you told me about? Well, I thought I could go help. I'll be gone for maybe a month. Ember promised she would watch over you while I'm gone."

Merlin pressed his hands against the trunk of the tree. He could feel the energy coursing through in the same way he felt the movement of water. "Are you taking care of her, Gaia? Tell her what I said. It'll make her happy. Tell her..." Merlin closed his eyes and laid his head against the bark. "Tell her I love her."

A sharp crack pierced the air. The bark under Merlin's hand split and sap came pouring out like blood from a wound. The sharp sting of panic rose in his throat. This was wrong. The winter thaw was long over, the bark shouldn't be splitting like this anymore. The split had made a long deep fissure into the wood. Panicked, he reached in trying to find what had caused the sudden split. Then something grabbed his hand.

The flow of the sap was slowing by the time Merlin pulled his hand back and Terra's body fell into his arms. She was perfect. Her chest rose and fell with soft breaths. Her dark curls were slick with sap. Her marks were faded with faint lines that connected them like the branches of a tree. "T-Terra!" He touched the side of her face, feeling the warmth of her skin, "Open your eyes. Please, Terra, please open your eyes."

She opened her eyes. Green as Gaia's power. "Mer—"

Merlin wrapped his arms tightly around her and fell to his knees with her cradled against him. "Terra...Terra..." His voice cracked and he buried his face in her neck.

She reached up and touched his hair, the small action made him pull back and look her in the face. There were tears in his eyes. "How long was I gone?" she whispered, with a soft voice like she had just woken from sleep.

"A year."

She laughed softly and it sounded like sunshine to Merlin's ears, "She kept her promise," Terra whispered. "My body was nearly destroyed. She kept me so I could heal." Her hand slipped from his hair to his face, "She told me the things you said. You never gave up on me, huh?"

Merlin's shoulders began to shake with a mix of tears and laughter, "I promised I would take care of the tree. I told you I would wait for you." Merlin pulled her close and pressed his lips against hers. She tasted like the sweet sap of Gaia mostly, but there was a little of her beneath that, like earth and sunlight. Terra giggled breathlessly against his lips and was smiling when he pulled back. "No leaving again, promise?"

Terra leaned forward, touching her forehead against his, "Promise."

ACKNOWLEDGMENTS

Many thanks to everyone who helped me while I wrote this book. Thank you to my husband Jeremy and your eternal support and to my daughter Sophia. Thanks to my editor Angela Churchill and your endless patience with my comma usage. Thanks to my beta readers Cyra, Scythe, Hope and Thomas and for putting up with my chaotic REEEE energy while I was writing. Thanks to the GWOAC for answering my questions whenever I needed advice from fellow writers. And thanks to you, the reader. I hope you enjoyed this book and all the others to follow.

ABOUT THE AUTHOR

Jodi Trask currently resides in Newfoundland, Canada with her husband Jeremy Trask and their daughter Sophia. She has always had a love for stories and has been writing from a young age.

Jodi studied at Memorial University of Newfoundland - Grenfell Campus and earned a degree in Environmental Biology.